SORCERESS OF DESTINY

SORCERESS
OF DESTINY

LAMORRA SAGA
BOOK ONE

ALEKSEI PARKER

*This is to those who read to escape and
have adventures in other worlds.*

*To my family and friends for their amazing support
as I pursued my dream to tell this story.*

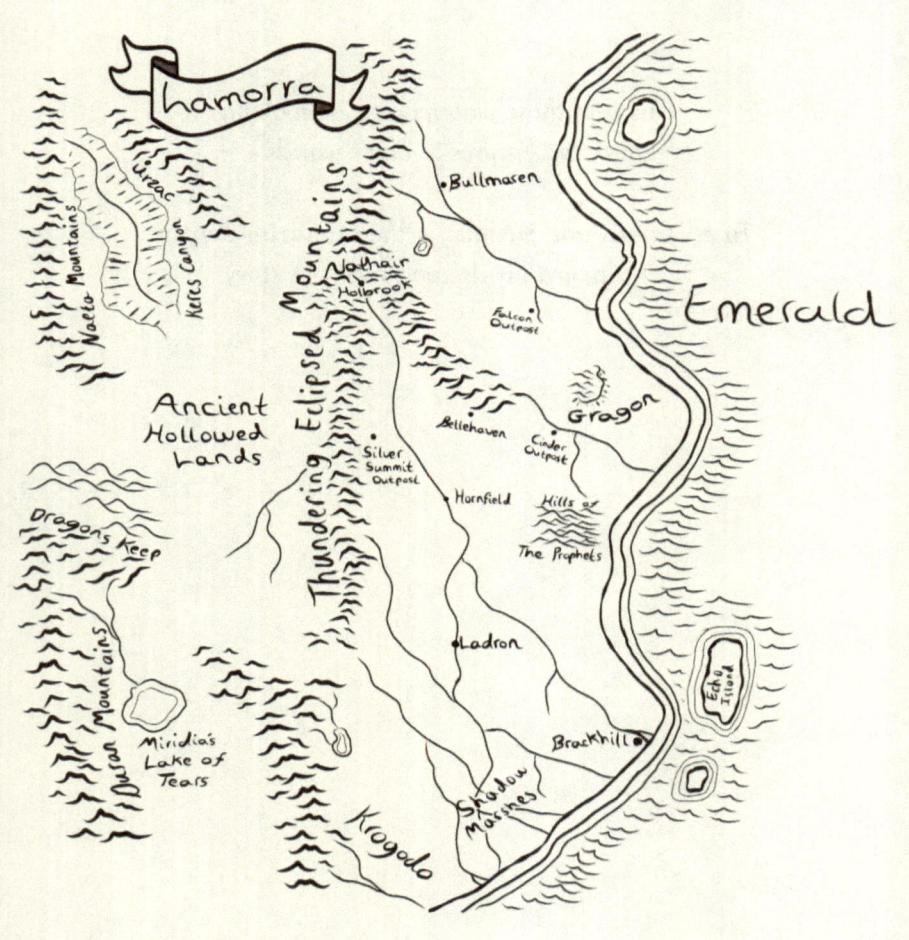

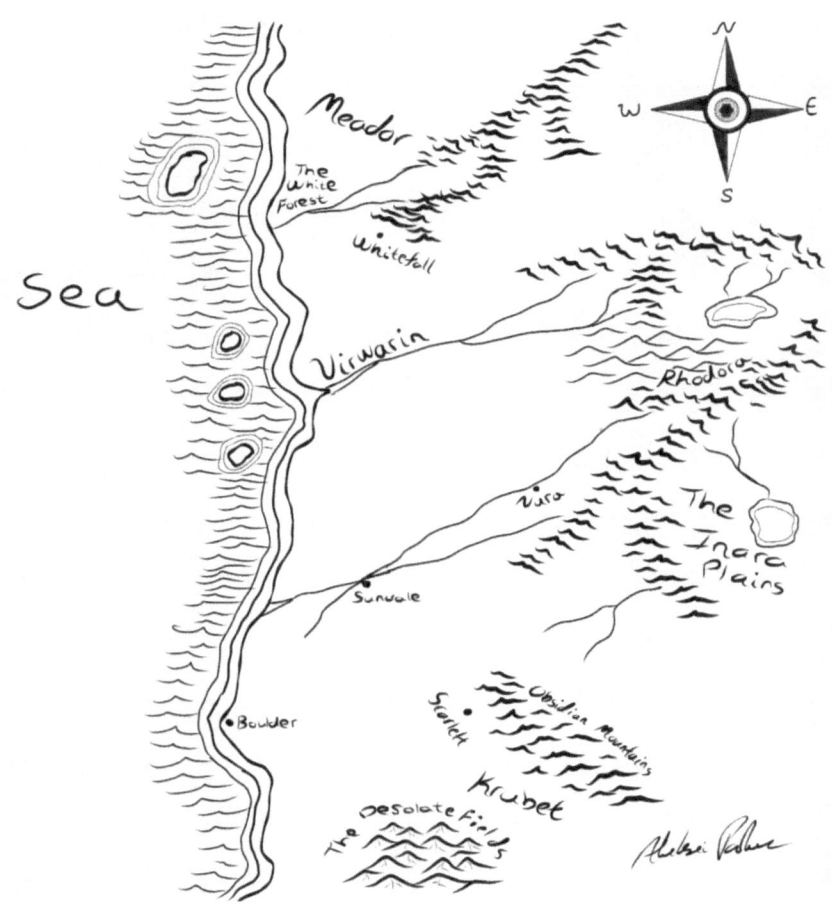

1

PROPHECY FORETOLD

Rain poured upon the soldiers fighting on the vast open plain surrounded by a forest near the base of a small mountain range. Many of them lost their footing on the slick, mucky ground as they fought. Atop a small cliff side some distance away stood trebuchets flinging large boulders, killing anyone in their path of impact. Fresh thick mud flew into the air as the large slabs of rock landed on the wet earth.

The war has lasted for a little over a year, with no end in sight. The realm of Lamorra was not ready for a war against an army led by the newly proclaimed Dark King of the Nathair Kingdom and his new powerful ally, Sorcerer Vaxar, the last surviving member of the coven of dark sorcerers. None of the kingdoms in the realm were ready for the kingdom of the mountains to declare war and seek to become the first empire in the lands.

Vaxar stood beside the trebuchets, watching the battle below. He wore a long, dark cloak draped over his simple battle armor that partially covered his dark green tunic, black pants, and boots. Despite the drenching rain, he kept his hood off with his long black hair slicked back so his enemies down below could clearly recognize him. Vaxar preferred to lead his battles from afar but would always be in sight of the enemy, hoping to strike fear into their hearts with his presence.

Should he be successful in the battle today, they will be within striking distance of the Gragon Castle and have felled a second kingdom under the power of Nathair. The battle today was a few miles south of the Gragon Castle upon a large hill with two small narrow canyons north and south of it, forming a low valley to its east. Its position upon this hill might prove to be a challenge, but Vaxar was sure he'd be successful in taking it. The small valley led straight down for several miles towards the eastern shore of the Emerald Sea. Conquering Gragon would help give a powerful position against the Elvish Kingdom of Virwarin and the southern kingdom of Krogodo.

Vaxar desperately searched for the Gragon king upon the battlefield below. The battle had lasted longer than he wanted, and his forces were dwindling, more so than his enemy's, much to his dismay. If he could find the king and if the circumstances proved fair, only then would he join the battle.

As he stood searching the battlefield below, Vaxar ordered the third and only remaining wave of soldiers to march onto the field and turn the tide of the battle in his favor. With his forces taking the lead, Vaxar finally found his target.

The Gragon king stood across the battlefield in his dirty armor with his hand stretched in the air, pointing right at Vaxar. Vaxar was curious and wondered if the king was signaling for the few archers left to attempt firing what little arrows they may still have.

A figure emerged from the forest behind King Gragon, dressed in an odd combination of green and silver armor. His blond, almost white hair gleamed in the small amount of light that shone through the thunderclouds above. It was the Elf King, Gantar Virwarin. King Virwarin looked right at Vaxar as he signaled his archers, hidden within the forest, to fire at the cliff side. The arrows flew. But before they could hit their target, the arrows suddenly shattered, as if smashing against a stone wall as they collided with the magical shield that Vaxar quickly conjured.

Vaxar looked at King Virwarin with a sneer as his eyes glowed with a dark, menacing red from his magic.

"Foolish elf," he said to himself.

King Virwarin smiled back at Vaxar. A loud crash from beside Vaxar startled him, breaking his focus on the elf. Large stones thrown by the Elves' mangonel catapults destroyed Vaxar's trebuchets. The Elves strategically positioned the catapults, concealing them within the forest among some trees spaced far enough apart for the deadly weapons to fire without being seen. King Virwarin knew the arrows would be pointless against magic but thought they would provide the perfect distraction to hit the true targets.

This quick blow of an attack, with the Elvish army now entering the battlefield, easily overwhelmed Vaxar's forces. Filled with rage, he reluctantly gave the order to fall back, ending the battle in defeat.

Gragon will be safe for another day thanks to those Elves, he thought.

Vaxar's forces fell back to the newly established Cinder Outpost on the other side of a river southwest of the Gragon Castle. It placed them further away from both the kingdom and the battlefield. However, with the Elves now within the Gragon kingdom, it would be a safer place to stay. The outpost would hold well enough defensively should their enemies attempt to attack.

Shortly after arriving in the outpost by horseback, Vaxar

received a message from the Dark King, delivered by the shadow journal, summoning him immediately. He promptly readied his horse and gathered provisions he would need for his journey to the castle. Before leaving, he gave one of his generals precise instructions to hold the line in the forest just a few miles away, between the outpost and the battlefield, along the river, until his return.

He arrived early in the morning several days later at Winterstone Castle of the Nathair Kingdom before the sun had yet peeked over the mountain tops. Even as early as it was, servants already saw to their tasks for the morning. He made his way towards his quarters that contained a large bookcase filled with tomes, vials, and bottles, next to a small table and chair, a fireplace and his bed. Turning down a couple of hallways and then down a small stairway, he stopped a young servant boy who crossed his path. He requested the servant to bring some food to his room. Vaxar wanted to take advantage of his early arrival to eat and rest before the king would wake.

Vaxar's room, according to his request on his first meeting with the Dark King, was to always be on the lower level, if possible. It was just around the hallway to the dungeons. The lower level of the castle was much colder than the upper levels, which he very much enjoyed. The room also provided an easy way for him to escape quickly if the need ever arose. One hallway near his room led towards a side door that spat him out into the forest against the mountainside. It was dark but for the light coming from the lit hearth and candles on the small table in the middle of the room, as the curtains to the three windows in his rooms were always shut. The room was spotless, with his potions, vials, bottles, and books neatly organized on his dressers and bookshelves. The room looked as if there was not a single speck of dust.

Vaxar promptly sat in his chair beside the fireplace to get a moment of rest. But no sooner had he shut his eyelids than a servant knocked and entered with his breakfast. It was not long after he finished eating that the king summoned him to his study. It was a surprise that he rose earlier than normal.

Vaxar walked down the elegant corridors of dark granite floors and stone walls, then up the large stairwell towards the king's study. The servants were making their way towards the kitchen when he passed them, carrying dirty dishes from the direction he was headed. He arrived soon at the cracked door to the study, letting some light from the room escape into the dim hallway.

Vaxar knocked on the open door and entered the room without waiting for a reply. As he approached the Dark King, who was frowning at a crumpled piece of parchment at his desk, Vaxar looked around the room as it disgusted him with how lousy his friend was at keeping things clean. The room held maps, books, and papers scattered across the floor, bookcases of disorderly tomes, and the king's desk. He marveled at how none of the papers near the candles on the desk or on the floor near the fireplace had caught fire yet.

Vaxar did his best to avoid the mess as he sat down in the chair that, surprisingly, did not have any papers on it. He guessed the king must have had a servant clean the chair before Vaxar's arrival. The Dark King continued frowning at the parchment well after Vaxar had sat down. He was in formal wear of a dark red shirt and black pants. His hair, nearly black and long enough to dust his jawline, was slicked back behind his ears. His rugged, shaggy beard clearly hadn't been trimmed for a few days.

"Take a look at this parchment. The guards found this posted on the front gate before the pathway to the castle from Holbrook several days ago. We may have a bigger problem with that other sorcerer than we previously thought," said the King.

Vaxar took the parchment and read it.

"Dark King, you will soon have not just one sorcerer, but two to deal with. Your reign will end, and your sorcerer will have no power against us. Against the uprising."

"It appears Sorcerer Krarick may be training a new apprentice. I thought you had said that you two are the last of your sorcery kind," continued the King after Vaxar finished reading.

"We are. I do not think that it could be a new apprentice, though, King Erebus," said Vaxar.

"Explain your reasoning," requested Erebus.

"I know for a fact that Krarick is the only other sorcerer alive from the Nightshadow War. There is no one left with magic to train, not even young boys. If this rebellion is speaking of another, then it only means that Krarick must have a child on the way," he replied.

Vaxar thought to himself for a moment. He stared at the parchment, reading it over again as his forehead wrinkled.

"I shall visit the Hills of the Prophets and use the magic there to learn the meaning behind this message. We need to gain the advantage of learning Krarick's secrets and end his annoying life," said Vaxar.

"Then go to the hills at once. Take care of this problem now while we can. And see what the prophets have to say about my son continuing our kingdom's legacy, ruling over the empire I am building. He may be two years old now, but he will be as great of a ruler as me," said Silas.

"Of course, Your Majesty," said Vaxar as he stood up and promptly left the study.

Vaxar headed back towards his quarters. He gathered some powders and potions for teleportation spells and other advanced magic into a bag as he prepared for his journey to the Hills of the Prophets. He wanted to leave immediately. When or if he got tired, he would set up camp and rest then. He would rather get to the hills as soon as possible to gather his information before things have a chance to change. A new sorcerer can make his plans much more difficult to achieve as it would mean yet another person he would have to face off against. It is already challenging enough against the last surviving sorcerer with no other dark sorcerer alive by his side. The Nightshadow War left them both the sole survivors of their opposing sides. After only a few minutes of preparation, his satchel was full of the ingredients he may need for his journey. He left his quarters for the stables to saddle his horse.

The Hills of the Prophets stretched over a vast area with many hills, each bearing entrances to the inner tunnel network and rooms underground. The hills contained prophecies with clues to the future, the history of the past, and powerful magic unknown even to those who studied the hills, as some were too dangerous to explore. The spirits of the hills are protective of their magic. The spirits would allow sorcerers to enter to learn only what was permitted. Should the sorcerer attempt to learn things the spirits did not allow, they would be trapped and become part of the hills. Many believed the spirits of the magical prophets held a close relationship with the higher spirits, Dusan, and creator of the land of the living, Meridia. The prophets built the hills over thousands of years ago and have remained a part of their creation as spirits. Those who visited this place were frequently challenged with riddles they must solve to uncover the knowledge they seek. However, in rare cases, trapped souls became prophets to convey prophecies through visions. The hills were both sacred and dangerous as some sorcerers in the past, who searched for knowledge within, lost themselves to the magic and the maze of the land, trapping their souls forever.

At the grand, moss-covered stone archway entrance to the hills stood Sorcerer Krarick Sloane. He wore a navy-blue tunic and dark brown pants with his caesious hooded cloak covering his short brown hair. He had a small satchel draped across his shoulder and resting against his hip. It carried a few potions and powders along with the sorcerer's codex book.

He carefully looked at a detailed map of the hills, searching for the one that contained the magic that would show the future or any prophecies that can help with fighting the enemy. He found the hill that he must go to and set out towards it, walking on the paths circling around the many hills. The pathway was filled with tall blades of grass with a large mixture of flowers and green bushed across the hills. His path wandered around many of the hills that blocked the view of the land beyond. He eventually made his way to the door of the hill he was searching for.

Krarick took what he felt was the safer route by following the pathways above the ground instead of the tunnels. The underground pathway was darker than a moonless night sky, making it easier to get lost.

"Morelio saci," he said, holding his hand out to unlock the wooden door in the hillside while his eyes glowed a deep green color.

It was pitch-black inside, with the only light coming from the doorway. He ignited the torches along the walls with a snap of his fingers. He hoped the spirits wouldn't mind sparing him some light. With the inner workings of the hill illuminated by the burning torches, Krarick could see that the hill was far larger on the inside than he had previously thought.

This was his first time at the Hills of the Prophets. He preferred to avoid the place, as he did not like to deal with powerful, dangerous magic. It was against the teachings from the Strometh Temple. Powerful magic is taught to lead to the darkening of one's soul and death. But things had changed recently, and he could not delay any further. He needed information on what the future held and how he could destroy the impending threat of evil.

He walked down the tunnel built with wooden frames and walls through which roots broke through with stone flooring. The tunnel appeared to go on forever, lined with closed doors, though he only needed to go to the first door on the right, which swung open on its own as he approached.

It was dark inside, much like the hallway except for the fire in the center of the room that ignited at his arrival. Above the fire hung a large cauldron. Krarick guessed that either the spirits or the magic of the hills ignited the fire for him. There was only one bookcase in the room, filled with a few bottles, vials, and books beside a table, on which knives, mortar and pestle of three different sizes, and spoons lay as if in wait, among other items needed for preparing potions.

Whispered voices surrounded him, even though he appeared to be alone. The trapped spirits, now one with the magic of the hills, were rarely ever visible to the living. They preferred to remain hidden in the dark, almost invisible. Krarick was not sure which spirits surrounded him, but he hoped it was the Dusan, the good spirits who served under the creator of the land of the living, Meridia. If he was surrounded by the Naeta, the dark spirits who served the ruler of the underworld, Keres, he would be in more danger than he would like to be.

"*I foresee a battle in our midst,*" said one voice.

"*What fun!*" another voice laughed wickedly.

"*The last two survivors of the war that has yet to conclude. Though an answer will be given in the distant future,*" said all the voices in unison.

Just as the voices spoke, he sensed a familiar dark magic that he knew all too well.

Vaxar! Why is he here? Does he know I am here, or is he searching for something as well? Either way, I must hurry and remain undetected, he thought.

"*You best hurry, sorcerer. If you wish to remain unnoticed, you will need to work fast,*" whispered a voice.

"*He will need to be faster than a spirit,*" laughed another.

Krarick hurried, grabbing a couple of the vials from shelves and pouring them into the cauldron at the center of the room. He shared the same fear as his former colleagues of the dangers that surrounded the Hills. To fight this fear of powerful magic, he studied everything he could as an apprentice in the Strometh Temple on all knowledge they had on the Hills should he ever have to visit.

Many of the vials from the shelves in the room contained liquid and some held solid objects, from plants to bugs to small pieces of various animals. Luckily, he did not need to slice anything, but he had to use the mortar and pestle on a few thin leaves. As he poured the last vial into the cauldron, the potion activated, sending a bright cloud of smoke into the air, just as Vaxar entered the room.

"No!" yelled Krarick.

"Krarick. What a pleasant surprise," said Vaxar.

Before either of them could say or do anything more, the cauldron erupted into a vibrant, multicolored cloud filling the room.

Black silhouette images formed in the smoke: a lone

hooded figure with magic flying from its hands as it fought against an army of some sort of tall creatures with pointy ears and vicious looking face with protruding front teeth and vile looking men. Behind the army stood a figure without a hood and red smoke surrounding them. This other figure cast spells against the hooded figure, to no effect.

Then the image changed: the hooded figure stood before someone wearing a crown of a prince that slowly changed to a crown of king. The silhouette of the crown became clearer until it looked like the crown of the Nathair Kingdom with four tall spikes like a small arrowhead and small point in between the spikes. The front of the crown bears the engraved symbol of the grimog creature's head. It is a clear sign this figure is the current baby Nathairian prince. The silhouette of the prince, now king, stretched into a bowing stance towards the hooded figure. The figure removed their hood, revealing long hair flowing down past the shoulders. It was a sorceress. All the images reappeared in the smoke and aligned with each other in the order they had appeared.

"*Should the first sorceress in over a thousand years live,*" the spirits said in unison, "*the true Dark King and his efforts to build an empire shall fail. The magical forces of Meridia and Keres shall once again renew their fight. Darkness will grip the lands of Lamorra and the sorceress's path. But should the sorceress gain the aid of powerful ancient beings, the flame of Keres will be extinguished. The rays of Meridia's sun will once again shine upon Lamorra.*"

The cloud of smoke decimated into a colorful flash, leaving the sorcerers face to face with each other.

Krarick was trying to think of a way to get out of there without having to go through a troublesome fight with Vaxar. He would like to teleport. However, the magic of the hills prevented him from doing so. The spirits control what magic is permitted within their hills. They prevent teleporta-tion spells as it would be too easy for those breaking their rules to escape.

"Our first sorceress of the realm in a thousand years. She'll be a marvel to see, won't she, Krarick? You remember learning about the last one back at that dusty old Strommeth temple, right? How powerful and dangerous she was. I won-der if she could be the same and how easy it could be to cor-rupt her path rather than kill her," said Vaxar.

"You won't succeed."

"Oh? What makes you so sure?"

"As the prophecy was just foretold, you and the Dark King will lose by the sorceress's hand," said Krarick.

"Prophecies can always change. Besides, aren't you al-ready forgetting that one little detail? 'Darkness will grip the lands of Lamorra and the sorceress's path.' There's a good chance I can sway her over or simply kill her and win over the realm that way," said Vaxar.

"You won't succeed with either! There's no chance you can turn my daughter into being a servant of Keres!"

Vaxar's eyes widened, and a small smile formed.

"Daughter? Now I don't remember the spirits of these hills saying that word. You have a child now, Krarick? I would very much like to meet her," said Vaxar with an evil laugh.

"No," whispered Krarick to himself. "You will never get that chance, Vaxar," he said, filled with anger as he discreetly reached into his bag hanging at his side.

"We shall see," said Vaxar, as his eyes glowed blood red.

Vaxar threw a fireball at Krarick. He narrowly dodged it while throwing a pale blue mist at Vaxar. The powdery mist stunned him, rendering him immobile as he flew backwards into the wall behind him. The powdered potion would only last a few minutes. Krarick quickly made his way out of the room and then out of the hill before making a run for the archway so he could teleport some distance away without Vaxar being able to track which direction he would go afterwards.

He was a short distance away from the archway when a fiery object flew past him, narrowly missing his shoulder. The spell on Vaxar had worn off quicker than expected. Krarick quickened his speed as more spells and fireballs flew around him, nearly hitting him several times as he tried to dodge and make it harder for Vaxar to aim.

"You can't hide forever, Krarick! I will find you! I will find your daughter!"

Krarick dived through the archway into the sunlight and immediately teleported, just as a fireball would have hit his head. He transported into the middle of a forest, safe from Vaxar for now. Though he was still not far away, as the simple teleportation spell could only teleport short distances. Krarick pulled out a green powder from his satchel.

"Transigeo," he said as he threw the powder onto his legs and feet.

The powder exploded into a cloud of thick black smoke and transported him to a cottage within the Nathairian Kingdom, the very one he had been helping other kingdoms fight against. He reflected often on his sadness and anger of the moment when the King of Nathair announced their allegiance with Vaxar and his plans to unite the realm under an empire. Since then, his cottage has felt less like the home it once was. The cottage stood at the edge of the village of Holbrook, near the woods against the mountainside.

Krarick took a moment to gather his bearings from the spell as it sometimes dizzied him. Once his eyes adjusted, he entered the cottage. It was small, with two bedrooms and a little kitchen that doubled as a dining room, a fireplace built on the opposite side of the kitchen. It was a cozy home that he and his wife shared with two elves.

The Elf woman, Gwyneth Elmenor, sat at the kitchen table, in her olive-green Elvish style tunic with her dirty blonde hair messily gathered in a bun. Sitting across from her was her son, Thallan, in his blue Elvish tunic. They were both drinking hot cider and eating some sort of muffins.

"Have any extra to spare?"

"Of course, Krarick. You know me and my baking. There's always plenty for everyone," said Gwyneth as she made to stand.

"No, I can get it myself. With all your baking and help around here, you deserve to sit and rest," said Krarick.

"You are too nice."

"How is Eleanora doing?"

"She is still asleep. Your little one is with her. Such an adorable girl, Krarick," said Gwyneth.

Krarick poured himself a cup of cider and used a small amount of magic to heat it before he grabbed a muffin and joined them at the table. They sat in silence for a while, enjoying the fire in the hearth and the delicious drink and food.

"You are back home early," said Eleanora as she entered the kitchen with a yawn.

"I teleported home. How are you feeling, my love?"

"Tired. Little one is so quiet, but she is always wanting attention when awake. Thallan here has been a great help in keeping her entertained to give me a nap or two throughout the day," said Eleanora.

"Just doing what I can to help," said Thallan.

"Have you chosen one of the names we were thinking of for her? We cannot all keep calling her 'little one.' I am sure no person would like that name when they are older," said Krarick.

"Lysandra. I can already tell it would be the perfect name for her," said Eleanora.

"It is perfect. Is Lysandra still sleeping?"

"She is, but I'm sure any minute now she will wake up and cry. The only time she cries is when she is alone."

"Come sit down. I'll get you something to eat and drink. If she wakes, I can go get her," said Krarick.

Not long after, Lysandra started crying. Krarick went into their bedroom, and the minute he picked her up, her crying ceased.

Krarick sat back down at the table with Lysandra happily in her father's arms. He made silly faces, trying to get Lysandra to giggle, when a faint knock came from the front door.

"I can get it," said Thallan.

He walked over to the door and cracked it open while holding a knife behind his back. Thallan didn't want to take any chances, given how late in the night it was.

"May I help you?"

"I must speak to Sorcerer Krarick right away, sir. I have urgent news regarding his encounter with Vaxar earlier this evening," said the man at the door.

"Step into the light first before I let you in. 'Tis late and I will not chance letting a stranger of a voice I do not recognize in," said Thallan.

"Of course, sir. My apologies. I am Lucas, son of Sorcerer's Krarick's old friend from the war, Clay Eryx," said the soldier as he stepped into the lantern light that hung by the door.

"Thank you, Lucas. I recognize you now. My apologies for not remembering you right away. You may enter. I shall get Krarick for you. Wait here just inside the entrance, please," said Thallan.

Thallan walked to the kitchen, where the others sat in curiosity.

"There is a soldier here by the name of Lucas Eryx, wanting to talk to you, Krarick. He says it is urgent," said Thallan.

"Thank you, Thallan. Eleanora, can you hold her for me, please?"

Krarick walked over to where the soldier stood waiting.

"Sorcerer Krarick. My apologies for the late-night interruption, but I felt the news I have is urgent and should not wait till morning," said the soldier quickly.

"It is quite all right, soldier. Please tell me this news you have," said Krarick.

"Vaxar has ordered a battalion of the palace guards to hunt you and the baby sorceress. He told us to kill you on sight and take the baby alive and unharmed. Vaxar knows you are living within this kingdom. He proclaimed he performed a tracking spell on you from your fight earlier today," said the soldier.

Krarick's eyes widened. He looked down at his clothes and quickly examined them to see if anything was missing. None of the clothes he was wearing appeared to be ruined, aside from some dirt.

"Krarick, there is a piece missing from the bottom of your cloak," said Thallan.

Krarick silently cursed under his breath.

"Thank you, soldier. This information is indeed urgent. I recommend you return to your station immediately. I am sure they will be on the lookout for anyone gone from their posts for too long and suspect anyone of being a traitor for trying to help those against the dark forces," said Krarick.

The soldier nodded and promptly left the cottage, making his way back to his post at the town gates that led up to the castle.

"What did the soldier have to say? Given everyone's

faces, it must be serious. The one time I wished I had Elvish hearing," said Eleanora.

"Vaxar tracked me back to the kingdom. All he knows is that I am somewhere within its borders. But he sent out soldiers to search for me and for Lysandra. He now knows of her," said Krarick.

"How can he know? She is only a few days old," said Eleanora, with fear in her voice.

Krarick explained all that had happened during his visit to the hills. Each of their faces showed a mixture of sadness and fear.

"What should we do? We must get Lysandra and you to safety," said Eleanora.

"I have a plan, but Eleanora, my darling, you will not like it. I shall leave and head for the Krogodo Kingdom. It is the safest kingdom that the Nathairian forces cannot attack and where I have the strongest of allies. Krogodo's forces are too strong for Nathair. They are strong warriors that know their land well. Gwyneth, I must ask you and your son to stay with Eleanora and my daughter. Your Elvish aura will mask her magical aura from Vaxar," said Krarick.

"Wouldn't it be safer if we all left? We could first go to Krogodo, then to Virwarin. Vaxar despises the strength of the Elvish kingdom and their strategic placement," said Thallan.

"I agree with Thallan," said Eleanora. "Krarick, are you sure your plan is the safest idea? Leaving us here in Nathair Kingdom so close to the people who are now after her? I don't understand how us staying here would be safe for her."

"Yes. You both will be safe. Elves can easily mask our kind of magical aura, as theirs is much stronger than a sorcerer or a sorceress. I can keep Vaxar distracted and looking away from here. I can make him think you are now safe in another kingdom, beyond his grasp. I know Vaxar. He would never suspect something under his own nose," said Krarick.

"Then we will go with your plan...for now. Should danger arise for her here, we will leave for the safety of Krogodo," said Eleanora.

Gwyneth and Thallan nodded in agreement.

Krarick began packing a bag of clothes and provisions for his journey to the southern kingdom of Krogodo. Thallan helped him as much as he could.

He stood before the door with his cloak on and bag draped over his shoulder. He walked up to Eleanora and gave her and Lysandra a hug.

"Give this to her when she is old enough to understand and know her destiny," said Krarick as he reached for a necklace with a pendant attached to it that he wore around his neck, underneath his tunic.

He gave Eleanora one last hug and kiss before giving Gwyneth a hug and thanking her for her bravery and loyalty. Krarick stood before Thallan.

"Look after them all. I know that's an enormous responsibility and puts a lot on your young shoulders, but I believe you are ready. I have seen for some time now that you have a lot of your father in you. Be strong for me, Thallan. Protect them," said Krarick in Elvish.

He gave Thallan a hug, like a father to a son. Krarick, filled with sorrow, left the little cottage with tears in his eyes. He headed into the forest, doing his hardest not to look back, for if he did, he knew he'd turn around and go to his family.

As he walked through the forest, Krarick thought to himself of other ways to possibly help protect his family from Vaxar. He remembered hearing of a family not too far away from the cottage that expressed wanting to leave the kingdom for somewhere safer but did not know how to travel through the mountain range safely. It was a couple with a little boy who was almost a year old. If they traveled with him, word might spread of people seeing him with a family and heading for Krogodo. He hoped his idea would trick Vaxar into thinking they all had fled the kingdom and would cease his search within the kingdom for his daughter.

He made his way to the family's home and explained his situation. To his surprise, despite the potential danger of coming across soldiers along the journey, the family agreed and quickly packed up their belongings and supplies. They left just before the sun peeked over the mountains. Krarick was ever so grateful to the family and wanted to keep them safe as he helped lead them to a new home.

2

EIGHTEEN YEARS LATER

I t was a brisk early morning, rain trickling against the window seal in front of her. She read the sorcerer's codex her father had left for her by candlelight, as the dark rain clouds kept the warm sun hidden, as it did most days in this valley tucked within the Thundering Eclipse Mountains. She had read the sorcerer's codex well over a thousand times now, but continued to study it at least once a day. It was all she had to help her learn how to use her magic, since her father was elsewhere in the realm, fighting dangerous battles against the Dark Sorcerer and his army.

She had learned of the prophecy that was foretold about her when she was quite young, despite her mother's attempts to keep it hidden to give her as much of a normal childhood as possible. Since her mother and the two elves felt that she was of age to learn as much about magic as she could, that was all she ever did. Then, when she got a few years older, she received combat training from Thallan, who she considered as an older brother as his mother, Gwyneth, had also come to be like a second mother to her.

The rain outside fell more steadily against the window seal when she heard a creak of the floorboard outside her door, followed by a gentle knocking.

"Come in", she said as she wrapped the blanket tighter around her shoulders.

"Lysandra, honey, why are you up so early again? Gwyneth told me she saw the flicker of your candlelight under the door," said Eleanora.

Her mother's face was soft and full of worry and care as she looked at her daughter, sitting in her chair before the window. A slight, cool breeze was blowing through, entering the room, adding a chill to the air.

"I woke up and could not fall back to sleep. So, I've been reading the codex," said Lysandra.

"Is there something bothering you? I'm sure Gwyneth may have something to help you sleep if you are having trouble," she said.

"No, thank you. I'm fine," said Lysandra.

"Very well. If you change your mind, just let me know. Well, anyway, it's time to get ready. Thallan will be here shortly for breakfast," said Eleanora as she gave her a quick hug before she left to go to the kitchen downstairs.

Lysandra always looked forward to seeing Thallan. She did not get to see him as often as she would like, despite living in the small town of Holbrook just a few miles away from the Winterstone Castle that her brother spent his time at as a general. The castle was slightly up the mountainside to the north of the valley where the village sat surrounded by the mountains.

Once Thallan, who was a high knight, became appointed as General of the Nathairian army, he started working more closely with King Keir Nathair. He joined the kingdom's forces when she was a young girl and made his way to his current position to ensure Vaxar and King Keir did not discover Lysandra. If they did, he could at least slow them down, buying time for her to escape to safety. Thallan has made it his duty to keep the promise he made to Krarick all those years ago. He not only protected her, but he trained her in combat, giving her needed skills in swordsmanship and archery. Lysandra never minded the training, as she liked the idea of being able to defend herself.

She dressed as quickly as she could in dark tan pants, brown boots, and a blue-grey shirt. She then grabbed her moss-colored cloak hanging on an old nail in the wall beside her door to wear later when making her deliveries for the bakery. Before leaving her room, she remembered she needed to do something with her hair, so she laid the cloak on her bed. She braided her brown hair into a half braid down the back. Then, with the loose hair, she divided it into two small braids down each side and used some string to tie all the braids together, holding them in place. It was the style she was most fond of, even if it may bother Gwyneth with her sometimes-messy braids since it was an elvish style.

She went to her nightstand and grabbed a necklace with a small pendant on it from a drawer underneath some fabric. Her mother gave her the pendant when she was ten years old and was told the hidden truth about her father and the destiny placed upon her shoulders.

Since then, there had not been a day when she had not worn it. It was a circular pendant with only the upper half of the dragon shown in the design. The dragon held a small, dark blue stone in its claws in front of its heart, and surrounding the magnificent creature was a nest of intricate geometric designs.

She'd studied the design of the pendant countless times, having some sort of inkling that it must hold some sort of importance, aside from being a gift from her father. She asked her mother and Gwyneth about it years ago. All they knew was that her father received it from someone known as Master Warlock of the order of sorcerers from Strometh Temple during a battle as he was dying. Other than that, her father had told her mother that it was just a simple trinket passed down between Master Warlocks for generations, using it as a reminder of what they and the sorcerers of the light were supposed to be for the people. A protector and a man of wisdom and power.

As she looked at it, Lysandra tested herself by remembering what she learned through the sorcerer's codex about the Master Warlocks.

A Master Warlock is the leader of the sorcerers. As the end of their life nears, they choose a new sorcerer to take the place and title. The position calls for them to guide, teach, and lead the noble sorcerers to stay in the light of good, of Meridia, to help protect and defend the innocent from the darkness of Keres and to ensure no one is to use or learn the dark arts of magic of the underworld, she thought.

She often wondered if her father was Master Warlock, since he had it before passing it on to her.

Lysandra put the necklace on before grabbing her cloak. She made her way downstairs as she tucked the pendant underneath her shirt to conceal it. Halfway down, she smelled the sweet aroma of the bakery starting up for the day. She loved Gwyneth's baking, for she could never tire of Elvish food.

She entered the kitchen to see Thallan standing in the entryway. He wore his uniform of brown leather boots that matched his pants with a blue tunic hidden underneath a brown leather vest and a green sleeveless hooded cloak over it. It was all held together by his belt, which held a sword and dagger. The green cloak had the Nathairian symbol of a creature called the grimog with an embroidered shield outline around it, showing his rank as knighted general. Other soldiers of the kingdom would have the claw and pawprint of the grimog painted on their armor, either on their chest or shoulder piece. His attire showed that he was prepared for battle, with his clothes, gauntlets, and a leather woven pauldron over his left shoulder that displayed the same symbol as his cloak.

His hair seemed to have gotten longer since the last time she saw him. It now hung just below his shoulders with half of it braided down the back. Lysandra took notice that his braid was far neater than her own.

Thallan stood watching his mother and Eleanora baking. They both wore simple gowns beneath already messy aprons. Gwyneth had her hair braided down her back and Eleanora had her hair in a braided bun.

"Tired of the castle food again?" asked Lysandra.

He turned and gave her a smirk.

"Just a little. I miss seeing my family," he said with a sigh. "There have been some disturbing things happening at the castle. Vaxar has been growing more impatient with the efforts of this war," he continued.

Lysandra had hoped he would have waited longer before talking about such things. She did her best to hide her irritated feeling so he would not notice. If he did, he would only stress to her how important it is to discuss such matters and then ramble on, and at some point, Lysandra would have tuned him out.

"Let his impatience grow. It just might cause him to act recklessly for once," said Gwyneth.

"Let's continue this conversation in the dining room for breakfast. Lysandra, help me carry some of this in there and

Thallan, be a dear and prepare the table as we make our way in there, please," said Eleanora, stopping the conversation.

Thallan grabbed plates and silverware and made his way into the room. The rest of them grabbed the food and followed him through the short, narrow hallway that connected the dining room to the large kitchen.

The house they live in doubled as the bakery that Gwyneth and Eleanora ran together. They gave Lysandra the job of delivering orders in the mornings and maintaining the front of the house just by the kitchen, where they had a small counter for when customers visited to buy any baked goods or place orders.

With Thallan working as the general, he earned plenty of money to build the house for them ten years ago. Before then, they were still in the cottage at the edge of the forest just outside of town.

The bakery provided the perfect cover for them all. It also gave them the ability to gossip with the other locals or overhear news that may be important to know.

They all sat down and filled their plates full of tomatoes, sliced ham, and bread with strawberry jam.

As they ate, Lysandra could not help but think. It was all she seemed to do when not training, studying, or working in the bakery. She picked up on her family's worries over the years and had grown to have the same fears as they did sometimes, along with self-doubt in her abilities with magic.

Thallan noticed Lysandra staring quietly at her plate as she slowly ate. He looked out the window and decided it was still early enough for him to spare a couple of hours before he would have to return to the castle.

"Lysandra, I have some time before I must return. We could do some combat training for a couple of hours, if you would like to," asked Thallan, hoping that would help perk up her mood.

"Sure. Although at some point, I would like a challenge. I wonder if you could spare Richard one day so he could visit," said Lysandra with a smirk on her face.

Thallan gave her a disapproving look. She chuckled at the expression on his face as she stood up and took her dishes to the kitchen. Once she knew she was out of sight, she let out a silent sigh and dropped the smile. She loved him dearly, but did not like how serious he was about all the training and preparing for a fight when all she ever did was lay low and hide.

She started getting her small satchel ready with some snacks and a canteen. Then she put on her cloak as Thallan finished his meal. Once he was done, they left the bakery and made their way towards the dense forest just outside of town as Gwyneth and Eleanora began baking the fresh orders for the day.

They had discovered a secret area many years ago alongside a river with a waterfall where they could safely practice archery and swordsmanship. Luckily for them today, they could use Thallan's horses to get there faster. No one in the town ever noticed or cared what they got up to because in this kingdom, unlike the Meador and Krubet kingdoms, woman may join the regiment if they wished as long as they could fight and had the skillset to be in the army. However, few women joined or even trained, as the kingdom still restricted women who join from achieving positions of power greater than men. The kingdom still considered men superior, unlike in Virwarin and Krogodo.

They rode on through the morning fog in the forest for roughly a half hour until they arrived at their little spot near the waterfall. They tied their horse to a couple of trees.

Lysandra loved visiting this secluded area simply because of its beauty. The river ran against a rocky terrain in a curve before straightening out and leading to a cliff where the twenty-five foot waterfall fell about a hundred feet away. Within the curve, a cove of water gave way to a small clearing. A perfect place with enough room for archery and sword fighting practice while having the safety of being hidden. Such a beautiful and tranquil area concealed within such a dark and dangerous kingdom.

The air was much colder next to the icy waterfall. There was a slight breeze that lifted the chill from the flowing water in their direction.

Beautiful fallen leaves littered the water's surface, adding color as they floated downstream. The trees reflecting in the water added more beauty to the serene cove. There was very little fog here, unlike in the forest. During the cold winters, the river and its waterfall froze, and thick, fresh white powder covered the frozen surface of the water.

Lysandra placed her bag down against a little bush next to a fallen tree. The color in her eyes changed to a dark blue as she muttered, "Levitaortia," in her mind. It was a simple levitation spell that was followed by the motion of her hand so she could lift the log into the air, revealing a small hole that contained a large bag. She used the same spell to lift the bag out of the hole and placed it next to the bush as she carefully motioned her hand and returned the log back to its place.

Once she was done with the levitation spell, her eyes returned to their natural color. With any sorcerer and certainly with her, the eyes will change into the color of that person's magic when using it. Each sorcerer has different colors and shades, though it is not uncommon for some to have the same. Magic flows through their body and when conjuring, the eyes show the flow of that magic. As for the colors, the sorcerers suspected that they resemble the soul.

Thallan watched her perform the spells with ease in astonishment, as he had not seen her use magic for quite some time. Lysandra had always preferred to practice in solitude without the judgmental comments of her family, as she already received that with practicing combat.

"You are most certainly getting stronger with your magic if you're able to perform two spells at once. I do not believe I have even seen Vaxar do that," he said.

"You probably just haven't noticed. And it's honestly not that difficult to do. Of course, it's easier when you do the same spell, but it's not that much harder when I do two different spells at once. Now, let's practice some fighting, unless you're wanting to try practicing some magic. I don't think you have the ability, but if you want to try, we can," she said.

Thallan chuckled. He then quickly pulled his sword from its sheath and immediately swung it towards her. Before he could hit her, she said in her mind, "Adaer," as she thought of her weapon, which rapidly levitated and flew to her hand in just enough time for her to block his attack. This stunned Thallan, causing him to lose his footing. His eyes widened as he worked to regain his balance and reposition his feet.

She had never mixed magic with her fighting before, at least to Thallan's knowledge. She practiced that alone as well, hoping to impress Thallan and gain his trust in her abilities.

"That was new," he exclaimed.

"Well, with all those stories you've told me of how Vaxar operates and fights, I figured it would be best if I learned how to combine my magic with a weapon. That way I can hopefully have a slight upper hand over him," she said.

She pushed off with her sword and quickly swung for his left calf, but he blocked the attack.

"I did not hear you say the spells, though. That was what really caught me off-guard," he said.

"I can perform the spells without needing to say them out loud. I have been able to do that...well for a long time now," she said.

Lysandra did partially lie to him, though. She used her magic by only thinking of the spell since she was very young and first started learning magic. She grew stronger in her ability to do so once she started practicing alone in her room or here beside the waterfall.

"Your skills certainly improved since the last time we practiced together. I am proud of you," he said.

"There's a lot more that I can do than just these simple spells. And besides, it has been quite a while since we last practiced," she said.

They continued with swords before switching to archery and then close-combat archery. After practicing that for a short time, they stopped for water, filling their canteens for a second time from the river.

"Let's switch back to swords. But this time, I want you to use your magic while fighting me. Do not hold back," he said.

"Are you sure? That would mean that there's a good chance I could beat you and knock you down into all this mud," she said.

"We shall see about that. Let us begin," he said.

If Lysandra has already been practicing her use of magic alongside swordsmanship, then I will help her become the best she can be. She is already as skillful a fighter as me, thought Thallan.

He swung for her and again, she magically brought the sword to her hands, but did not use it to block his attack. Instead, she quickly thought of the spell defenetta, blocking his attack with a magical shield. She tossed her bow and quiver against a bush as she readied herself.

Her quick reflexes shocked Thallan. He found it hard to contain a smile. He was immensely proud of her and how far she had come since she was a little girl, learning how to even hold a sword.

Their swords clashed together, first starting off as an ordinary swordfight, until Thallan thought he had the upper hand. Lysandra wanted the fight to feel like normal until the moment came for her to add magic to throw off her brother. She thought of the spell anambulo and pushed him back several feet with nothing but air as her free hand made the motion towards his middle. The sudden push threw him backward into a tree. The force of the spell knocked his breath from his lungs for a moment before once again charging back at her.

As he was about to get close, Lysandra gave him a small smirk as she thought of the spell arboradix. Then, unknowingly to Thallan, she controlled the roots arching above the surrounding ground to wrap around his ankles, causing him to fall onto his back. She used the other roots to grab his sword and drag it to a nearby tree out of his reach while keeping some roots to hold him down.

His eyes were wide as he looked up at Lysandra standing over him as he lay motionless on the muddy ground. Shock filled him as he realized how easily she had outsmarted him.

"All right...you win. I officially do not know if there is anything else that I can teach you. You have moved on beyond my skillset. All I can think of is to keep practicing whatever you just did," said Thallan.

Lysandra laughed. She let go of her focus on the spell and her eyes returned to their natural brown color instead of the magical dark blue. She helped him up as he wiped mud from his clothes.

"I am sure there is always something new to learn, especially from a wise old Elf," she said, laughing.

"Again, with the old jokes," he laughed. "I am not that old, as I am the youngest of my siblings. Now, I think it is about time we headed back to Holbrook. You have deliveries to make soon, and I must return to the castle," he continued.

Lysandra nodded and went to retrieve her bow and quiver from the bushes. She used her magic and returned her weapons to their hiding spot beneath the log. She could easily keep them in her room, but years ago Thallan insisted she keep them out here just in case someone with the right mind asked the right questions. Lysandra agreed then, not wanting to draw attention or argue with him. However, as time carried on, things changed and people in Holbrook believed she was loyal as possible to the Dark King, thanks to Thallan being the knighted general. People in the town suspected that Thallan had been training her after hearing of Thallan having the blacksmith make a sword for Lysandra, but the people only guessed that he was doing so to prepare her for joining the regiment and following in his footsteps.

"You know, despite your eyes magically glowing, I could not expect what spell you were to use or when it was going to happen. It is quite effective in putting worry into a person's mind as you fight them," he said as he mounted his horse.

"That's good to know, especially after I knocked you on the ground for once," she said.

Thallan could not help but hide his laugh.

"You are getting better but still have much to learn and practice. The world is rough and dangerous. I think you are almost ready but not yet. Keep practicing," said Thallan.

Lysandra mounted her horse, and they rode side by side, back towards town. Throughout the ride, Thallan did most of the talking, and she listened quietly. He talked to her about ways to improve and continue practicing using magic alongside the use of weapons. She secretly wished that she did not show him her new skillset because now it would lead to more practicing and not actually putting them to the test and getting more involved in the fight against the dark forces of the king and Vaxar.

As they arrived back at Holbrook, Thallan bid his good-byes as he made his way north towards the castle. She made her way to the bakery, passing by only a few people strolling in the early morning. In a couple more hours, the streets would be busy with people and merchants going about their day-to-day activities.

The smell of rain filled the air as clouds moved closer to the valley. She hoped that the rain would remain a light drizzle. At least until she was done with her morning deliveries. It was dreadful walking through the thick mud in the streets with a heavy downpour of rain. The air still felt as it did during the night as the clouds had kept the air cool and damp despite the moment of the morning sun peeking over the mountains before the thick clouds returned. She was happy that she at least got to see the sunshine upon the red and gold leaves in the valley and mountains.

Lysandra loved fall, with the colder temperatures and wonderful color changes of the world around her. She preferred the colder weather over the heat of the spring and summer months. Her favorite time of the year was after the harvest celebrations, when winter began. The soft, white snow always amazed her with its sparkling beauty. The cold, delicate powder that concealed dangers when combined with other forces of nature. She loved the feeling of being cold and eating warm food and drink, heating your body alongside the comfort of a roaring fire. Lysandra longed to have the fire roaring in her room beside her as she would sit in her chair and look out the window to watch the snow fall ever so lightly upon the ground. She had many fond memories of fall and winter where her worries seemed to disappear with the soothing weather.

3

THE ATTACK

Lysandra walked throughout the town, making her deliveries while trying to keep the parcels dry and warm in the steady drizzle of rain. With the weather, she was glad that many of the people she delivered to did not bother her with the daily gossip. The older couple on the edge of town insisted she hurry home and expressed their concern for her health working in the cold, wet air.

Her last delivery of the day was to the family who managed the stable in the town. The father and his two children were outside in their cloaks, shoveling fresh hay in the barn.

"Good morning. I'm sorry it took me a little longer than usual to get your delivery to you. We had a few extra orders this morning. Though I believe that your order is still quite warm," she said to the owner of the stable.

He stopped shoveling the hay as she approached. Lysandra handed him his order that contained two loaves of bread and four muffins wrapped nicely in some flour covered cloth.

"That is quite all right. Allows us time to work up an appetite. It sure smells good. Thank you, Lysandra," he replied.

"Yes! Fresh bread!" yelled a little girl as she ran up to them.

She was about to reach out and grab the bread, but her father stopped her in her tracks.

"Not yet, little one," he said as his son approached to hear what his sister was yelling about. "You and your brother will have some with lunch after we finish shoveling this hay," he continued.

They both let out a whine of complaint, but the father gave them a stern look.

"You know, if you hurry and get your chores done, the sooner you get to eat the fresh bread while it is still warm," said Lysandra.

The kids looked at each other and sprinted back to the piles of hay, working to finish their chores as fast as they could.

"I might have to use that trick from time to time just to get them to help around here. So, I may place some orders more often," he said, laughing.

"I'm sure it will work every time."

"You should hurry and get home before this weather worsens. As soon as we have this hay moved, we'll all be spending the day inside. It looks like a more serious storm is on the way. I wouldn't want you or my children to get sick from this weather. Thank you for the lovely bread, as always, Lysandra. Get home safe," he said before taking the bread inside his home.

She left the stables and walked through the center of town, heading back home. More people were out now. Luckily, no one seemed to acknowledge her as she walked through the town. She also noticed the increase in the quads that consist of a small group of four high ranking soldiers walking throughout town along with some on horseback that looked to be heading towards the western trails in the mountains out of town.

As long as they don't seem focused on me, I'm fine. But I wonder why there are so many of them here in town and why quads are heading towards the trail, she thought to herself as she continued walking.

She turned down a street off the main road to get home a little quicker. A young woman suddenly came rushing out of a cottage. Her hair was in a tangled mess and her clothes wrinkled, with her dress falling off her shoulders. Then an older man ran out chasing after the woman, who looked to be in his forties, and was only wearing loose pants, boots and no shirt.

Lysandra paused for a moment to assess the situation. She wanted to make sure the man had no weapons on him before approaching.

"Leave me alone! I told you no, Declan!" yelled the woman.

"Get back here, woman! I did not say we were done," said the man, apparently named Declan.

"I am not your woman! Leave me alone!"

The man grabbed hold of the young woman. She tried to pull away, but his grip was too strong for her.

"Get your filthy hands off of me!"

"Shut up, Briella! Remember your place, woman! I have chosen you and it is your duty to serve me," said Declan, gripping her arm tighter.

Lysandra had to think of something quickly, and then she remembered the dagger that she always kept in her right boot.

"The woman said no! Now kindly let her go or else," said Lysandra.

Declan turned towards Lysandra and let out a small chuckle.

"What are you going to do, baker girl? Have your rotten Elf brother arrest me? He won't. It seems that I must remind you two women that in this kingdom, you are beneath a man. Whether it is out in the open or in the bedroom," he said.

"That so? I know about the status of hierarchy of authority, but I haven't heard of anything going beyond that. Women are respected here, unlike the pit you crawled out of," said Lysandra.

Declan let out a growl of anger. With his grip still on Briella's arm, he flung her out of the way, causing her to fall to the ground. He then walked towards Lysandra, ignoring Briella's cries of pain.

"I ought to teach you manners, girl! It appears no one has taught you how to respect a man."

"I would give you respect, but I do not see a man in front of me."

"Declan, don't!" yelled Briella.

Declan raised his right hand to slap Lysandra across the face. He swung, but Lysandra grabbed hold of his arm with her left hand. Then, with her left foot, she swung it behind the back of his right calf. Lifting his leg up with her foot, she knocked him backwards into the ground. As he fell, her right hand grabbed the dagger out of her boot. He landed in the mud with a thud, causing his head to bounce. Lysandra placed her left knee on his groin as she brought the dagger to his throat.

"Now, you listen carefully. You will apologize to... I'm sorry, what was your name?" asked Lysandra as she looked up at the woman.

"Bri-Briella," she said.

"Thank you, Briella," she replied before turning her attention back to Declan. "You will apologize to Briella for your absurd behavior this morning. You will never touch or harm another woman ever again. If you do, I will personally make sure that you lose something very dear to you," she said as she placed more weight on his groin.

"Also, I am sure that my brother, who is the Master General Knight might I add, would gladly lock you up should you continue to attack the women of this town," continued Lysandra as she adjusted her knee again.

He winced in pain but had nothing to say, mouth opening and closing like a fish on a dock.

"Now, if you understand what I have just said, I recommend you apologize to Briella right now."

He made a slight nod, with the knife still pressed against his throat.

"I-I'm sorry, Bri-Briella," he said.

Lysandra put all her weight on her knee before standing up. As soon as she took a step back from Declan, he began trying to get up. He said nothing to either of them except moaning in pain as he tried walking away, hunched over.

"Are you all right, Briella? Did he hurt you?" asked Lysandra.

"I'm okay. Just a little shaken up. Thank you for saving me from him. I don't know what came over him this morning. I was just returning something my father had borrowed from him. He was always so nice," said Briella.

"Some men are just pigs. They try to hide it, but eventually the truth will come out. You should go home and get some rest. Stay safe when you're out here alone."

Briella nodded and began to walk in the opposite direction from Lysandra. As she walked down the road, before she turned down the next street that led to her home, Lysandra looked behind her to make sure that the man did not come back out and attempt to follow the young woman.

Thankfully, Briella was already reaching the main road with nobody following her.

Lysandra made it home just in time before the rain began to pour. As soon as she stepped through the front door, her mother grabbed hold of her, pulling her in quickly while also slamming the door shut. Eleanora looked through the window beside the door before turning around.

"What took you so long to get back home?" asked Eleanora in a panic.

"I had more deliveries than usual, you knew that. What's wrong?"

"In a moment. First, hang up your cloak and go into the kitchen. I want you to stay beside Gwyneth for the rest of the day."

"Mom, what's wrong?" asked Lysandra again, while she hung up her cloak on the rack against the wall behind the door.

Eleanora grabbed hold of her daughter and led her to the kitchen, where Gwyneth was still working.

"All right, I'm in the kitchen. Will someone tell me what is going on?"

"Someone attacked Vaxar in the forest on his way back to the valley. Richard told us just as he was passing by, heading quickly to the forest trails to find Vaxar," said Eleanora.

"Vaxar sent word out for aid. He only reported being attacked. We don't know who, but someone somehow injured him. Given that he is still alive, whoever attacked him is sure to be dead," said Gwyneth.

"We want you to stay here for the time being, near Gwyneth, until things calm down. We are afraid that Vaxar may be on edge and will be on the lookout for anyone or anything while he is back," said Eleanora.

"No arguments here. I agree with you both," said Lysandra.

"We already have the excuse, though, that you are learning some baking skills while I'm resting from falling sick," said Eleanora.

"That should work. It's believable, and people will be fine with picking up their orders. After all, it is a small town," said Lysandra.

"Good. Why don't you get cleaned up? I'll have some lunch ready for us in a few," said Gwyneth.

The rest of the day went by quietly. Very few people visited to purchase or place orders with all the rain, which worked out perfectly for Lysandra as Gwyneth started teaching her some of the easier recipes to bake. By late afternoon, Lysandra had learned how to make loaves of bread and rolls. By the third batch, Lysandra was making them on her own as Gwyneth made a few pastry orders for the next day.

Lysandra was cleaning the front counter when she heard a commotion from outside. She walked up to the window and adjusted the curtain to peek out. Several soldiers, some on horseback and some on foot, passed by. Following the quad of four high ranking soldiers, Vaxar appeared. Lysandra felt herself freeze in place, fear flooding her as her pulse quickened. Vaxar looked directly at her. The left side of his face was bloody from a large gash that started just above his left eye and stretched down to the middle of his cheek in a nearly straight line. There were two smaller gashes, one near his nose and the other on the far side of his cheek. Lysandra felt like he looked at her for an eternity, but his gaze was only brief.

Gwyneth approached Lysandra and laid a hand on her shoulder.

"What is it?" she asked.

Lysandra couldn't find her voice to answer. Gwyneth peeked around her and saw the dreaded sorcerer. She immediately pulled Lysandra away from the door.

"Get away from there," she whispered harshly.

Gwyneth peeked outside once more. Vaxar was already halfway down the street, with several soldiers following behind him.

"What were you doing? If he had sensed you, I fear you would be dead right now. You are very lucky that he didn't. I keep telling Thallan that we should leave this awful place. It is too dangerous for you, but that darn boy listens to your father's advice more than my advice these days. Go see if your mother needs help with anything. And stay away from windows for the rest of the day while you are at it too, please," said Gwyneth.

Lysandra, still quiet from seeing Vaxar, did as she was told and headed towards the dining room to help her mother package up some orders for tomorrow.

The next day, as Lysandra cleaned up after baking the last batch of rolls and Gwyneth prepared dinner, someone knocked loudly on the door moments before it opened. Gwenyth grabbed Lysandra's arm to pull her closer.

A sigh of relief escaped from Lysandra when she saw Thallan walk around the corner.

"Hello! Could I and a friend join for dinner?"

"Of course, you and I'm assuming Richard are always welcome," said Gwyneth.

"Actually, it's not Richard. He is on his return from the forest. May not get back until late," said Thallan.

A figure, face covered by their muddy hood, appeared from around the corner and stood by his side. The person reached up and removed their hood. A woman with dark red hair gave Gwyneth and Lysandra a smile.

"This is Valda. She is visiting from Krogodo. I was hoping she could stay here until Vaxar leaves. If that is all right, Mother?"

"Of course, my dear. It is an honor to meet you, General Valda. We know of your strength and valor against the Nathairian forces, from what Thallan has told us. You are welcome to stay here as long as you need."

"Thank you. It is an honor to meet you all. Especially you, Lysandra. No need to worry. I am an ally, and your secret is safe with me," said Valda.

Lysandra gave her a smile.

"It is an honor to meet you, Valda," said Lysandra.

"Dinner will be ready in a little over a half hour. Introduce Valda to Eleanora. I believe she is in the dining room getting a fire going. Lys, you might need to give her a hand. I think the firewood got wet in the rain earlier," said Gwyneth as she returned to cooking.

Thallan and Valda followed Lysandra through the small hallway to the dining room. Eleanora was struggling to get the fire started.

"Mother, I can get this going. Thallan is here, and he has someone to introduce you to."

"Oh, thank you, dear. That wood isn't soaking wet, but it's putting up a good fight," said Eleanora as she stood.

"Eleanora, this is Valda. She will stay here for a few days, or at least until Vaxar leaves the valley again. I asked Mother, and she said it was all right. I hope it is with you as well," said Thallan.

"Oh, yes, of course. You are more than welcome to stay

here, Valda. It is so nice to meet you. We have heard many good things about you from Thallan."

"Thank you. It's an honor to meet you," said Valda.

"Make yourselves comfortable. I am going to go help Gwyneth with dinner," said Eleanora.

Thallan grabbed both his and Valda's cloaks and left to hang them on the hooks by the front door. Valda sat down on one of the chairs by the fireplace.

"Need a hand?" she asked.

"No, thank you. This wood is just being stingy. I think all it needs is a touch of magic, but don't tell Thallan. He gets bugged when I do simple tasks through magic. And luckily for me he is not in the room at this moment," said Lysandra with a chuckle.

Lysandra turned to the fireplace. In her mind, she spoke the spell, "Pirocaust," while focusing her attention on the wood. A spark at the center of the firewood ignited the wet wood into a roaring fire. Lysandra couldn't help but smile, even though it was one of the most basic spells she had learned.

"I could have gotten the fire going with no magic. You must not always rely on it," said Thallan, breaking the silence.

"I thought you liked me to practice my magic as much as I can?"

Valda chuckled. "She has a point. And besides, there was no way you could have gotten the fire going. Unless you doubt what Eleanora had said about the struggle of starting the fire as well?"

Lysandra laughed. Thallan gave her a scornful look, quickly followed by a smile.

"Of course I don't," he said.

The three of them sat in front of the fireplace.

"Lys, would it be okay if you shared your bedroom with Valda for a few days?"

"Yeah. I was already thinking about sharing my room with you, anyway. You can have my bed, and I can sleep on the rug with some extra blankets."

"Oh no, I'm not kicking the sorceress out of her own bed. I can take the floor. I am used to it with the amount of traveling I have been doing. Plus, your floor and rug are going to feel amazing compared to the cold, hard, rocky ground out there."

"Are you sure? I really don't mind. I've slept on that rug so much over the years when studying up on my magic."

"Absolutely. You stay in your bed. I'll take the rug," said Valda with a smile.

"All right, but we can trade spots anytime if you need something more comfortable."

"Thank you, Lysandra."

They gave each other a sweet smile as Thallan chuckled at their brief argument.

"Dinner is ready, everyone! Thallan, can you come here, please? Darn wine is too high in the cabinet for either of us to reach. I think you stored it there anyway," yelled Gwyneth from the kitchen.

"Sorry! Your cabinets are always so full I didn't know where else to put it," said Thallan as he headed towards the kitchen.

Lysandra grabbed the silverware and plates from the pantry in the dining room and proceeded to set the table.

The others entered the dining room, hands filled with dishes of food containing cooked pork, potatoes, carrots, berries, and rolls. Everyone helped themselves as Thallan filled their glasses with wine. The crackling fire and scraping silverware filled the silence as they ate.

"Gwyneth, Eleanora, this meal is delicious. This is the best meal I have had in such a long time. Thank you so much," said Valda.

"You are very welcome, my dear. We are so glad you like it," said Gwyneth.

"You know, I may not want to leave this place. Everyone here is so kind, and the food... Words can't even fully describe how delicious it is," said Valda, as she ate a slice of pork.

Everyone laughed and continued eating their food. The room was silent for some time except for the scraping of silverware on the plates and the crackling of the fire.

"So, are you ever going to tell us what happened to Vaxar? Richard said something attacked him. I saw him walking through the streets past here and his face had a large wound," said Lysandra.

"He was... Wait, he was here?" asked Thallan.

"He was just walking by with soldiers all around him. Gwyneth was beside me the whole time. Clearly, he didn't sense my magic," said Lysandra.

"That may be, but still too dangerous having him that close. You were lucky."

"Yeah, I know. What exactly happened to him, though? Do you know who attacked him?"

Thallan gave her a stern look.

"Well, he oddly hasn't said who attacked him. I think maybe it wasn't a some*one* but a some*thing*, since it was in our forests."

"That's possible. If it was a person who attacked him, he would send every soldier to hunt them down if they got away. Unless he killed his attacker," said Valda.

"If he killed his attacker, wouldn't he have said that or at least boasted about it? Has he said nothing about the attack?" asked Lysandra.

"He has not. Not even to the King, who Vaxar told it was no worry and soon taken care of. Whatever that means. Vaxar has been acting odd, and has for sure been grumpier than usual," said Thallan.

"All we can do is speculate until more information reveals itself," said Gwyneth.

There was a moment of silence as everyone ate their dinner.

"We considered often of traveling to your Kingdom, if things ever got too dangerous here or Lysandra was ever discovered. So far, my husband's plan has proven to work well. Vaxar has not suspected her living under his nose as my husband stated," said Eleanora.

"It is a good idea. But in my opinion is too risky. If you ever change your minds away from the sorcerer's plan, it would be my honor to help you get to the safety of my Kingdom," said Valda.

"Thank you. After the close encounter with Vaxar, I am thinking of considering leaving this dreadful kingdom," said Eleanora.

"Of course," said Valda.

Once everyone finished dinner, Lysandra helped Gwyneth and Eleanora clean up. Thallan and Valda sat by the fireplace and talked for some time until the others returned.

"I should return to the castle before it gets too late. Thank you so much for dinner. I will inform you of when it would be safe for you to continue your journey, Valda. In the meantime, enjoy the wonderful baking and cooking from my family," said Thallan.

"Thank you, Thallan," said Valda.

Thallan gave his family hugs before leaving for the castle.

"Would it be all right if I took my things up to your room, Lysandra? I might also try to go to bed early to get some much-needed rest. Traveling to this little village is no easy trek," said Valda.

"Of course, the bedroom is up the stairs. Let me grab you a pillow and blankets, too," said Lysandra.

"With that said, it may be a good idea for us all to get some rest. It has been a long day," said Eleanora.

"I agree. I am exhausted. Have a good night, everyone. Valda, if you need anything, do not hesitate to ask," said Gwyneth.

"Thank you. Have a good night."

Valda followed Lysandra to her room. As Valda set her things down beside the desk, Lysandra grabbed several blankets and a couple of spare pillows.

"Are you sure you're fine with sleeping on the floor? I really don't mind lending you the bed while you are here."

"No, you sleep in your bed. I will be perfectly fine on the floor. Trust me. It is no bother, though you are very sweet and kind for offering."

"Of course, but if you change your mind, I will be more than happy to let you have a much more comfortable sleeping arrangement."

Valda laughed. "I will let you know."

"Good. I am going to give you a moment to change into sleep wear...that is, if you have any."

"I do, but there is no need for you to leave the room unless you want to. I grew up with two sisters. Really is no bother to me changing in front of another woman."

"Oh, all right... I think I will still give you some privacy, though."

"I'll be quick. I will swap places with you so you can change to your sleep wear as well."

"All right. Thank you."

After changing, Lysandra climbed into bed. It was a new

feeling having someone else in her room. So far, she liked Valda very much. Lysandra was planning a way to learn as much as she could from a warrior and general from another kingdom.

Valda fell fast asleep as soon as her head hit her pillow. Lysandra fell asleep sometime later after planning and imagining how the next days might go until her new friend had to leave.

4

A NEW FRIENDSHIP

While everyone was still sleeping the next morning, Lysandra quietly changed into her usual clothes and cloak. After getting dressed, she braided half of her hair, as usual. Lysandra was not too worried about how nice the braid might look since she was heading out to the forest, and she could hear the drizzle of rain hitting the outside of her window. She wanted to sneak in some training before working in the bakery.

After gathering her things, she quietly opened her door to not disturb Valda. Lysandra tip-toed as lightly as she could down the wooden stairs that would let out a small squeak with almost every other step. She had done this so often that she knew where to avoid stepping to not wake up someone, most likely Gwyneth, with her heightened Elf hearing.

Lysandra made her way to the kitchen to grab some provisions and her water canteen. She stuffed them in her pack, then left through the back door.

The sun had yet to peek over the mountaintops, but

there was just enough light for her to see her way through town and into the woods towards the little cove to practice.

The air was cold enough for Lysandra to see her breath faintly in the air. The mostly broken clouds, which had hung over the valley all night, let the frigid chill enter the valley. A low fog blanketed the ground as Lysandra traveled through the forest. The fall leaves were in full bloom with their colors of fire dancing on the tree branches.

As Lysandra approached the cove, she had a sudden feeling that she was being followed, hearing a subtle sound of the crunch of leaves. She knelt beside the fallen tree and sat her pack down next to the bushes. Saying the spell, "Levitaortia," in her mind, she ever so slightly lifted the tree an inch above the ground, giving enough room for her to reach down and use the spell adaer to bring the weapon into her hand. The sword in hand, she pulled it from underneath, and she gently lay the tree back down with her magic.

"I know you are out there. Reveal yourself. If you were an animal, you would have attacked me with my back turned," said Lysandra.

She faced the forest, taking a defensive stance with her sword, looking for where the person was hiding.

A figure stepped out from behind the tree and into the faint light, with their hands partially raised. It was none other than Valda, in similar clothes to the ones she had on the day before.

"I surrender," said Valda.

"General Valda! My apologies. I didn't know it was you," said Lysandra.

Lysandra used the spell adaer to bring the rest of her weapons out of the little hole towards her pack before carefully placing the log back to the ground. Valda noticed the flash of magic color in Lysandra's eyes.

"I am a light sleeper, so when I heard you getting ready this morning and figured you were up to something, I pretended to be asleep. I wasn't sure what you were up to and wanted to make sure you were safe," said Valda.

She paused for a moment as she glanced at the log and then at the bag of weapons.

"However, it looks like you can handle yourself. I assume this must be where you can safely practice?"

"It is. This is where Thallan started taking me years ago to train and practice magic. It's tucked far away from any trails and close to this waterfall that hides a tiny cave behind it, if I ever need a quick hiding spot. It's the perfect place."

"I don't think you could find a better place. Quite a gorgeous little cove, too."

Valda walked around, looking about the area until she stood beside Lysandra's gear.

"Lysandra, would you mind if I join you in your training today?"

"It would be an honor to learn from you, General Valda!"

"Great! And you don't have to call me General. You can just call me Valda."

They both removed their cloaks, draping them over the log. Lysandra walked towards the shallow water of the little cove, giving space between Valda and herself. Valda removed her sword from its sheath and turned to face Lysandra. They stood a few feet away from each other, swords at the ready.

Lysandra made the first move to strike Valda's shoulder. Valda parried, then pivoted as she stepped away, putting space between them. Valda's speed surprised Lysandra. Advancing, Valda feinted an attack on the left, then swung her sword to the right. Lysandra sidestepped, using her sword to deflect Valda's attack.

They continued to spar for a while longer, Lysandra blocking nearly all of Valda's swings until Valda surprised her.

Valda swung her sword at Lysandra's shoulder. As Lysandra blocked, their swords clashed, and Valda pushed forward, bringing their faces within inches of each other. Lysandra fought to keep her focus this close to Valda. Valda knew she had the element of surprise. She used her foot and wrapped it behind Lysandra's leg, holding her steady for a quick moment before she pulled on the back of Lysandra's leg up and forwards, causing her to fall backwards. Valda kept the force on the swords until Lysandra fell. Lysandra fell hard onto her back, knocking her head against the cold, wet sand on the riverbank. Lysandra did not have time to react to the blow and think of a way to defend herself as Valda had already knelt, straddling her with the sword against her neck and a smile curling up one side of her mouth.

"You're good. But always expect the unexpected. Always maintain focus and strength in a fight. Also, don't give them any signs of weakness. They'll be looking for that as you search for theirs," she said before removing the sword as she stood up.

Valda extended her hand to help Lysandra up. Lysandra rubbed her head before wiping off some of the sand. She knew that for the first time in a long while, she would have some bruises from training.

Valda noticed Lysandra rubbing her head a little as they both walked towards their bags to grab their water canteens.

"Is your head all right?"

"Yeah. I'm fine. Just a slight bump, nothing to be worried about."

"Good. I didn't mean to knock you down that hard."

"It's all right. It's good practice. As Thallan tells me,

'The enemy will not be your friend. They will do whatever it takes to kill you.'"

"He's not wrong. However, we are sparring, and it does not need to be that aggressive."

"That is also true. I guess he has the training more on the aggressive side."

"Why don't we change it up a little? Thallan told me last night that you had recently surprised him by weaving magic into your fighting. I would like to see your skills there, if you're all right with that?"

"Sure. I need to practice more using my magic alongside combat. However, between you and me, I was holding back some with Thallan."

"And you still knocked him on his ass!" she laughed. "Then I really look forward to seeing how powerful and skillful you are. So, please don't hold back on me. I have seen what Vaxar can do in battle, as well as your father. Neither of them combines magic with combat."

They both stepped back to the open area beside the cove. This time Valda went on the offensive, charging Lysandra. "*Arboradix*," Lysandra thought in her mind and used a vine to grab onto Valda's foot while Lysandra swung towards her chest. Valda dodged the swing, rolling on the ground, causing the vine to twist tightly around her foot even more. She slammed her sword down on the vine to cut herself free. Once she was back on her feet, facing Lysandra, Valda wore a smile like that of a child when having fun.

Nearly every time Lysandra attacked or blocked, she used the vine spell or the spell anambulo to send a controlled gust of wind to lift Valda slightly off the ground and throw her back a few feet. Every time, she recovered quickly and continued with another attack.

Valda quickened the pace of her attacks, along with the

intensity. After a few quick blocked strikes from Valda's attacks, Lysandra slightly lost her footing as she blocked the latest strike. Valda took notice of the slight stumble.

Valda aimed her swing towards Lysandra's middle. As her sword moved, she had her foot once again knock out Lysandra's dominant leg. Lysandra fell onto her back harder than before. Valda swung downward. Lysandra instinctively used the spell miraculum, creating a translucent blue shield that stopped Valda's strike in an instant.

Valda stood shocked, with the sword resting on the magical shield after hitting it. Lysandra smiled. She controlled the shield to push Valda off, flying into the air and landing in the river. Valda, still in shock, got up and looked towards Lysandra with wide eyes.

"Well, that was unexpected. You, my friend, are most certainly skilled with your magic. You are more than ready for battle if you can stand your ground against me. It would be an honor to fight by your side."

Lysandra couldn't hide the smile from the confidence she was feeling from Valda's compliment. "I'm sure there are a few things I need to practice on some more. Since you knocked me on my back twice."

"Ha! Twice. That's better than all the men I have trained back in Krogodo. You can only practice so much before you're forced into battle. The genuine test and greatest practice are fighting the enemy head on. You will surely grow further in strength and skill then. Not to mention catching the enemy by surprise with what you just did here today."

"Thank you, Valda."

"Of course! And thank you for the honor of sparring with you. That was the most fun I've had in a while."

"Well, I'm afraid that the fun must come to an end. The sun is just above the mountains now, which means it's time to be getting back to the bakery. I must be back before it opens to help with chores."

"Of course."

Lysandra placed her weapons back in their bag before using her magic to raise the log.

"Why don't you take your weapons home? I believe this kingdom, like mine, does not frown upon women fighters. There is no need to keep them hidden all the way out here. If someone sees them and questions them, you can simply tell them they belong to Thallan. People will believe it because they see you as his family."

"You make a fair point. It is probably time I keep a sword at home with me from now on, anyway. Got so used to keeping them here, I never considered otherwise."

They gathered their belongings. Before leaving the cove, they used the river to help wash off the thick mud from their clothes and boots and dusting sand from their hair. Once they were mostly mud free, they began their quick journey back to the little town of Holbrook. They should be dry from the water and mud by the time they arrived at the bakery.

They walked in silence through the forest for a short time. Most of the fog had faded away. Though the air remained cold, it felt refreshing to them after working up a sweat.

Finally, Lysandra summoned her courage. "Valda, there is something I would like to ask you."

"Yeah? You can ask me anything. Can't imagine being cooped up in that village of yours for your whole life. Ask away."

"You mentioned earlier about knowing how my father fights. Have you met him?"

"Oh! Yes, I have met him. I first met him many years ago when I was still training to be the warrior that I am now. I had never really gotten to know him, though, until the short time that we worked together a couple of years ago. He is a kindhearted man with a great deal of courage and bravery. He is quite good with magic, but between you and me, I think you're more skilled."

"Hopefully, one day, I will get the chance to meet him," she said with a small smile.

"It must have been difficult growing up without a father. I'm sure you two will have the chance to meet."

"May I ask about the time you two worked together?"

"Oh, of course. Ah, what a great story, too. He came to Krogodo, seeking a ship to sail him to Krubet. He received a message that Vaxar and a small army were there to take the kingdom. My queen and king immediately granted him a ship and entrusted me to lead the army of soldiers by your father's side to help Krubet against that evil man. It was my first ever mission as a leader of other soldiers."

So, my father has traveled outside of Krogodo? I thought he only hid there and never left, thought Lysandra.

"How long did he stay in Krogodo before traveling elsewhere? I thought he was living there."

"I'm not sure. He remained in Krogodo until he grew tired of Vaxar trying to get through our forces, trying to reach him."

Valda thought to herself for a moment.

"I think he may have only lived in Krogodo for a year or two before leaving. Krarick has an old friend from my kingdom, a soldier. They knew each other from before that war among the sorcerers. They developed a plan to keep Vaxar busy. Krarick gave his friend some sort of magic powder and sent him off to Gragon, under Vaxar's nose, and then used that powdery substance. I remember something about it, helping his friend pretend to be Krarick to draw Vaxar away from Gragon to chase after the false Krarick. Since then,

Krarick and his friend have been playing a game of cat and mouse with Vaxar across the lands, keeping him occupied and away from you."

"Vaxar hasn't discovered my father's trick?"

"I don't think so. Krarick has been trying to distract Vaxar from Krubet, but he has not fallen for your father's trap. Krarick suspects Vaxar is after something hidden within Krubet, if he's ignoring your father."

"Any idea what it could be?"

"No, but we're sure it isn't a good thing if he's so focused on it."

They walked through the dense forest, making their way to the path to take back to the village. A light drizzle of rain fell as a slight cool breeze from the oncoming storm gave them a sudden chill, pulling their cloaks closer to themselves.

"Anyway, the story of your father and I working together. One scout working with Krarick saw Vaxar's forces heading towards the mountains near Krubet kingdom. My king sent me along with some of our forces to help Krarick fend him off," she said, pausing for a moment to drink water from her canteen.

"As Vaxar's forces began their attack on the town, Sunvale, near the palace of Krubet, Krarick noticed Vaxar wasn't doing a full attack on the town and that he was nowhere in sight. We realized the attack was a distraction. I sent some scouts out to search for Vaxar, and they discovered him with a small force of soldiers traveling alongside the Obsidian Mountains. He appeared to be trying to go around the kingdom. Krarick and I took some soldiers to cut him off."

"So, Vaxar was trying to attack the palace?"

"No, he wasn't after the kingdom at all. As we got closer and saw for ourselves, Vaxar was heading towards the mountain directly."

"The mountains? That makes no sense."

"That's what I was thinking. To this day, I still wonder why. I suspect something is hidden there. Anyway, Krarick was very smart and had our archers head up the mountain off to the side, away from Vaxar and his troops to get some higher ground and start firing upon them. As the battle began, Vaxar was throwing balls of fire at us. In fact, I missed seeing his first fireball, and Krarick saved me from being hit by pushing me out of the way."

I think I remember Thallan saying that Vaxar loves using fire-balls in fights, thought Lysandra.

"Then, out of nowhere, Vaxar created a powerful gust of wind that threw us all, even his own men, into the forest at the mountain's edge, pelting us with dirt and branches as he quickly ran further up the slope. Krarick got back onto his feet faster than I could. He used his magic to protect us both, along with a few of my men from some of the large branches breaking off that nearly fell upon us.

"Once the burst of wind subsided, Krarick chased after Vaxar. Later, your father mentioned ancient tales of dragons that used to live in the Obsidian Mountains. Krarick worried that there may be some dragon magic Vaxar was after, but he was vague on that point when explaining the situation of keeping Vaxar away from what he's searching for."

"Were you able to catch up to Vaxar?"

"We were right on his tail until that rat turned around and dragged the coming rainstorm over our heads. It made it hard to see where Vaxar was standing. Luckily, I could see Krarick running ahead, so I followed right behind him. I figured he was using magic or something and could see Vaxar."

"He most likely was. There are some spells that could help with seeing through a storm."

Valda nodded. "We followed Vaxar to a large cave.

Krarick told me to stay outside in case Vaxar might slip past him and try to head back out. So, I had my bow ready with an arrow notched. They were in there for only a few minutes before Vaxar ran out."

Lysandra's eyes widened in surprise as they continued walking, with Holbrook almost in sight.

"Before he could start using his magic, I had shot as many arrows towards him as I could. Then I realized that none of them had hit him. He stopped every arrow I had shot. They were just floating in the air, still pointing at him, but they quickly changed their direction. Before I could have time to react, the arrows were already flying towards me. I got an arrow right here in my right shoulder and one skimmed past my abdomen as I attempted to dodge the others," she said as she pointed to where the scars would be under her clothes. "I fell to the ground and hit my head hard after being hit by one of my arrows. Next thing I know, I'm waking up in the town, Sunvale, with Krarick sitting in a chair in the corner of the room, asleep."

"What happened to Vaxar?"

"Annoyingly, the rat got away. But he failed to get whatever he was searching for."

"Thank you for telling me."

"Of course. I'm grateful for your father saving me and for all the help he has given. He has sacrificed much in the fight against the Dark King and Vaxar. Not to mention, I always enjoy telling the tales of my past battles. I am also both grateful and honored for the chance of befriending Krarick's daughter."

"I am honored to befriend a courageous general."

Valda gave Lysandra a smile.

When they arrived at the little bakery, Valda returned to the dining room beside the lit fireplace as Lysandra got things ready for her daily tasks. She was not looking forward to her day of delivering orders to those who have grown to be rude to her more recently. They received no word from Thallan of when Vaxar was planning to leave the Kingdom to return to the battlefield. They knew based on his routines, if he was not set on leaving, then he would be at the castle. He rarely ever passes through town, preferring the trails outside the town closer to the mountainsides.

Throughout the day, as Lysandra made her deliveries, Valda tried her best as their guest to help in the bakery. However, baking was not one of her skillsets. Valda nearly ruined several batches of pastries while trying to help with the baking. Once Gwyneth had enough of trying to teach her, she instructed her to help Lysandra by wrapping and preparing the baked goods for delivery when Lysandra came back to deliver another round of pastries and bread to customers.

Lysandra escaped to her room when the day ended, diligently memorizing every spell in her sorcerer's codex. Valda, bored from the lack of excitement in running a bakery, tried to turn in for the night early, only to find Lysandra studying.

"Surely you must know all those spells by now."

"I do, but it doesn't hurt to always study. I want to make sure that I am more than confident with remembering anything I may need if I'm ever in any kind of trouble."

"Would you like some help? I was going to turn in early for the night, simply because I was bored. I am not used to the sort of excitement found in a bakery."

"Sure. I'm not sure, though, how much more exciting this will be than the bakery."

She had had no one to help her with studying her spells and potions for a long time. Since her family knew little about magic, they never offered to help after the few times they tried when she was young. Gwyneth would try with the little she knew. Elves only know herbal magical remedies and slight elemental magic. Like humans, only some Elves are born with full magical abilities and become sorcerers, training and living in the Strometh Temple. Since the Nightshadow War, there are no Elf sorcerers alive. They stopped, though, because of the challenge it created by trying to understand magic enough to help her practice it.

Lysandra handed the book to Valda. She looked at the black leather cover bearing intricate geometric designs with the engraved lines crossing over one another on the entire cover. The pages looked old but were deceiving as Valda, initially trying to be delicate with them, soon discovered they were in fact as strong as fresh paper. She flipped a few pages before landing on a spell to test Lysandra.

"All right, let's start with this one," she said as she scanned the page. "Explain the details of the spell, anam... anambulo."

"It is a spell used to control a burst of wind to throw someone back at a distance."

"Correct. May I ask you something before we continue?"

"Of course."

"With using these spells, such as anambulo, are you able to control the intensity of the spell, or is it just how powerful the spell is?"

"I can control all the spells. For instance, with that spell I used on you this morning and on Thallan the other day. Both times I controlled the wind so as not to throw you too far back or too harshly."

"Interesting. I noticed you can conjure magic or spells without saying them out loud. Your father and Vaxar can do that as well. However, I noticed it was only with some spells. I'm guessing it was the less complicated ones. Although, both use their hands to control the magic. But as I saw today, you seemed to do it with just your mind. I thought that was impressive."

"I hardly use my hands with magic. I just simply think of the spell I want to use and imagine what I want it to do."

"That would take a great deal of focus then! Does Thallan understand how powerful you are? I have gotten the impression from him of the importance to protect you from everything and that you are not ready to fight Vaxar."

"He has always been protective of me. All of them have, really. I feel like I am ready, but I have my doubts because of how they respond to my request to take part in the fight."

"Hmm. I may have to be subtle and tell Thallan it's time to let you take charge in this fight. After all, the prophecy says that it is you who defeats the evil forces, not them. I hope I am there when you prove them wrong and show them your strength."

"Thank you."

"If I may ask, why do your eyes change color when you use your magic? I noticed yours changed and I've seen Krarick's as well, though his were green."

"I'm not entirely sure. From my understanding, magic just simply reveals itself a little through the eyes. Magic is constantly flowing inside me, and I think it's one way for magic to be visible to a person when I tap into it. In relation to the different colors and their meanings, my only guess is that it must represent either our personality or souls. Could also be the level of power, but I am not sure. The book I have doesn't cover that subject very well."

We shall ask Krarick one day, then. He may know the answer. Shall we continue studying?

Lysandra nodded. Valda continued helping her study the magic of the sorcerer's codex for another hour, well after the sun had set. Then Valda asked Lysandra to light the candles with her magic to practice. Valda had always been curious about magic and enjoyed her evening learning things from Lysandra.

Lysandra also enjoyed having a friend eager and excited about magic and was more than willing to help her study.

5

JOURNEY TO BELLEHAVEN

A few days later, a bird arrived with a note from Richard informing Valda that Vaxar had left the kingdom and advised her to wait to leave till the next day. Not long after receiving the letter, Valda checked through her supplies and began preparing for her journey.

The next morning, dark thunderclouds blanketed the valley, covering the peeking rays of sunlight above the mountains. The air was crisp with the light drizzle of rain. Lysandra's room was lit by candlelight alone.

Valda was gathering her things and preparing for her travel with Thallan towards the Cinder Outpost between Nathair Kingdom and the Gragon Kingdom. She packed the last of her things as she found a letter in the small side pocket of her pack.

"Lysandra, I almost forgot that I have this for you. Just before I started my journey here, your father sent me a letter to give this parchment to you. You can also read the letter if you like. He heard I was traveling here," said Valda.

With the letter in hand, Lysandra struggled to control

her shaking from nervousness and excitement about what it contained.

As Lysandra read the parchment that contained a spell, Valda removed a brown leather necklace hidden beneath her clothing. The necklace had a pendant of a small black arrow with thin brown leather wrapped around its shaft.

"Here Lysandra. When I was younger, a loved one owned it, but he died in battle a few years ago, and I have worn it ever since. I have always kept it with me, so I'm sure ownership will clarify it as myself. Would that communication spell should still work with this, if you need to reach me?"

"It should. But this is valuable to you. I could not take something with so much meaning to you. Is there not something else that would work?"

"This is all I got. Think of it as holding on to it for me for safekeeping, just for a little while. I'll be back as soon as I take down the Cinder Outpost by Gragon Kingdom for Gragon soldiers to take back their home. I'll be back before you know it and then you can return it to me then."

Lysandra nodded in agreement as she held the necklace and parchment.

"Don't worry. I'll be back before you know it. I read the parchment and wanted you to have something you can use for that spell to reach me instantly, if you need anything."

Valda gave Lysandra an unexpected hug.

"Let's go see what you family has cooked for breakfast. Food always lightens the mood."

Lysandra quickly placed the items with her codex before following Valda downstairs. The smell of food welcoming them into the kitchen.

Thallan arrived as they ate breakfast.

"Vaxar is heading towards the Cinder Outpost. Apparently, he needs to speak to me and got word of me traveling to do an inspection of the outpost. It won't take him long to get to Cinder since he is currently at the Falcon Outpost. I suggest you stay in Bellehaven until I send word for you of when it is safe," said Thallan.

"Of course, that rat is going to the outpost. He better not stay there long," said Valda.

"He never stays long at any of the outposts. He's always on the move. Also, I'm afraid you're going to have to change into these."

He slid a large pack towards her. Valda knelt and opened the pack, revealing Nathairian armor. She looked at him, puzzled.

"Might I inquire why?"

"We will have a couple other soldiers traveling with us and one is quite loyal to the King's father and Vaxar. He is being transferred to the outpost since, apparently, he angered the Queen yesterday. I already have an excuse for you when it comes time to separate so you can stay in Bellehaven and not look suspicious to him. Also, your name shall be Elara, as I am sure he would recognize your true name."

"Fair enough. Just give me a moment to change into the armor."

Valda grabbed the large pack and made her way to the stairs to use Lysandra's room to change. She stopped halfway up.

"Lysandra, would you mind helping me get this armor on? Oh, and could you grab my pack that I left down there?"

"Of course."

Lysandra grabbed Valda's pack and followed her upstairs. Lysandra placed the pack on the bed.

"Let me change into one of my other shirts. I don't want to feel the cold metal of the chain mail through some holes in this worn one."

Valda grabbed a dark shirt from her pack. She laid the shirt on the bed before removing her cloak. She then took off her pauldrons and breastplate.

With her armor removed, she pulled off her worn shirt and placed it on top of her pack. Lysandra could not help but notice the number of scars on her back. She recognized the scar on Valda's shoulder from where the arrow hit her from the story that she told the day before. There were five other scars across her back, and when Valda turned with the shirt almost on, she saw a scar on her abdomen. Lysandra then noticed how toned Valda's arms and abdomen were. She had never seen a woman so fit and yet so beautiful, even with all the scars.

"Never seen so many scars on a woman before, have you?"

Lysandra shook her head, cheeks flushed as she looked at the ground.

"It's all right. Few don't. I've earned these fighting in battles. My only hope is you don't have to get this many to take down the Dark King and his sorcerer."

Lysandra helped Valda get into the armor once she changed into her other shirt.

How could such a beautiful woman have so many scars and still be fighting? How many times has she nearly died fighting in this war? Is this how she became a general? By earning those scars from battles? I wonder how many scars Thallan could have because of this war? Could he have more because of his age? I hope this all ends soon. Valda and Thallan and so many others are getting hurt in this battle, while all I have been doing is hiding here. It's time I join the fight. But I don't know how. Maybe when Valda returns, she can help, thought Lysandra.

The room remained in an awkward silence until they were done, and they went back downstairs. Lysandra, Eleanora and

Gwyneth all gave their goodbyes to Valda and Thallan as they left. Once they were gone, the three of them began preparing the bakery for their usual business for the day.

I need to figure out how to fulfill this prophecy. I need some kind of plan. Maybe that is what Thallan is waiting to hear from me. To hear me say that I am ready. I hope, thought Lysandra.

Valda rode on her horse with Thallan and three other Nathairian soldiers. The two loyal to Thallan were next to each other, riding behind her. The other soldier loyal to the King's father rode beside her.

They rode along a path within the Thundering Eclipsed Mountains. With rain already falling so early in the morning, it would take a fortnight to reach Bellehaven and then another week of travel towards the Cinder Outpost. It was best not to ride the horses fast through the mountain trail. The pathway to Bellehaven was dangerous, with steep cliffs, rocky and muddy hills, and parts of the path being covered in the thick, dense forest. Thick fog often fills the forests in the fall and spring, limiting visibility.

The day wore on. At nightfall, they made camp near a shallow and damp cave. Valda tended to the horses as a soldier grabbed a bundle from the side of his horse that contained a few dry logs for a small fire. Another soldier attempted to find any additional dry wood to help keep the fire burning for the night. Thallan was going over his map to calculate how much further they would have to travel through the forest based on their current position.

The frosty night crept in, and they each took turns keeping watch and the fire lit. No one hardly spoke a word to one another and mostly kept to themselves. By morning's first light, they packed up their gear, doused the fire, and began their journey once more. The weather for the new day was already proving to be difficult, with blistering icy winds blowing against them, sending a chill to their bones.

They camped for another few nights, finding small caves along the mountains just some ways from the trail. The nights were far colder than the days. The caves provided shelter from the rain and wind while also helping keep the warmth of the fire in the room around them as it heated the rocky walls.

When the trail moved along the cliffside, it became more dangerous than they expected because of the gusts of wind. The rocks were wet from the night's rain, making the trail slippery. They all dismounted their horses and proceeded as slowly as possible, careful of their steps. Each of them needed to be extremely cautious with the added elements to the trail next to the sheer drop down the mountainside.

Not long after starting their journey's most dangerous trek, worsening weather forced them to make camp along the path near the cliff. The wind and rain made it too dangerous to continue or return to a safer area to rest.

The next day, the weather was calmer, giving them all a sigh of relief as they started on the last part of the cliffside trail.

As they ambled along the last part of the path, one soldier slipped on a loose rock. He desperately reached to grab whatever he could on the ground to stop his fall. His horse fell over the ledge. The soldier grabbed hold of a root sticking partially out of the ground, but it cracked from his weight. Thallan quickly grabbed the rope from his bag and tied it around a tree against the trail before tossing it to the fallen soldier. The others got on their hands and knees, carefully trying not to slip as they crawled closer to the soldier to help pull him to safety. Valda and Thallan could have easily let the soldier fall to his death, since it was the one loyal to the King's father. However, it was not in their hearts to be so callous, even to someone that in the face of battle would fight against them.

They successfully helped the soldier up and back onto the trail. Before they continued the journey, each of them took a moment to rest and calm their nerves. After a few minutes, they began once more, even more cautious than they were earlier in the day.

After their troublesome day traveling against the cliff, they made camp in another cave. It was another cold and quiet night as they rested.

The rest of the trail was far easier to travel. Their journey had finally started to descend in elevation as they grew nearer to their destination. The only danger now would be the creatures that lurked in the forest.

They arrived in Bellehaven just after midday, already tired and dreary from their journey. The town was just slightly smaller than Holbrook. Thallan, Valda, and the three soldiers made their way to the Misty Cavern Inn and Pub to get rest and nourishment.

The Misty Cavern was busy inside, filled with townspeople eating and drinking ale. When Thallan, Valda, and the soldier entered, the room went silent at the sight of them. Thallan ignored the stares as he searched the room for a table. Some townspeople got up and gave their table to him. Either out of generosity or fear, Thallan was not sure of. Thallan still gave his thanks to the people giving them the table. Once they sat down, the room returned to its loud bustle from before. There were some, though, who kept a watchful eye on them. Unsure and afraid of their business in the town.

They all stuffed their bellies full of warm food and drink. Once they were done, they left the Misty Cavern and went back to their horses tied to posts outside. Thallan, in his head, quickly thought through the excuse once more that would help Valda stay in Bellehaven without causing unnecessary curiosity.

"I have instructed Elara to stay behind here for a while longer. There are rumors that a scout from either Krogodo or Gragon is within the kingdom, attempting to approach the castle. Rumor has it this scout will arrive here before going to the valley. Elara's orders are to identify and eliminate the scout. The rest of us will continue our journey at first light tomorrow," said Thallan.

"Yes, sir," said all the soldiers and Valda in unison.

Thallan had gotten them all separate rooms for the night. He had trouble falling asleep, despite the comfortable bed. His mind wondered about the task at hand with getting Valda safely to the outpost as soon as Vaxar left. His other worry was her plan of escape and possibly fighting off soldiers in the destructive chaos of the outpost. He didn't know her escape plan, but he had overheard her telling Lysandra before leaving that she would return after completing her mission. After running things over through his mind endlessly, he eventually drifted off to sleep.

With the sun barely visible over the horizon, Thallan and the three soldiers mounted their horses and rode southeast towards the outpost. Valda moved to a new room in the Misty Cavern that Thallan had secured for her while she and the others were eating breakfast.

The room was small. The bed was in the middle, with the

headboard against the wall and dressers on both sides. A small window allowed some light in from outside. On the dresser were two candles, wax dried down their sides. Valda placed her packs against the bed as she sat down. She hoped this plan would work, and that she wasn't putting Thallan at risk. For if he got caught sending her the message by bird to head for the outpost, then his family would be in danger.

Then Lysandra would be in danger.

6

FORGETTING THE FIRST RULE

Two weeks have passed since Valda and Thallan left. For two days Lysandra took a break from studying and training. She hadn't felt like getting up as early as usual and wanted to get some rest for once. She didn't know why, but she was feeling exhausted.

Lysandra was also not in the mood to deal with the usual townspeople. They tried to gossip with her as she did her deliveries, but she hardly said a word. Once she was done with her chores for the day, she remained in her room. She sat at her window, wrapped in a blanket, watching the sunset until dinnertime.

She hid how she was feeling from her mother and Gwyneth to avoid worrying them. Lysandra figured it could be the lack of sleep she'd had since Valda left. She had trouble falling asleep and would wake up often throughout the night.

The next day, she woke up early with determination to finally leave the house after days inside. With much thought, Lysandra decided to go out to her hidden spot in the forest and practice her magic.

She slowly got ready and gathered her things. After she made her way down the stairs and into the kitchen, she put a few provisions in her pack. With her sword attached to her belt, bow and quiver strapped across her back, and pack draped over her shoulder, she put her hood on from her cloak and stepped out in the chilly morning air.

It was still dark out, as the small amount of sunlight was not strong enough to peek through the dark clouds. Lysandra spotted lightning far off in the distance to the south, followed by rolling thunder that echoed off the mountainsides. She hoped the storm was moving slowly and she could get some practice in and be back home before its arrival.

Thoughts overran her mind as she hurried through the forest. She kept her eyes focused on the path ahead to make sure not to miss the turnoff from the main trail that was just as wide as a traveler's wagon with engraved tracks from their wheels. She walked in silence, finding herself wishing that Valda was with her. Lysandra had not realized how much she enjoyed her company until she was gone. Valda never critiqued her like her family and gave Lysandra a newfound confidence in herself. Now she had to figure out how to not lose it.

Out of the corner of her eye she saw two trees growing together from the root but split in half a few feet above the ground, the mark of the turnoff. As she stepped off the main trail, Lysandra kept her focus on the forest around her. There was not a creature in sight.

By the time she arrived at the little cove and placed her pack against the fallen tree, darkness had covered the entire sky, and thunder and lightning seemed to come from all around her. The air felt much colder next to the river, so she kept her distance. Opening her hands, palms facing up, she ignited fireballs using the spell pyrocaustrusphere. After the story Valda told her of Vaxar's specialty with it, she wanted to practice throwing them into the river.

Lysandra had tried the spell a few times before. The ball of fire had always grown a few sizes too big just as she would throw them or extinguish midair because they were too small. Her challenge today would be to keep the fire small enough to work for throwing and practice merging the fireballs from each hand into one and throwing a constant flame.

Lysandra made the first attempt at throwing the fireball from her right hand into the river. The fire managed to only grow slightly larger, though she successfully threw it into the river. When she created the fireball in her left hand, it grew too large. Taking a deep breath, she decreased its size and threw a similar fireball as she had with her right hand. She did this a few more times until a branch snapped behind her.

Before turning around, she quickly ignited a fireball in her left hand as she pulled her sword out of its sheath with her right. Knowing they had just seen her practicing magic, she chose to use it to intimidate whoever has been watching her. She faced the forest, scanning from left to right, but saw nothing. Her heart pounded in her chest. Fear gripped her mind that it could be a grimog, as she could see nothing through the light drizzle of rain.

Lysandra took a deep breath to calm her nerves—and then spotted a hint of a brown cloak partially hidden by a wide tree trunk.

"I can see your cloak. Step out of the shadows and reveal yourself!"

The stranger stepped out from behind the tree with a sword and shield in his hands. His armor shimmered in the dim light. The Nathairian coat of arms upon his chest caught her eye.

Lysandra's mind raced with fear and worry at how the

soldier followed her. Then she remembered. Ever since leaving home this morning, her guard has been down. She assumed that with the weather, there would be no one out in the town so early. As she traveled to the cove, she didn't stay aware of her surroundings. She broke rule number one that Thallan had established for her with training out here and at home.

"*Be mindful of your surroundings and those around you. Never let your guard down.*"

"You are the sorceress! Thallan's sister! You are both traitors to the crown! Stand down! I shall take you to Vaxar myself for you to receive justice by his hands. If you resist, I shall kill you myself!"

"You stand no chance fighting me. You do not want to do this. Please let's just talk about this. There's no need for violence," said Lysandra.

The soldier stood for a moment, contemplating his options. He looked at the fire still floating in Lysandra's hand. Then he started running, back the way he came.

Lysandra quickly diffused the fireball in her hand and used the spell adaer, bringing her pack and bow and quiver to her almost instantly. She started running after the soldier as she draped the pack and quiver over her head and onto her shoulder. She returned her sword to its sheath so she could grab her bow.

The soldier was far ahead of her, beyond the distance for her bow. He had too much of a lead on her and was running at a much faster pace than she could run. Her mind raced with fear at all that could happen if he got away.

The soldier had such intense fear running through his mind that he ran right over the road and kept running through the forest, missing his turn to take the trail that led straight back to Holbrook. He kept looking behind himself, hoping that he had lost her, but she was still there chasing after him. He nearly tripped twice in his haste.

Seeing him trip, Lysandra got an idea. She concentrated harder than ever as she ran faster to close the gap between them. Her eyes flashed a powerful, vibrant blue color as she used the spells arborexo and arboradix together. She controlled a tree branch to lower itself a few feet in front of the man, causing him to slow his pace some. As he ducked to avoid the branch, roots from the surrounding trees clutched his ankles. He fell to the ground on top of his shield, attempting to use it to help break his fall.

She finally caught up, as he was frantically attacking the tree roots. He stopped and pointed his sword at Lysandra as she neared him.

"Please stop. I just want to talk. I don't want to hurt you. Can you lower your sword?"

"Never, sorceress! I do not want to hear whatever it is you have to say. Your words will poison my ears and place me under your spell. Kill me, for if you remove your spell from these roots, you best pray to the spirits that your death will be quick and painless either from myself or Vaxar."

"I don't want to kill you, but I cannot let you go to tell the Dark Sorcerer about me."

"Then let me make the choice easier for you."

She looked at him, confused. He then grabbed a knife hidden in his boot and threw it at her. Instinctively using the spell miraculum, she created a shield. The dagger collided with it, then fell to the ground.

Lysandra, mistakenly at the same moment, lost her concentration on her spell controlling the roots. Her momentary distraction allowed the man to rise quickly. She ended her concentration on the shield to control the roots again as she saw him stand. Then the soldier lunged towards her.

Without hesitation, Lysandra, using the spell arboradix, used the roots as if they were spears and impaled him through both of his shoulders while he was in the air. He dropped his sword with a cry of pain.

"I pray to the spirits that Vaxar will give you the most painful death imaginable, sorceress!"

"I am so sorry then."

She readied her bow and arrow, aiming it at his chest. She hesitated for a moment before releasing the arrow. The soldier's lifeless body fell to the ground as she released her control of the roots.

Now what am I to do? Others may come looking for him. I must hide his body somehow, but where? It will need to be somewhere no one knows about...maybe the cove would work, at least temporarily, she thought.

She grabbed the man's sword and placed it back in the sheath on his hip. She placed her bow over her head and shoulder.

Lysandra took a deep breath and then levitated the soldier just slightly above the ground with the spell levitaortia. She carefully made her way back to the cove. This time, she followed Thallan's rule, observing her surroundings. She kept the body floating in the air behind her low enough for it to be hidden by the bushes should she come across another person in the forest. She wasn't sure how far they were from the cove and did not know how long she could drag him before tiring out.

Once she made it to the cove, she hid his body in the hole underneath the tree. To her surprise, she did not need to use magic to make the hole bigger since the soldier could fit.

Then she quickly began heading home. She ran for a short while before walking at a quickened pace the rest of the way. Her mind wondered how to make sure no one would suspect her or go looking for the soldier. Thallan was away, and she did not want to tell him what happened, as it would cause instant worry. She decided to not tell the rest of her family for the same reason. Her only option was to send a bird to Richard asking to meet right away, as it was an emergency.

Richard Rivers was her longtime best friend, and only a few years older than her. They had always looked out for one another and been there for each other, no matter what. She was always happy around him. He never judged her and often shared her same views with how to handle the prophecy and that she is ready to face it.

They had met when they were children, when he lived with his family in a cottage on the edge of town. She had been learning to ride a horse when something spooked the animal, and she was only eight years old. She wasn't supposed to be outside alone. Richard heard her cries for help and rushed in to calm the horse. The horse had bucked her off, and she was on the ground, too scared to run away as the horse was slamming its front hooves against the ground. When Richard approached, he saw it was a snake that startled the poor horse.

The horse distracted the snake, so Richard carefully and quickly grabbed the slithering creature by the head, squeezing its mouth shut. It wriggled and squirmed, unhappy at its capture. Richard threw it into the bushes far away from them.

Then he calmed down the horse to keep it from possibly stomping on Lysandra, who was still curled up on the ground, scared.

"It's all right. You're safe now. That snake spooked your horse. Are you all right? I hope you have broken nothing." He extended his hand to help her up.

"Th-thank you."

"My pleasure. The name's Richard Rivers."

"I'm Lysandra."

Ever since that day, they had been best friends. A few years after they met, Richard stumbled upon her sorcerer's codex when helping Lysandra and her family move from their old small cottage to the bakery. That marked the moment that Richard would learn everything dealing with the prophecy and his friend. Richard was close with his father, who was friends with Krarick, and without question, took up the promise and oath to keep Lysandra's secret hidden and help protect her.

Lysandra and Richard used to combat train together in the forest with Thallan as their teacher. So, it was no surprise when Richard joined the kingdom's military, following Thallan's footsteps. Then eventually, he too could not visit as often as he used to. Lysandra enjoyed his company any chance she got, though, since he was her only friend growing up. She wished she were reaching out to him for better reasons than because of what happened in the forest.

She arrived home to find her mother and Gwyneth busy in the kitchen.

"How was training this morning?" asked Eleanora.

"It was all right. Cold and wet out there."

"Looks like it. Your cloak is filthy," said Gwyneth.

Lysandra looked down at the bottom of her mud-stained cloak. "Oh. When I was practicing, I slipped and fell into the mud. I should go clean up. I'm sorry for bringing in the mess."

"It is all right, dear. It's that time of year. Cannot avoid bringing in the mud, no matter how hard you try. Go hurry and clean up. These deliveries will be ready soon," said Eleanora.

After she cleaned up as best as she could, she got some paper out and her quill to write her message to Richard. Then she went downstairs towards the back of the house, where they had a few ashen raoks in cages. The birds are the size of a small hawk, with ashen feathers, and large talons. Ashen raoks are among the most intelligent birds, alongside their cousins, the kamari. Raok are believed to have the magical ability to understand all languages among the people. They can be trained to learn its owner's friends and family and by simply saying the person's name, the bird will carry the letter to its given destination and then return home. Only a small number live in the wild in clusters as these birds tend to gravitate towards people to make their homes.

Lysandra grabbed a raok and gave it the rolled-up message for Richard with his name written on the outside. She opened the window above the cages and told the bird where to go, releasing it to fly to the castle.

Eleanora quietly watched Lysandra from the other side of the room.

"Who was that for?" she asked, startling Lysandra.

"Richard. Wanted to see if he could give me some pointers with fighting in mud or weather like today."

"I am sure he has some advice, and if not, Thallan would certainly have some for you when he returns," she said.

Lysandra let out a silent sigh before following her mother to the kitchen. She got her basket ready to hold the orders and a piece of cloth to keep the rain off them. She made her deliveries for the day as quickly as she could.

When she got back from making her last of the deliveries, the raok had returned with a note from Richard. Gwyneth handed the note to Lysandra. It remained rolled as it had been when attached to the bird.

Richard instructed her to meet a mile outside of town off

the very trail that she took to get to the waterfall. He said to meet just after nightfall, when the town was usually empty, and everyone was inside to escape the chilly night air.

After dinner, she gave her excuse to Eleanora and Gwyneth. They both agreed that it was safe enough for her to go out to meet up with Richard. She grabbed her sword and hid it beneath her cloak. She chose not to bring the bow; it was difficult to hide. Eleanora and Gwyneth said they would wait up until she returned to make sure she arrived home safely.

She walked through town with her hood up against the light drizzle. Once she made it to the woods, soft white flurries mixed with the light rain. The air and wind grew colder the further she went into the forest. Winter would arrive in just a few weeks.

Lysandra was getting closer to the turnoff from the trail when she saw a torch light just off the side of the trail. As she got closer, she could recognize that it was Richard wearing his armor with his hood partially covering his head.

"Looks like we're getting our first snow. Autumn is leaving and winter is arriving to greet us," said Richard.

"It seems so. Earlier than last year, if I remember correctly."

"Possible. Now, what is so urgent that we had to meet?"

"Something happened this morning when I went to the waterfall to train. I think it'd be best if I show you."

"The let's hurry. I do not want to tempt fate and stay out here with the first signs of snow. I am not sure of what kind of mood the spirit of nature is in tonight," he said, looking to the sky.

"I agree."

They both walked at a quick pace towards the waterfall. With one torch in hand, they kept their guards up, watching the forest around them. It was extremely dangerous to travel at night with the creatures that lived in the mountains and descended to hunt for food at night.

After some time, they arrived at the waterfall. The flowing water added an extra chill to the air, making it feel like the dead of winter. Using her magic, Lysandra lifted the tree into the air, revealing the hole.

"Bring your light here," she said.

Richard moved closer and paused. "Is... Is that one of our soldiers?"

"Yes. I didn't notice that he had followed me early this morning until I heard him step on a branch while I was practicing magic. Richard, he *saw me*. I had to chase after him. Once I caught up to him and captured him...he tried to kill me."

"It's all right, Lys. You had no choice. You did this in self-defense." He rested a comforting hand on her shoulder.

"What should we do? Surely someone would notice his disappearance, right?"

"Someone might. I do not recognize his face. Though I am sure he has some friends or family that would notice."

He thought for a moment, trying to figure out a way to hide the true meaning of this soldier's death. In the meantime, Lysandra lowered the tree to the ground a foot behind the hole.

"I have an idea that could work. I can make it look like some kind of vicious creature attacked him. We'll need to take his body somewhere else in the woods away from here. Somewhere closer to town. In the morning, I can send a soldier to search for this soldier who failed to appear at his post. That way someone can find his body with the signs of an animal attack. It should be believable," said Richard.

"Sounds like a good plan to me. I can use magic to carry him so we can keep our focus on the forest."

"I'm not sure if you should use it. Even if it would make things easier and a little safer for us both. I do not wish to come across someone in the forest close to town seeing you use it."

"It would be the same spell I used earlier to bring him here. I had him floating only a few inches above the ground to hide behind the brush. So, if someone comes across the path, then I can simply drop him with no one noticing. I can have my hood pulled down to conceal my eyes. No one would notice."

"All right. I trust you. Let's hurry while the night is still young, then."

With the spell levitaortia, Lysandra lifted the dead soldier out of the hole and placed him on the ground behind them. She returned the tree to its usual place before levitating the soldier again.

They walked through the dark forest with their swords drawn and the soldier floating a few inches above the ground behind them. They kept watch around them, each taking turns looking behind themselves to make sure nothing was following.

When they reached the trail, Richard had them pause to make sure the road was empty. After a few minutes, he deemed it safe to go on but had them stick to the forest to the right of the path to keep the body hidden.

They continued through the forest until they could see the town in the distance, a tiny speck of light. She followed Richard further away from the trail, deeper into the forest for a few minutes.

"This should be a good place. It's a suitable distance from the trail. To our luck, the weather will have our tracks covered by morning. The rain is slowly picking up."

"What do you need me to do?"

"Hold the torch for me and keep it right here so I can see. I need to make it look like something mauled him. Close your eyes. I don't want you to see this. Don't worry. I will keep an eye out on the forest as I work."

Lysandra nodded. With her eyes tightly shut, she stood beside him, holding the torch. Although she had her eyes shut, she heard Richard cut into the soldier's lifeless body. She wished she was not holding the torch and could cover her ears to block out the sounds of the flesh being cut open and the fabric of the clothes being torn. The cold weather caused his body to be stiff and frozen, making the task quite difficult.

She tried to focus on the sounds of the surrounding forest to avoid listening to Richard's work. It was then that she heard the hoot of a creature related to the owls, the kamari. It was larger than the common wood owl. However, unlike ordinary owls, they had a long feathery tail, front feet with sharp talons and muscular hind legs. They flew slightly slower than their cousins, but they could hunt on the ground rather than just from above.

It felt like forever as Richard worked on making the body look like an animal killed it. She kept her focus on the kamari, trying to determine how far away it was. Lysandra wondered, if she opened her eyes, if she could see the beautiful creature with its dark brown and black feathers and tail, along with its bright yellow eyes.

When he finished, Richard took Lysandra's hand and turned her around before she could open her eyes.

"It's done. I just need to find some rodent to kill to add blood on him to make it more believable. No need to worry. No one will suspect a thing. Not even Thallan," he said as he hugged her tightly.

"Thank you, Richard. I don't know what I would do without you."

"Of course. You're my best friend. I shall always be here when you need me. You probably would have been in countless amounts of trouble throughout the years without me."

They walked around the forest for a few minutes until Richard found a small burrowing hole against a tree. He tried reaching inside but was unable to find or reach the small animal. Lysandra took the torch and used her magic to blow its smoke into the burrow, engulfing it. A small squirrel came scurrying out, rubbing its face with its paws, unaware of Richard and Lysandra standing by. Richard threw his knife quickly, pinning the poor creature, killing it instantly.

Lysandra followed Richard back to the body. He removed the knife from the squirrel and had the blood pour onto the body around the fake animal wounds he placed. After a few minutes, Richard nodded to Lysandra that it was done.

They began their journey home. For a few minutes, they walked in silence. Richard threw the dead squirrel deep into the woods off the trail for an animal to have. Both were shivering slightly from the wind that left a chill through their thick cloaks, down to their bones.

"So, you have not confirmed it, but I guess you did not tell your mother or Gwyneth of what happened this morning?"

"No. Though, to be fair, they noticed how muddy my cloak was from my chase. I lied and told them I slipped. Then my mother noticed me sending the bird, so I made up another lie that I was asking for advice on how to fight in slick mud."

"And I am sure that us meeting tonight was me answering the fake question. Well, you already know the answer to that. Check your balance and how you plant your feet. They should believe that. Just add a bit more of us doing some light practice of footwork to cover for the time you've been gone. They don't need the added worry. I've always agreed with you they worry too much about you."

"Thank you so much."

"Of course, Lys. We always have each other's back."

When they arrived at the edge of the forest, they hugged and bid their goodbyes before going their separate ways. Lysandra was ever so thankful for her friendship with Richard.

She arrived home to her mother and Gwyneth sitting in front of the fireplace. Eleanora was crocheting as Gwyneth sketched in her journal. Neither of them had done their hobbies for some time. It was refreshing seeing them returning to the things they loved.

They asked how her meeting with Richard went. Lysandra gave them the rehearsed lie that she practiced in her head. They believed every bit, just as Richard said they would. As she grew up, she had a feeling that the ease that Richard had with lying to both of their families was a bad influence, but it kept her out of trouble, so she let it be. She would take the consequences of the lies if it ever came to it. Though for now, she was happy to avoid any trouble she would be in.

7

A DANGEROUS MEETING

Night was approaching by the time Thallan and the soldiers arrived at the Cinder Outpost. There was a brisk breeze blowing in as the sun fell beyond the horizon. They entered the outpost through the tall wooden fence to see fire pits lit throughout, providing warmth and light to the many soldiers there.

At some of the fire pits, large slabs of meat were cooking, while others had massive pots of boiling stew. The light breeze carried the smell of food throughout the outpost, making its way to Thallan and his men, inviting them in with the sudden realization that they were all quite hungry.

Thallan instructed his men to settle in and eat before he made his way towards Vaxar's office across the outpost courtyard. It was best to see Vaxar immediately. He hoped the meeting would not take long so he could eat before the food was gone.

He paused as he reached the office before knocking, when unexpectedly, the door magically opened itself, revealing the Dark Sorcerer standing over a large table. The room was faintly lit by only a small array of candles spread around. What little light there was outside could not penetrate through the sealed window. Vaxar preferred the darkness. If he did not need light to read or see by, his room would surely be black as the night sky.

Thallan walked up to the opposite end of the table across from Vaxar. On the table was a large map of Lamorra detailing where the outposts of the Nathair kingdom were, as well as other outposts belonging to the other nearby kingdoms. Thallan noticed markings on certain areas that seemed to detail a plan for ideal attacks on the Krogodo Kingdom. He studied the plan so he could relay a secret message of Vaxar's plan.

"I need you to send a quad to the Silver Summit Outpost to gather enough troops to attack Hornfield while I lead troops to a small village just northeast of Ladron. I have already instructed your general how to begin the attack," said Vaxar.

"Why are we attacking them with separate forces at once? You know how strong the Krogodo forces are. There are rumors that many of the Virwarin forces have been living in Krogodo to help protect their allies. This plan seems too risky, Dark Sorcerer," said Thallan.

"Yes, there are risks, but the general traveling with me to attack Ladron will lead as I take a small quad to keep those Elves occupied in the Shadow Everglades."

"Why not keep the forces together and take Hornfield first, then move to Ladron?"

"I have received information that General Valda is currently away from the safety of her own kingdom. According to my sources, she may be near Bullmaren. I want to take both villages at once. It will give a nice blow to their forces and back them into a corner without their fearless leader to guide them. She won't be able to stop me this time with her being foolishly out of her own kingdom. Besides, I have a small quad heading for Bullmaren to find her."

"That's most odd, for her to be near Bullmaren."

"My guess is that Meador might finally try to plan an attack against us, which is why I want you to stay here, if it comes to that. They have kept to themselves all this time. We must be careful how we deal with them. I do not know the size or strength of their forces."

Thallan nodded in agreement. "It would be best to avoid gaining another enemy if possible. They could prove to be a great ally and would provide an advantage of having land across the sea."

"Indeed. Our biggest threat across the sea is the Virwarin Kingdom and possibly its longtime ally, the dwarf kingdom of Rhodora. We must separate their forces if we are to conquer both," said Vaxar. "Our opportunity to have the Krogodo Kingdom finally fall to their knees is now. Their general has made the most foolish mistake of leaving her kingdom, thinking we would not find out. She was the reason we could not take them down, she and her father before her."

Thallan realized he was right. Valda should have never left her kingdom. He'd have to make sure his general—who, like him, was against the Dark Sorcerer and Dark King and loyal to Sorcerer Krarick—lost this battle in a believable matter. It shouldn't be that hard. The general was nearly Thallan's equal in battle strategy.

"Now, to the other matters at hand. How well do you remember the Virwarin Kingdom? I understand you and your mother left when you were still young, for an Elf, at least."

"I remember it quite well. Might I ask why?"

"You do not still hold loyalty to their king, Gantar Virwarin, do you?"

"My loyalties are to King Nathair, sorcerer. Are you really questioning my loyalties once again?"

"Merely checking. You are an Elf who grew up in the Virwarin Kingdom. I am asking if you remember the kingdom because, once I return, I would like to discuss a plan of attack on them. Those Elves appearing out of nowhere in battle and driving our forces back have annoyed me long enough. I want to prepare for our attacks before traveling across the Emerald Sea."

"I shall begin drawing up plans."

"Good. In the meantime, stay close to the castle and have your men keep a sharp eye out for that general. I wouldn't hold it past her to sneak into our borders."

"Of course. She won't get through our forces, and even if she manages, she won't make it to the castle, or even Holbrook."

"Good. I have this feeling that she is up to something with her being so close and away from her kingdom. It is out of character for her."

There was a moment of silence as Vaxar continued looking at the map on the table. Thallan was about to walk back towards the door, thinking the meeting was done, but had a small feeling that there was something else Vaxar wanted to discuss.

"Before you go, in your room you shall find a package on the floor beside your table. Be sure that it gets delivered to the King. It is his medicine," said Vaxar.

Thallan nodded. He knew the King took something daily, like clockwork. He had always assumed it was a potion to strengthen him or make him more powerful. It had never occurred to him it was medicine.

Vaxar must have noticed Thallan's confusion.

"The medicine is for his illnesses, passed down by his

father. It is an illness he does not know about. His father and I told him the lie that it's an illness in his lungs. However, it is something far from it. If he should stop taking his medication, then his mind will lose its clarity and he may become more violent than he already is," said Vaxar.

Normally, Vaxar would like to continue keeping the secret but decided to tell him now, despite having proven his loyalties time and time again to him. This would also ensure the delivery of the medicine. He always had a bad feeling about the Elf. Then again, it could just be because of what he was, since Elves could throw off a sorcerer's magical senses.

"I will see to it personally that the King receives his medication," said Thallan.

"You're dismissed so you can prepare to journey back to the castle at first light," said Vaxar.

Thallan gave a slight bow, then left while taking one last peek at the table. As soon as he stepped outside, the door magically slammed shut behind him.

He walked towards a fire pit with a large pot that still had plenty of stew left inside. Even though he was hungry earlier, he lost a bit of his appetite after his talk with Vaxar. He grabbed the bowl off the small table sitting just a few feet away from the fire pit and scooped stew into it.

Thallan went to his room to be alone, worrying about the earlier discussion. His room was in the building behind Vaxar's quarters, as well as the armory. He entered his room to find the candles had already been lit for him and his packs were sitting against the wall opposite his bed.

The room was small, only containing a little table in front of the closed window and a simple bed. Beside the table was the pack of medicine.

He sat down at the table to eat the beef and vegetable stew. He was not fond of beef but ate it, anyway. Unlike many people in the kingdom, he didn't want to waste the food he was fortunate to have.

Valda should have never left her kingdom. With her gone, Vaxar has a greater chance of attacking the Krogodo Kingdom and winning the battle. There must be a way for me to get a message to her, thought Thallan.

He looked down at the pack beside his table with a worried expression as his forehead crinkled.

Was Vaxar really telling the truth? If the Dark King does not get this medication, will he really become more dangerous than he already is? So dangerous that even Vaxar is using his magic to keep him under control? After all, his father is still worse, so I guess it makes sense if his son could be far darker than the father, thought Thallan.

After he finished eating, he removed his armor and decided he was too tired to change into cleaner clothes. He laid down on his bed and swiftly fell asleep. However, a knock on his door woke him only a couple of hours later. He got up and opened the creaking door, revealing a young soldier.

"Sorry to disturb you, sir, but I must speak with you immediately. I have urgent news from Holbrook," said the young soldier.

"Come in," said Thallan with a slight yawn as he closed the door.

"I have received a bird from General Rivers. He has received information that someone within the castle is going to kill the royal family soon, sir," said the young soldier.

"Did he say who might try this or how he knows?"

"A merchant overheard a man speaking with a woman about planning an attack and informed General Rivers immediately."

"Do we have this man and woman identified?"

"We do not, sir. All the general said is that it may happen

soon while the Dark Sorcerer is away," he said as he held the letter out to Thallan. "General Rivers has enlisted your sister, Lysandra, to question the merchant discreetly, alarming no one or scaring them like a soldier would. You are being asked to return immediately, sir."

Thallan took a moment to think. He knew Vaxar had to have already teleported out of Cinder Outpost to meet with his army heading to Ladron.

"Alert a small quad and have them prepare to leave within the hour. We must get back to the castle at once. Send a bird with a message for General Rivers informing him of my journey back to the castle," said Thallan.

"Yes, sir," said the soldier as he promptly left Thallan's room.

Thallan shut the door and put his armor back on as quickly as he could.

If this person is successful in killing the King or Queen, Lysandra may be in far too much danger to stay hidden within the kingdom. Richard has too much trust in her. She is not ready to face the dangers the world has to offer. How can I have her leave without drawing attention? Many soldiers know about my family. If Lysandra disappears right after a royal assassination, they'll certainly find out who she is, thought Thallan.

8

THE QUERY OF AN ASSASSIN

A small, hardcover book flew through the air, narrowly passing Keir Nathair's head. However, he failed to dodge the boot.

It was nearly midnight and his wife, Seraphina, who was already in her dark purple nightgown with her brown hair flowing down to the middle of her back, was arguing with him. Like most nights, they argued over something he may have done that his father or Vaxar would not approve of. This time it was over Keir taking his medication nearly an hour late.

"I did not expect to be in the forest for that long, but the rainstorm delayed my travel back to the castle," said Keir.

"I don't care what your excuse is, Vaxar has clarified that you must take it on time! How can the Dark King be so stupid to put off taking important medicine all for a simple stroll through the forest? If Erebus wasn't already asleep, I would tell him how pathetically irresponsible his son is," said Seraphina.

"You do not need to remind me. But need I remind you

I am your king? You do not speak to me in such a tone, Seraphina," said Keir.

"I am also your queen. You may be the Dark King to all of Lamorra, but you do not speak to me with such insolence. Carrying your medicine with you is a must. You're like a child. So stupid and unable to think clearly," she said as she stormed into the other part of the room where their bed was, slamming the door shut behind her.

Keir ran his hands through his thick, black hair that sat just above his shoulders, then left his room for the small royal garden outside.

A brisk breeze brought some sprinkles from the last bit of rain. He walked over to the bench beside a large tree that could provide some cover. He sat down on the cold bench, unbothered that it was wet from the rain. The summer's dead plants, unable to survive the fall and winter, filled the garden. He noticed a guard stationed at the door in which he had come out of just moments earlier. He waved at him to go back inside, as he preferred to be as alone as he could after fighting with his wife. His mind wandered, remembering when things started between them.

He has tried to make her happy, but she never was. He had also tried to find love for her, but there was none when all she did was try to command him as if he were a mere servant.

When they first met, Keir's father instantly fell in love with Seraphina the moment he heard her speak to a servant, like a future Dark Queen would. She was a princess from the neighboring kingdom of Bullmaren. Keir and Seraphina's marriage united the two kingdoms, having Bullmaren under the control of Nathair Kingdom, further expanding Keir's father's dream of an empire.

Keir looked at the stars above peeking through the break

of clouds, lighting up the night sky over the valley below. He could see the small village of Holbrook lit up from torch lights in the streets and glistening lights that peeked through shutters of windows. Even without the beautiful flowers from summer, the garden was still his favorite place to sit and think because of the view it had over the valley.

I understand the urgency to take the medicine...but for the time I did not take it, I did not feel like I was having trouble breathing. In fact, I felt different...better, actually. I was feeling more myself. I don't know how, but I felt better without Vaxar's medicine. Maybe at some point I shall speak to him about it, thought Keir.

Keir stood up and left the garden as it was getting far too cold for him to continue sitting outside. He made his way towards the second, smaller royal chamber. He knew by now to give Seraphina her space when she was angry. Besides, he preferred sleeping alone than with her.

As he turned the corner down the hall, he came across a young female servant with food approaching the door to the royal chambers.

"Food for the queen, I presume?" asked Keir, as the servant bowed.

"Yes, sire. Is there anything I can bring for you?" asked the servant woman.

"Maybe a slice of bread and cheese. Just a small plate, though. It is late. And perhaps a glass of cider along with it," said Keir.

"Yes, Your Majesty. I shall have it brought to you at once," said the servant, as she bowed.

As the servant entered the royal chambers, he turned down another hallway, then entered his second royal chamber. It was smaller than its main chambers, but a perfect size for one person to sleep in and be alone.

Keir sat in his chair by the lit fireplace and grabbed the book on his side table.

Moments later, a loud rattling noise from his door made Keir jump to his feet. The door continued to rattle. Someone was trying to get in. Keir thanked himself for locking his door. He stood back, looking around the room for something to use as a weapon. Everyone in the castle knew to knock and wait for him to answer. The rattle of the door stopped.

Then a loud scream erupted nearby. It ended suddenly, followed by sounds of someone running. Keir carefully opened the door, peaking into the hallway. There was no one in sight.

Keir stepped out into the hallway. Worry and fear filled him. He thought the scream must have come from his wife, so he turned down the hallway when a servant girl was leaving the royal chambers. Her clothes were blood-soaked as she held a bloody knife.

"Servant! Stop! What happened?" asked Keir.

The servant girl froze. She then threw the knife at Keir. He pivoted, dodging the knife, as the woman bolted as fast as she could down the hallway. Keir took off after her but came to a stop when passing the door to the room she had left. He thought about checking on his wife, but he did not want to give the servant woman a chance to escape. He continued running after her. Keir hoped the guards placed throughout the castle also heard the scream and would soon come to his aid.

He trailed the servant as he yelled for guards, running through the hallways and down the servant stairs. The servant woman rounded a corner and ran into a guard with his sword drawn.

"Please help, I am being chased by a madman," said the servant woman as she moved behind the soldier, then kept running.

Keir turned the same corner, moments after the woman, and collided into the guard.

"You fool! Get her! I want her alive!" said Keir.

The guard quickly joined Keir in chasing the servant. They followed her outside to the pathway that led to the side gate as more guards appeared to help in the chase. Keir started running faster than the guard. He wanted to cut her off from her escape through the gate. The chase will become more challenging if she makes it into the forest.

Keir watches her getting closer to the gate as he tries to run as fast as he can. A guard stepped out from the other side of the gate into the walkway.

"Guard, stop that traitor from leaving! I want her alive!" yelled our Keir. As he ran, he saw that blood covered the guard's armor and sword.

"Hurry! There's too many of them!" yelled the guard to the servant woman.

She tried to run faster while glancing behind, hoping no one was close enough to grab her.

Keir stopped running. He became enraged that there was not just one traitor in his castle, but two. A guard with a bow and arrow stopped next to him. He grabbed the weapon from the soldier, notched the arrow, and aimed it at the traitorous guard. He released the arrow, hitting the man in his right shoulder. Keir notched another arrow, then aimed it at the girl, hitting her in her upper left thigh. She stumbled and fell, allowing the guards to grab her.

Soldiers made their way to the traitor in the guard's clothes at the gate. The traitor fought off his attackers. Another soldier arrived with a bow and arrows and fired at the man. An arrow hit the man in his left calf. He fell to the ground, surrounded by guards.

"Long live the sorceress! Down with the Dark King!" yelled the man.

Then, without hesitation, the man grabbed a dagger from his side and slit his own throat.

Keir slammed the bow into the soldier's hands before he walked towards the servant woman.

"Take her to the dungeon. No one is to question her. Leave the bolt in her thigh. She won't receive any help until we get a clearer picture of what is going on," said Keir to the soldiers.

"For now, it appears you are a traitor. We will treat you as such. It's unfortunate that we cannot question your friend now. So, you will also pay for his traitorous actions," said Keir to the woman.

The guards lifted the woman off the ground and began taking her to the dungeon. Keir made his way back inside the castle and then to the royal chambers.

How can anyone be so bold as to betray me within my castle? thought Keir.

He entered the room to see Seraphina's personal servant on the floor, crying beside the door to the bedroom. A guard approached Keir, blocking him from walking any further into the room.

"Your Majesty, are you sure you want to enter? This is not a sight for anyone to see. The assassin was merciless," said the guard.

"Let me see what has happened," said Keir.

The guard stood aside, letting Keir pass.

Keir entered the bedroom. He saw the torn bed. The torn canopy and scattered feathers from the pillows lay strewn about the floor. His wife's lifeless body lay against the bed on the floor. He stood there, expressionless at the sight. He should have been feeling grief or anger, but he felt nothing.

An old servant woman approached Keir and bowed to him.

"Your Majesty, I am so sorry," said the older servant woman.

Keir approached the lead guard who oversaw things when Thallan was away.

"Have the prisoner prepared for questioning. And when Thallan returns, have him see me immediately," said Keir.

"Yes, Your Majesty. I have instructed two guards to stay with you. If there were two traitors, I worry there may be more within the castle. The man killed was not a member of our guard. He stole the clothes off of the dead guard that we found just outside the wall in the forest. I shall send word for Vaxar to return and begin questioning the loyalties of everyone in the castle," said General Richard Rivers.

"No. Do not send for Vaxar. Alert him of what has happened, but tell him we can handle it here. It is more important for him to be where he is. We must show that this kingdom is still strong and that our enemies do not stand a chance against us," said Keir.

"Of course, Your Majesty," said General Rivers.

Keir made his way to his closet and grabbed a fresh set of clothes before heading back to his separate quarters. Two guards stood on either side of the doorway outside his room as he shut the door to change into the clothes he grabbed.

After changing, he took his medicine. He realized it had been some time since his last dose. He rarely had to take medicine at night, but he could tell that tonight was going to be long. Once ready, he left his room and headed down to the dungeon.

Keir entered the cold, torchlit dungeon. He passed dark cells holding criminals that Thallan's men had captured in Holbrook and countless other battles. He walked down a hallway leading to a circular room where the servant woman stood against the wall. Her hands were bound with the chains leading down to the floor.

A guard stood next to the table with knives laid out. As Keir entered the room and walked to the table, the woman trembled in fear.

"To save yourself the trouble and pain, you could answer my questions right away. Hold anything back or lie to me, and that is when the pain comes. Do you understand?" asked Keir.

The servant girl remained quiet, except for the rattling of the chains. She was shaking with fear even more.

"Don't bother being kind to this traitor, Keir. She is not worth it after what she has done. Let's just start torturing her. It won't be long till she squeals on her friends," said Erebus, as he entered the dungeon.

"Father, let me try my way to get her to talk. You can stay here but I will lead the questioning," said Keir.

"Fine. But if she stays quiet, I will step in for your failure," said Erebus.

"What is your name?" asked Keir.

The woman stayed silent, shaking in fear. Her eyes fixed on Erebus.

"Now come on. I just want to know your name. There is no harm in that, now, is there?" asked Keir.

"A-Ava," she said.

"Ava. See, that was painless. Can you tell me why you and your friend assassinated my wife?"

"T-to end the royal line. To be rid of you. It was my companion and I's plan alone to kill you all. We have grown tired of waiting for that sorceress to do it. So, we tried ourselves," said Ava.

"Well, you failed to kill my son, the King. You'll suffer

for your crimes against the crown for murdering the queen, servant girl," said Erebus. He stalked towards the table, grabbing a knife.

"Wait, she's talking. We can ask her more questions without slicing her up first," said Keir.

"If I don't, then you will. Or are you still a weakling and I must torture another person and have these dungeons guards yet again only speak of you doing my work? Man up, Keir. You are the Dark King now. Don't be weak," said Erebus as he held out the knife.

Keir let out a sigh as he dropped his head. He grabbed the knife from his father.

"Where is this sorceress hiding who you are so tired of waiting for? None of my men have ever come across her. It is as if she does not exist. Like a myth or legend never truly seen," said Keir.

"She is no myth or legend. And you will see her soon enough, at the time of your demise," said Ava.

"You did not answer the question, girl. Keir, quit stalling and teach this girl a lesson," said Erebus.

"Where is the sorceress hiding?" asked Keir as he took a step closer, rotating the knife in his hand.

Ava remained silent, this time not shaking and with her head held high, attempting to show courage rather than fear.

"Guards, tighten her chains. We would not want the traitor to move drastically or something fatal could happen before we get anything from her," said Erebus.

As the guards chained her closer to the wall, Erebus maintained eye contact with her as he stepped closer, beside Keir.

"Now, one last time, Ava. Answer the question," said Keir.

Ava, though shaking again with her hands above her

head and her feet spread in their shackles, maintained her silence. Keir shook his head and sighed, then sliced a gash onto her thigh just below where the arrowhead remained in her leg. Then he grabbed hold of the arrow's shaft.

"Where is the sorceress?" asked Keir.

Ava shook more now but kept silent with only a slight whimper escaping.

With her silence, Keir twisted the bolt in her thigh, and she cried out.

"Will you tell me now?" asked Keir.

"N-never," said Ava.

Keir shook his head. Erebus walked up beside Keir, then grabbed hold of the arrow and quickly pulled it out of her thigh as she yelled in pain and cried uncontrollably. He then slammed the arrowhead into her other thigh.

"Answer the question. You know where that blasted sorceress is hiding," said Erebus.

Despite the pain, Ava remained silent, causing Erebus to grow even angrier. Erebus pushed Keir out of the way. He then pulled the arrow out again and slammed it through her upper left arm. She yelled louder, dropping in her chains.

"Where is the sorceress? Who else in my kingdom are traitors?" asked Erebus.

"N-n-never," said Ava through her tears.

Erebus took the knife from Keir and sliced the inside of her left thigh. He then did the same to her forearm. After letting her cry for a moment, he delicately glided the blade across her sternum. As the blood seeped out of the thin cut, he placed the point of the knife under her chin and tilted it upward so she had to meet his eyes.

"Where should I hurt you next?" said Erebus.

Before he could move the knife, Ava swung her head back and with enough force, slammed her head into the knife, causing it to be lodged into her upper throat under her chin. Erebus filled with rage at what she had just done. He forced the knife the rest of the way into the bottom of her skull before forcefully ripping it out in a gush of blood. He threw the knife onto the floor as hard as he could with his anger.

The nearest guard started ordering the dungeon servants to clean the mess. Erebus walked to the table and grabbed a rag to clean his hands off.

"Have her and the traitorous guard displayed for their friends to see what happens to those who defy the crown," said Erebus. Then he looked at Keir. "Do not fail me again. I grow tired of your weakness."

Erebus promptly left the dungeon as guards followed him in silence. Keir sighed and left, too, back to his personal chambers.

9

THE MOST UNEXPECTED
DAY IN HOLBROOK

It has been more than a week since the Queen's death. People in Holbrook had been cautious with each other, those loyal to the king observing their neighbors, as if trying to find any other traitors within the kingdom.

By the middle of the day following the murders, both traitors hung on the archway of the gate on the road between Holbrook and the castle with a parchment attached to them that read: "This is what happens to traitors of the Royal Crown of Nathair."

Later that day, soldiers hunted down, questioned, and executed the assassins' families, finding them guilty of treason. Soldiers later hanged them with the traitors.

Since the assassination, soldiers had apprehended more and more people for questioning from Holbrook, nearby small villages, and even the minor kingdom of Bellehaven. Many did not return alive. A small pile of bodies grew beside those that were hung.

Lysandra had not seen or heard from Thallan since he

left with Valda. But Richard sent a bird letting her know Thallan had returned safely and had been by the Dark King's side because of the assassinations.

Between her morning fight with the soldier and the extra patrol of soldiers throughout the town, Lysandra had decided not to risk going out to the forest to train or practice her magic. She had instead used her spare time to study the sorcerer's codex. During the last couple of weeks, she had practiced the movements of various spells without using her magic to cast the spell. She wanted to be ready for whatever was to happen in the coming days.

Lysandra also used her mornings to get extra sleep since she hadn't been training in the forest. Strangely, as time moved on since that morning, she had been sleeping in more and more. She has been feeling defeated, helpless, and a sense of hopelessness since the two people she knew killed the Queen.

Eleanora knocked on Lysandra's door, but there was no answer yet again. Just like the past few days. She slowly opened the door and peeked inside to see Lysandra sound asleep. She walked to Lysandra's bed and gently stroked her shoulder to wake her.

"Lys...Lysandra. It's time to get up, my dear. I'm sorry. We wish we could let you sleep, but we need to keep up appearances with the added soldiers watching everyone in town. I have your breakfast ready downstairs. Did you hear me, dear?"

Lysandra mumbled as she rubbed the sleep from her eyes. Eleanora made her way back down to the kitchen as Lysandra slowly dressed.

Then she made her way down to the kitchen. She could tell the baked goods were almost ready by the wonderful smells lingering in the air. She entered the kitchen and grabbed her baskets and began prepping them for delivery in the cold air. Winter would be upon the land any day now.

She focused on the spells rather than her anxieties. She finished preparing the first set of deliveries in her basket and was about to leave when her mother grabbed hold of her arm.

"You need to eat, darling. You have not eaten yet this morning," said Eleanora.

"I will eat when I get back," said Lysandra.

She tried to leave again, but this time Gwyneth stopped her by standing in front of her.

"The deliveries can wait. You have plenty of time to eat," said Gwyneth.

Lysandra sighed and nodded. She set her basket on the counter, then sat down at the little table in the kitchen. Eleanora handed her a plate with a couple of small grugalberry muffins and a glass of milk. She had not realized how hungry she was until she started eating. The fresh muffin tasted delicious as grugalberries were her favorite. Grugalberries were a very light blue berry with the texture and size of strawberries, with the taste so sweet like candy.

"Please do not blame yourself for what that man chose to do. You did your part to question him for Richard. He had his chance to change his mind and chose otherwise," said Eleanora.

"I just can't believe how successful they were with killing the Queen. They had to have been planning for a long time. That poor woman used to work at the inn before working at the castle. But your mother is right. They made their choice," said Gwyneth.

"Airik and his family were so kind when I would deliver to them. Their son was just a child, and they murdered him for what his father did. I was friends with Ava. She found out only a few weeks ago that she is expecting while her husband was in Bullmaren trading goods from their small farm of chickens and goats...and now they're gone," said Lysandra.

"I know dear. I wished they had considered the consequences. They were brave though for what they did but still foolish as it is dangerously affecting others. But it is not on you what others decide to do," said Eleanora.

"With this though I am, aren't I? They went after the royal family, the Dark King who I am prophesized to take down along with the Dark Sorcerer. Instead of fulfilling that prophecy you guys and Thallan have me sitting here, hiding and pretending to be a bakery girl! So, others are trying to dangerously take matters into their own hands. The prophecy was specific that only I can save the realm from darkness. Not my father, not Airik and not Ava! Nor either of you or Thallan," said Lysandra.

Eleanora sighed as tears filled her eyes. "I know. Thallan says it's too dangerous right now though dear," said Eleanora.

"Thallan is doing all he can along with your father to make your job as less dangerous as possible. You are not ready yet as you still have much to learn and practice with your magic and combat according to Thallan. You just need to be patient," said Gwyneth.

Lysandra sighed and remained silent. She recognized where the conversation was going. She has had plenty of arguments with them about the prophecy and that she is ready. Lysandra turned her focus on finishing her meal instead.

Others are clearly not patient and more will try to do drastic actions to rid the realm of the darkness, she thought.

She finished her breakfast, then was out the door.

Luckily, she would only have two rounds of deliveries today. Orders had slowed down in the past week due to the recent events in the kingdom.

Once she finished the first round, she made her way back to the bakery and looked up at the sky. There were a few clouds floating above, showing signs of a clear day, providing a break in the near-constant sleet. However, despite the sun now shining, the air was still chilly, with a slight breeze that made it feel far colder.

Standing outside in the castle garden, Keir looked out at the small village of Holbrook, glistening in the morning sun with last night's rain. He'd received a letter a few days ago from Vaxar giving his condolences on his loss, while also stating that he should begin his search for a new wife. Keir did not want to think about finding a new wife yet, but he decided he should start looking to avoid arguing with Vaxar upon his next arrival along with putting an end to the same argument with his father.

Keir heard a knock on the door of the garden and found Thallan standing in the doorway. Keir motioned for him to approach.

"I'm sorry to disturb you, Your Majesty. You asked for updates on any more traitors to be found and friends of those we have apprehended?"

Keir motioned his hand for Thallan to continue as he put his cloak on.

"There have been two additional people found near the Silver Summit Outpost. We have also received word from Vaxar. He has yet to find General Valda," said Thallan.

"I expected that. Just have some men continue looking.

More traitors will eventually slip up, and we will find them. In the meantime, I would like you and a small quad to accompany me today. I wish to visit Holbrook and walk around the town and show my loyal subjects that I am still strong as ever... And possibly find a new wife. We both know Vaxar and my father already want me to start the search," said Keir.

"Yes, Your Majesty. I shall have the quad ready at once," said Thallan.

After spending some more time in the garden, Keir ate lunch with his father. Neither said a word to each other as they ate. Once he finished eating, Keir made his way down to the castle stables. Thallan and the quad were ready on their horses.

Keir mounted his horse, and they began making their way down the short path to the archway leading to Holbrook. The main road went through the center of Holbrook, leading to the other side of the town where there stood an archway matching the others. Then the road led out across the small valley and into the narrow path that would eventually lead out and alongside the Thundering Eclipsed Mountains.

Keir looked up to the mountains as they entered Holbrook, where clouds covered their peaks, with parts of the clouds stretching downward as if to touch the ground. He knew those clouds would bring either afternoon rain or snow, judging by the brisk air blowing in the slight breeze.

They rode through town, with many people bowing and giving their condolences to him. With each bow and condolence he received, Keir smiled and slightly bowed his head in thanks. He stopped by the blacksmith and watched as a young apprentice was observing how to craft a fine sword.

"I advise you to pay close attention to the making of such fine weaponry, young man. Our kingdom is always in demand for such fine weapons," said Keir, startling the boy who hadn't noticed him.

"Master General Knight Thallan has told me you are a very skilled blacksmith and have made many weapons for our soldiers," said Keir to the blacksmith.

"I want to ensure that we equip our protectors with strong, valiant weapons and armor, Your Majesty," said the blacksmith with a bow.

"And you do a magnificent job in doing so. Thank you, blacksmith Vicar. And to you, apprentice, learn well to gain the skill of becoming another fine blacksmith like your teacher," said Keir.

"Yes, Your Majesty. Thank you," said the boy.

Keir started walking down the road again, leading his horse by the reins. He had not visited Holbrook since he was a small boy with his father and Vaxar. He enjoyed seeing his loyal subjects who lived so nearby the castle until he remembered he must keep an eye out for any women who may look suitable to become his wife and queen.

Suddenly, a woman entered the main road from one of the side roads that led to a cluster of small cottages. She carried a basket and wore a moss-covered cloak. Her hood was down, and her brown hair was half up in an Elvish braid. He could glimpse the side of her face before she started walking away from him, unaware of his presence. From the moment of seeing her face, she looked like a ray of sunshine to him. He followed her as he hoped to catch up to her and start up a conversation, or at least see the rest of her face.

She stopped along the main road. Before Keir continued walking closer, he noticed she was making deliveries of what looked like pastries and decided he would follow her at a distance until she had completed her duties. He found himself not wanting to disturb her as she worked. Keir pretended to look around at the area of town that they were in until the woman walked down the main road again, then off down another side road.

"Let's get off the main road. I would like to see more of the village," said Keir, giving his excuse to follow the woman.

To his luck, none of his guards took notice that they were following her. They followed until she entered a two-story building with a wooden sign that read *Bakery*. Keir assumed that this must be where she worked. Then he remembered Thallan, his top general and loyal knight, owned a bakery where his family lived. He must have laid eyes on Thallan's adoptive sister, and this must be the bakery. Keir made his way towards the door to see if his suspicions about the woman and bakery were true.

Thallan was unaware that they were following Lysandra, until he saw her ahead of them just a small distance, as she was entering the bakery. The horrific sight instantly filled Thallan with fear.

Lysandra was setting her basket on the table when she heard the door open behind her, followed by a brief gasp and then the words "Your Majesty" from Gwyneth. Her mind raced as she turned around to see the Dark King himself in the doorway, with Thallan just behind him.

Lysandra immediately dropped into a curtsy as she said, "Your Majesty," while holding back the panic in her voice. Fear gripped her body as she found herself unable to step further away from the king.

"Your Majesty, what can we do for you?" asked Eleanora.

Keir broke his gaze from Lysandra.

"Forgive me. I did not mean to startle any of you. I was

taking a walk through the village to get a break of scenery from the castle walls and the forest until, I must admit, the beauty of your delivery woman drew my attention," said Keir.

"Your Majesty, if I may interject, this is the bakery and home that I own. This is my family. My mother, Gwyneth, and our close family friend Eleanora and her daughter, who is much like a sister to me, Lysandra," said Thallan.

"It is an honor to meet you all. And I apologize for following you, Lysandra. I am afraid I let my distracted mind forget about formalities," said Keir.

Lysandra, still frozen in fear, fought hard to find her voice and think of a reply.

"That...that is all right, Your Majesty. Is there anything we can do for you? We have many fresh pastries today," said Lysandra.

Her mention of pastries made Gwyneth gasp and sprint to the oven to save the muffins. The smell of the fresh grugalberry muffins filled the room. Keir's eyes gave away a hint of hunger. Lysandra noticed his change of focus to the muffins.

"Would you like a fresh grugalberry muffin, Your Majesty?" asked Lysandra.

"That would be delightful. But only if you have an extra to spare. I assume these are for orders from your customers and I would not like to take away from them," said Keir.

"Oh, we have all the orders made today. These muffins are simply a special treat. You are more than welcome to have some, Your Majesty," said Gwyneth.

"Please, come in and have a seat, Your Majesty," said Lysandra as she led him to the small kitchen table.

Lysandra grabbed a fresh cloth to hold the muffin and placed it onto a small saucer plate. She then filled a glass with wine. She placed the plate with a cloth napkin beside it and the glass down on the small table for Keir. He gave her a sincere smile.

"Thank you," said Keir.

Gwyneth and Eleanora resumed working in the kitchen. Lysandra stood awkwardly by the table, not sure of what to do with the unexpected guest.

"Please sit. You are not a servant. I'm sure you are tired from walking around the town delivering these amazing pastries," said Keir.

She nodded and promptly sat down, not knowing what else to do.

"These muffins are delicious. Thallan, you did not tell me your family are exceptionally talented bakers." Keir turned to Thallan as he wiped around his mouth with the cloth napkin. "Are you the only man in this house?"

"I am," said Thallan.

"Where is your father, Lysandra?" asked Keir.

"He died when I was a baby. Drunk men wishing to cause trouble killed him in Bellehaven."

It was the lie she was told to use if anyone ever asked that question.

"I am sorry to hear that. I am sure it must have been hard growing up without a father. But I am glad that you still have your mother and this fine man here in your life," said Keir.

Keir thought to himself for a long moment.

"Lysandra, I would like to offer you a chance to become my queen. I know this must be unexpected. There is no need to worry about not being of royal blood. Thallan has earned the honor for this family to have the opportunity of such formalities as this. I know it is sudden, but I cannot think of anyone more perfect than you. I also hope this will strengthen the bond with my people rather than find someone from another kingdom to unite with," said Keir.

She sat across from him, stunned at what she heard. *Did the prophets see this coming? If so, a forewarning would have been nice. I can't think of a way out of this predicament,* thought Lysandra.

She realized she had not said a word and tried to think of something formal.

"It would be an honor, Your Majesty," said Lysandra as she bowed her head to him.

"I'm glad. I would like to invite you all to dinner tonight to celebrate. Please don't worry about looking so formal. It will be just us. Thallan, I may need your help with having a few soldiers keep my father away. I will tell him the news tomorrow," said Keir.

Thallan nodded in agreement, knowing that Keir's father would be quite unhappy with who Keir chose.

"We shall be there, Your Majesty. Thank you for the invitation," said Gwyneth as she and Eleanora bowed in a curtsy.

Keir stood up and placed the empty cup on top of the plate with the napkin to the side, attempting to clean up after himself.

"Thank you so much for your hospitality. I look forward to this evening."

He walked just outside the door but stopped to take one last look at Lysandra and give her a smile. Then he turned and left, heading toward the castle.

Thallan followed but gave a quick look to Lysandra and mouthed *"Don't worry."*

Gwyneth and Eleanora noticed Lysandra still standing by the door, frozen in place. Gwyneth gave a nod to Eleanora to go to her to ease her worries, letting her know she could handle the baking.

Eleanora stepped in front of Lysandra, blocking her view

of the door. Lysandra's mind was racing with worry and fear on the inside while she tried to hide it on the outside.

"Darling, you mustn't worry. I saw what Thallan mouthed to you. Listen to him. The king has no reason to suspect you of being the sorceress. Think of this as a blessing in disguise. You will get close to him without Vaxar there. Losing the Dark King will weaken Vaxar and make it easier to take him down," she said while rubbing Lysandra's shoulders.

Lysandra did not respond, as she was overthinking the situation.

"Don't forget, you won't be alone. You have us, Thallan, and Richard. In fact, I'm certain Thallan will never leave your side while you are at the castle," she continued.

Eleanora stepped closer and looked into Lysandra's eyes, seeing fear and worry. She instantly hugged Lysandra tightly, wanting to take away what her daughter was feeling.

"Oh, my dear. I wish you did not have to deal with this prophecy. But no matter what, I will always be by your side to help you with anything. I will never leave you," she said into Lysandra's hair.

"You will always have me and Thallan, too, my dear," said Gwyneth as she placed a comforting hand on Lysandra's shoulder.

Lysandra pulled away from the hug and held both her mother's hand and Gwyneth's hand in comfort as she tried to remain strong on the outside.

"I know. I see your point on what you've said, but it also increases the chances for Vaxar to discover who I am. He is unpredictable with his travels from the castle and the battle-fields. He is more than likely to make the trip back to the castle for the wedding. That would make things harder for Thallan to always have an excuse for being by my side. For the wedding ceremony, it would help with you there by my side, Gwyneth. But if Vaxar stays past the ceremony, things could get difficult quickly," said Lysandra.

Eleanora slumped her head as she sighed, hearing the bitter truth her daughter had spoken. She wished she could keep her safe and far from harm's way. She wished that there was no prophecy to begin with, or all this evil in the realm of Lamorra.

"We will still be by your side. We will figure out how to get through this. I pray the Dusan Spirits will guide and protect you," said Eleanora.

Eleanora and Gwyneth both hugged Lysandra.

"We should get this kitchen cleaned up before we have to get ready for dinner with the Dark King," said Gwyneth.

All three of them worked tirelessly to distract themselves from their thoughts of Lysandra becoming the bride to the Dark King and being that much closer to the dangers that come with fulfilling the prophecy.

10

THE FIRST DINNER

Keir, Thallan, and the small quad of soldiers arrived back at the castle. Thallan ordered the quad to return to their posts as he followed Keir inside. They headed to the library in which Keir spent much of his free time.

Thallan promptly lit the fireplace, providing light and heat to the room. A servant man entered and bowed.

"Your Majesty, is there anything you need?" asked the servant.

"Yes. Can we get some food and drink, please? Bring a plate and a cup for Thallan as well. Thank you," said Keir.

The servant bowed before leaving the small library. Keir sat down in a chair before the fireplace.

"Take a seat, Thallan. I was hoping we could talk before you return to your duties," said Keir.

"Yes, Your Majesty," said Thallan and sat in the other chair by the fireplace.

"Thallan, you are my most trusted general. So, I feel I should explain to you my intentions with your sister and why I have made such a rushed decision."

Thallan nodded, waiting for him to continue.

"I know my father and Vaxar would remind me of the importance of having a queen by my side and an heir to the throne. However, I have no intention of making your adoptive sister worry about that second part anytime soon. I want to get to know her and create a friendship with her. That is more of a formality to appease my father and Vaxar," said Keir.

"I understand the formality. It is an honor to have Lysandra become the future queen of Nathair Kingdom."

The servant man returned with a tray of sliced bread and cheese with two goblets of mead. The servant placed the plates and goblets on the low wooden table between Keir and Thallan.

"Is there anything else you require, Your Majesty?" asked the servant.

"No. That will be all for now. Thank you."

Thallan grew tense with fear and anger over the situation he found himself in. His fear attempted to overwhelm his mind with trying to figure out how to keep Lysandra safe. He never once thought in a million years that the events happening now were even possible.

"I noticed in our brief talk with each other that she is a very kind and strong woman. She shall become a wonderful queen and hopefully a kind friend to have," said Keir with some sadness in his voice.

Keir was hopeful about his choice. He felt drawn to her from the moment he saw her and only hoped she would at least become a close and kind friend as time moved on.

Once they finished their bread and cheese, Keir left for the garden. Thallan made his way to the guard headquarters within the castle to have Richard gather two additional soldiers to help with escorting his family to the castle safely.

The late afternoon sun peered through the low clouds over the valley. Ever since King Keir returned to the castle, many people visited the bakery asking questions about his visit.

After a few people left, Lysandra's mother suggested she rest before dinner, so she eventually disappeared into her room upstairs. Eleanora noticed the villagers were getting on Lysandra's nerves with all the questions. She was happy this was one of the few things that she could help her daughter with. They told everyone a lie as they were all not ready for the truth and the gossip that would follow.

Eleanora and Gwyneth were cleaning up the kitchen as Lysandra joined them. She had used the time when she was avoiding the villagers to study the sorcerer's codex and practice some light defensive maneuvers with her dagger. But she was restless, so she grabbed a rag and helped where she could.

It was nearly time for them to depart for the castle as they finished cleaning. Three castle guards entered through the front door after a brief knock. All three of them were good friends of Thallan. Lysandra immediately recognized one of them.

"Richard! It is so good to see you again, my friend," said Lysandra as she ran up and gave him a hug.

"It is good to see you as well, Lysandra. Are you ladies ready to go?" said Richard.

"Is what we're wearing acceptable? We all changed earlier into our best clothes," said Eleanora.

"Yes, you all look lovely. He is not expecting you three to be in formal attire. You will impress him."

"Not a bad idea, in my opinion, to start things off on his good side," said one guard.

Lysandra wore her one Elvish dress with brown fabric

underneath a dark blue covering. The brown fabric piece fell to her feet and had sleeves stretching down to her elbows. The blue covering draped from her shoulders to her waist before ending just below her knees in a separate wide stretch of fabric, allowing it to flow freely and give way to the brown dress underneath.

Eleanora and Gwyneth wore similar outfits, since neither of them owned fine dresses, either. Many years ago, they sold their dresses to pay for Lysandra to have a nice bow and for the armorer to teach Lysandra how to make her arrows should she ever need to.

Cloaks on, they rode in the carriage followed by two guards on horseback down the main road of the village towards the direction of the castle. As they sat in the carriage Gwyneth noticed Lysandra's messy braid.

"Lys, how do you make such a mess of a braid every time?" asked Gwyneth. She moved to sit next to Lysandra. "Keep still and face that way. I shall fix your hair quickly before we arrive. I will allow no one there to see such a terrible half Elvish braid when you have two Elves present by your side."

Lysandra rolled her eyes and decided not to protest. Eleanora and Richard could not help but chuckle at Gwyneth's displeasure. Lysandra was not as worried about how she looked, but knew both her mother and Gwyneth cared about appearances.

It was not long before they approached the front gates of the castle, which Lysandra examined in awe. The design of the stone walls with small window openings protected archers while enabling them to defend against intruders. The Winterstone Castle was a couple of miles away from Holbrook, up the slightly inclined pathway. Nathairian Kingdom strategically built their castle against the mountainside at a higher elevation for defensive measures against any enemies.

The enormous castle had its own kitchen, dining hall, extravagant ballroom, a small library, a large room that Thallan called a war room, and at least twelve bedrooms, along with the royal chambers. On either side of the castle were two large, rounded towers. Similar gates stood on the front, left, and right side of the castle. All gates opened into the forest, providing a quick escape route and ample cover should invaders besiege the castle.

They entered through the large wooden front doors to the castle to see polished flagstone flooring, large travertine columns, and grand juniper-green tapestries alongside the many windows. Lysandra, Eleanora, and Gwyneth were all in awe of the exquisite beauty of the inner workings of the castle.

Richard led them down a few hallways until they arrived at the dining hall. A fire roared at the far end of the room and candles glowed from the walls and down the table. The entire room was so well lit from the sunset that it did not need the candles yet.

"You may take your seats. I shall inform the King and Thallan of your arrival," said Richard.

"Thank you, Richard," said Lysandra.

The three of them walked towards the table as servants stood at the ready to scoot their chairs in and begin serving them wine and fruit. Lysandra sat on the chair to the left of the head of the table, assuming that it would be where the king sits. Her mother sat next to her and Gwyneth took the seat across from Eleanora, knowing that Thallan would sit beside the King and across from Lysandra.

With the sun nearing the horizon, two servants began closing the curtains. As the last curtain was closed, Keir entered, followed by Thallan.

The three of them stood to curtsy to Keir. He sat down at the empty seat at the head of the table. Thallan naturally took the empty seat beside his mother. Two servants immediately served Keir and Thallan their glasses of wine before making their way back to the servants' hallway that led to the kitchen.

"I would like to thank you for inviting us to dinner this evening, Your Majesty," said Lysandra, breaking the silence.

Thallan's eyes widened in surprise. He was expecting her to be much shyer and quieter instead of confident and sociable.

"Of course. You all look elegant and lovely this evening. It is a pleasant change to have dinner with someone other than my father. But don't worry, he should not be joining us."

Servants entered through the servants' entrance carrying dishes with food and placed them each on the table setting in front of each person. Their first course was vegetable soup.

"I hope my chefs do not disappoint our kingdom's best bakers. Your muffins earlier today were delicious," said Keir.

"It all looks lovely, Your Majesty," said Eleanora.

"I am sure your cooks are very talented," said Gwyneth.

Once they finished the first course, servants entered, removed the dishes and placing down the second course of pork and roasted vegetables.

Only a few minutes passed, but Lysandra felt the room had been too quiet for ages. She wondered if Keir would ever talk or even bring up his idea of marriage. She glanced at him and gave him a small smile, and that was when she noticed something about him. He had not mentioned the notion of marriage because he was nervous. She noticed small signs of sweat on his brow and how his cheeks blushed when she smiled at him. She decided she may need to be the one that would have to break the ice.

"Your Majesty, I have been told by Thallan that you have an elegant garden. According to him, it is a great place to see the stars shimmering brightly in the night sky across the valley," said Lysandra.

"Yes. Our garden is quite beautiful. I spend a lot of my time there. It is a wonderful place to watch the sun and moon shine over the valley," said Keir, seeming relieved she spoke.

"Then I look forward to the marvelous views that your garden offers," said Lysandra.

"You shall, and soon. In fact, I thought of sending Thallan with some servants tomorrow to help you gather your things to move into the castle. We must begin preparations for the wedding. I would also like to keep you safe after recent events. Thallan has increased the guard and safety here. In fact, Thallan, I would like you to stay by her side. You can have Richard take your place of your temporary guard duties on me," said Keir.

As they spoke, servants entered with the third course dishes of roasted chicken and warm rolls.

"When shall the wedding take place?" asked Eleanora.

"Four days' time. Vaxar should be back by then, after using his magic to quicken the journey. Once you're settled in, Lysandra, you and I will begin working together on the wedding preparations," said Keir.

"I understand. It shouldn't take too long to gather my things to move," said Lysandra.

"As for your mother and Thallan's mother, you are both invited to move into the caste as well, but I understand if you wish to stay in Holbrook and continue running your lovely bakery. You are welcome to come to the castle whenever you like," said Keir.

"Thank you, Your Majesty. May we discuss upon the offer and inform you of our decision at a later time?" asked Gwyneth.

"Of course. There is no rush on the matter. It will remain an open invitation," said Keir.

As they continued talking about the wedding preparations, the fourth course of roasted fish and potatoes and the fifth course of roast beef with vegetables was served. After their fifth course, servants brought out slices of chocolate cake with fresh berries on top.

As they ate the chocolate cake, the doors sprung open to reveal Erebus.

"What is this? I thought you were too busy to have dinner, son? Who are these people? Why is General Thallan sitting at the table beside you?" asked Erebus, as he approached the opposite end of the table from Keir.

"These lovely ladies are Thallan's family members. I was going to inform you in the morning, but the lovely lady to my left is to become my new queen. Thallan has earned the honorability and formalities for her to be considered per tradition and laws," said Keir.

"If she is part of Thallan's family, then why is she not an Elf, or at least a half-Elf then? I see no pointy ears," said Erebus.

"His family took her and her mother in. Her father died years ago when she was a baby. She counts as his family. You have no say in who I am to marry. A marriage with her could help strengthen the bond with our subjects, especially after recent events. You yourself said our people do not appear to be as loyal as they used to be. This could help," said Keir.

"Hmm. You make a fair point. I just hope you have chosen wisely with someone who grew up with an Elf," said Erebus as he stared at Lysandra.

"I have chosen wisely, Father. Is there something that you need, since you are here?" said Keir.

"I was hoping for dinner, as I have not yet eaten. I suppose I should have a servant bring it to my chambers. Good night," said Erebus, as he quickly left the room, slamming the door shut behind him.

"Apologies. He...well, he is not the nicest person. I will be honest, he has a nasty temper. Servants should have brought him his dinner as we were being served. I advise staying away from him as much as possible, Lysandra. His attitude can easily ruin a day," said Keir.

"Thank you for the advice," said Lysandra.

Once they finished eating dessert, Keir bid his goodbyes to Lysandra, Eleanora, and Gwyneth before retiring to his chambers. Richard followed Keir, staying by his side as his personal guard with Thallan having been reassigned as Lysandra's guard.

The four of them made their way back towards Holbrook. Their path was lit by the bright moonlight and the few torches they carried. A crisp, cool breeze slipped throughout the valley, and the town was eerily quiet as everyone was indoors, staying warm.

Once they got home, Thallan started a fire to warm everyone. No one had spoken a word since they left the castle. But Lysandra didn't linger before slipping away to her room, needing the solitude.

She sat on the edge of her bed and pulled out her necklace hidden beneath the collar of her dress. She studied its fine details. The necklace always helped ease her mind from worry. After some time, she eventually fell asleep.

Eleanora quietly entered Lysandra's room sometime later. She saw her daughter fast asleep and grabbed the blanket draped on the chest in front of the bed and laid it across Lysandra to keep her warm. She then placed a small kiss on her forehead.

Before she left, Eleanora stopped to look at Lysandra sleeping. Now more than ever, she wished for her husband to be here to help their daughter. She knew why he left, but she had always hoped he would make his way home to rescue them or for them to have left the kingdom to find him and live somewhere safer, far from evil. She wished they could leave, far, far away from the kingdom, so that her own daughter did not have to marry the Dark King.

11

THE LIFE OF A ROYAL

The next day, a flurry of servants and a quad of soldiers helped move Lysandra into the castle. But it was Thallan who helped her hide the spellbook among her clothes.

They also moved her weapons to the royal chambers, which surprised Keir. Thallan explained to Keir that he trained her in combat to defend herself. Keir was glad that he was to marry a woman who believed knowing how to fight and defend herself instead of relying on guards and soldiers to do so. This helped put his mind at ease a little, knowing that if someone should try to harm her, they would have more of a troublesome feat doing so compared to Seraphina.

Throughout Lysandra's first day in the castle, seamstresses and servants surrounded her. The seamstresses spent their time getting measurements, draping her in layers of fabric to find the right colors for her hair and skin. They were to make not only the wedding dress for Lysandra but gowns or other clothes she may request. She took advantage of this and asked for a few gowns for formal occasions but also clothes like those she already wore as she was most comfortable in them. While packing, she realized she needed to replace many worn-out clothes.

Lysandra felt like she would never get used to having a servant always beside her. She was surprised that the servants helped her, even with simple tasks like choosing her clothes for the day or brushing her hair. Although, she did not mind having someone there to clean up her dishes or wash her clothes.

By her second day of life in the castle, Lysandra was becoming more aware of Keir's behavior of being unusually kind when he was around her compared to the stories of how mean he could be. Even Thallan thought Keir was much kinder than he had seen in the past. Though, Keir still spoke to her and acted in a very formal matter—perhaps that would change after the wedding. Lysandra and Thallan both wondered if Keir really did fancy her and was trying to impress her or was simply nervous around her, unlike with his former wife. Nearly everyone in the kingdom knew Keir and Seraphina had never gotten along.

Lysandra finished her breakfast with Keir before she walked beside him towards the royal chambers where four seamstresses awaited them to make the final preparations for the wedding clothes. Keir and Lysandra found them hidden behind changing screens. The four seamstresses focused on Lysandra while the others attended to Keir. Then they made their final adjustments and were done with Lysandra and Keir within the hour.

Once they were done, Keir took Lysandra's hand and tucked it into the crook of his arm. He led her out into the hallway, and they walked side by side towards his study, where a servant was waiting, standing beside a table covered in fabrics of different colors laid about neatly across its surface.

"Which color do you fancy, my dear?" asked Keir.

Lysandra approached the table, with Keir beside her, as she tried to get a better look at the fabrics on the table. The fabrics were all of extravagant, beautiful colors: midnight blue, emerald green, burgundy, sage green, rosy red, and a bright silver shade.

"They are all so lovely. I am finding it difficult to choose one," said Lysandra.

"Yes, they are. I'm torn between the two green colors. But I'll be honest, green is my favorite color," said Keir.

"Green is one of my favorites as well but blue is my most favorite color. I'm thinking of either this midnight blue fabric or the emerald green fabric," said Lysandra.

"Then we have our decision. We will do the midnight blue and the emerald green," said Keir.

"What are these fabrics for?" asked Lysandra.

"For our formal wear and the like, for us both to wear when we are together. I noticed as your things were being moved that you could use some new clothes without tears and holes," said Keir.

She blushed at the mention of her old clothes.

"Thank you, Your Majesty. My clothes have gotten quite old. I asked the seamstresses yesterday to make me more clothes other than dresses. If that is all right?" asked Lysandra.

"You are soon to be queen. If you are ever in need of anything, don't hesitate to ask for it," said Keir.

"Thank you," said Lysandra.

He smiled back at her. Keir was not used to hearing anyone thank him but servants, who only said it as a formality. He was becoming very grateful for her kindness and realized just how horrible Seraphina had been. He couldn't imagine Lysandra throwing a book or a boot at his head.

I never knew it was possible to find someone as nice as her. Am I deserving of this? Am I worthy? My wish is for us to become great, close friends. I promise to her and to myself to spend more time with her, for us to get to know each other...to bond. I will not be like my father or my former wife. Lysandra shall only receive the purest kindness, compassion, and support, thought Keir.

"Would you like to see the garden?" asked Keir.

"I would love to," said Lysandra.

He offered his arm to her and led her from the study down to the doors to the garden. Keir saw the low-hanging clouds through the window to the left of the doors. He realized it may be quite cold outside for what they were wearing. He turned to his personal servant, who was already there, offering a cloak.

Once the cloaks were draped around their shoulders, Keir led Lysandra into the garden. They walked through the garden, dead though it was, as Keir led Lysandra towards the terrace that faced Holbrook and the valley. Keir first looked out at the view, then at Lysandra, who stood in awe of the scenery, her eyes wide. She glanced at Keir and realized that he looked genuinely happy. His eyes looked at her softly as he gave her a small smile.

How can a man, known to be cruel and coldhearted, show so much kindness to me? Was this how it started with his previous wife, or did they always fight with each other? Why is he being so nice? thought Lysandra.

"May I ask you something, Keir?"

"Of course."

"How did you and your late wife meet?"

"Seraphina and I met when my father took me to visit the small kingdom, Bullmaren, on the other side of the mountains, just past the Falcon Outpost. Our fathers arranged our marriage to unite the kingdoms."

"I'm sure her home is angry at what has happened. Might I ask what the late queen was like?"

"They are certainly grieving their only princess but are glad her murderers were dealt a swift justice. From the moment I met Seraphina, she was a woman who wanted to take command and make it known, even towards me. Seraphina was nowhere near as kind as you are, Lysandra. I know I am known as cold and cruel to our enemies, but I think she was much crueler than I could ever be."

Keir paused for a moment as he looked out to the valley.

"And I am sure Thallan must have told you about her, so you know she and I fought often," said Keir.

Lysandra was afraid to answer for Thallan's sake, for she was not sure how Keir would react if she told him the truth.

"It's all right if he did. It was no secret that we had never gotten along from the moment we met," said Keir.

"I am sorry you had a wife who you did not get along with, Keir."

"It is all right my dear. I only hope that you and I can be friends, at least to start with. Even though we are getting married, I don't want to rush you into the more intimate things. I'm sure this is very nerve-wracking for you," said Keir.

"I would very much like to get to know you and create a friendship with you, Keir," said Lysandra.

He gave her a sweet smile.

After some time out in the garden, Keir led Lysandra throughout the castle, helping her learn about the royal duties that she would help with. She also helped with the occasional questions from servants regarding the wedding details.

As dinner approached, Thallan let Lysandra and Keir have the dining room to themselves, except for the two guards posted just beside the door inside the room for protection. Thallan wanted to use the time to meet with Richard.

Thallan made his way to his quarters to find Richard waiting in the hallway. They both entered the room, shutting the door behind them.

"So, what's the plan? Any idea on how Lysandra can take down the Dark King and the Dark Sorcerer?" asked Richard.

"I have hardly had the chance to speak with Lysandra. She has been by the Dark King's side all day," said Thallan.

"Hopefully, you shall get the chance to discuss things with her soon."

"I am sure we will this evening. In the meantime, I have a plan for keeping her safe during the wedding."

"What's your idea?"

"Vaxar will arrive in two days' time. I need some way to cause him to leave the kingdom before the wedding, or at least during the opening portion of the celebrations. I am afraid that neither I nor my mother can stay beside my sister to mask her magical aura from him for very long."

"I suppose you have already come up with an idea on how to get rid of him?"

"I was thinking of somehow pulling an attack somewhere in the kingdom, making it look like the enemy's handiwork. I am afraid, though, that our men, who also despise the Dark King and Dark Sorcerer, would be recognized. It would be too risky for them if Vaxar was the one chasing them."

"That is far too dangerous to ask of our men, but you are on the right track of an idea. Maybe Lysandra can use her magic to help us quickly contact members of the other kingdoms that could help us?"

"It is possible. I shall speak with her later this evening about this. Valda may be our closest friend who could help with this problem... There is also something you should know about the king. I have told no one yet. It must stay between us."

"I will tell no one. You have my word."

"Vaxar informed me on my latest trip to Cinder Outpost the purpose of the medicine that the king has been taking all his life. Apparently, he can easily lose his temper and become violent. The medicine is to help keep him from being far more cruel and violent than he already is. So, if Vaxar is having him take that, then we should make sure he keeps taking it I do not trust his word but it makes me wonder if Vaxar is trying to contain Keir's darkness, then maybe, just maybe, he is telling the truth."

"Agreed. I don't like Lysandra being so close to him now. This is too dangerous for her, hiding right under their noses."

"I dislike it, too. But I cannot think of a way to get her out of here without risking discovery of who she really is," said Thallan right as someone knocked at the door. "Enter," he called, hand on his dagger.

A guard entered and bowed his head to his commanders. "Sorry to disturb you, sir, but the king has ordered me to tell you that dinner has finished and you can join them now," said the guard.

"Thank you," said Thallan.

The guard's disturbance broke off the conversation. Thallan promptly left his quarters and made his way towards the dining hall where Keir and Lysandra waited for him to join them as their personal guard. When he entered the dining hall, he saw Lysandra smiling her sweet smile and giggling, much to his surprise.

"Ah! Thallan, good, you're here, now we can go to the library," said Keir as he stood up from the table and walked towards Lysandra.

Keir helped move her chair out of the way as she stood up and extended his hand out to her. After they stepped away from the table, they shifted to having their arms linked, leaving the dining hall.

Thallan was uneasy about how close they were getting to be. It seemed too fast for his liking. Every bit of this situation felt too risky. He wondered what her plan was and hoped it would explain the way she was acting around him.

"I was just telling Lysandra all the trouble I used to get up to when I was younger and how often I angered my father. According to her, she was similar with her own mother and yours, Thallan. I don't believe her, though, with how kind she is. Tell me, is she speaking the truth?" said Keir.

Thallan did not know how to react to how kind and genuine Keir seemed. *Could he really be in love with Lysandra?* Thallan thought to himself.

"Yes, it is true, Your Majesty. She was a little rebellious as a child," said Thallan.

Keir laughed as he led them down three different hallways to a pair of doors propped open to a library full of books, parchments, and what might be artifacts scattered about. The library looked lovely to Lysandra, as her eyes were wide and her lips spread in a smile. Multiple large bookcases lined the walls, filled with books and rolled parchments. A window to the right of a fireplace against the wall overlooked the forest and mountainside. She wanted to read every book and discover their secrets, whether it was fictional stories or tales of myths and history.

"It's nothing grand, but it has plenty of knowledge," said Keir.

"This is lovely. It's more books than I have ever dreamed of reading," said Lysandra.

"Read anything that you like in here. Oh! There is a desk over there where you can read, if you choose, but you are welcome to take the books anywhere about the castle," said Keir.

"Thank you, Keir. I have always been fond of reading and learning new things," said Lysandra.

"Well, there is plenty to learn from these dusty old books," said Keir.

Lysandra chuckled softly at his remark. She hoped she could get some time to look through the library before anything of the more serious matters became precedent. She knew for now that she was safe, and the king was no real threat to her. Something felt odd about him to her, and she was keen to discover it, but wanted to be careful doing so. Something in her gut told her it had to do with magic somehow, but she was not sure. So far, her only real threat currently in the castle was Keir's father.

Lysandra wandered around the room, looking at all the books. Many caught her eye. She perused until she found the first book she wanted to read: a book on ancient tales of Meridia, the Dusan, and other spiritual beings. She'd heard stories from her mother and Gwyneth but wanted to read and learn more about them. After all, it was spirits who issued the prophecy.

"That is a good book. All the information on our ancient spirits you can find. It is getting late. May I take you to your room?" said Keir.

"Of course," said Lysandra as she took his arm.

"I will continue to stay in the second smaller main chambers until our wedding day to give you some time to adjust to living here," said Keir, as he led her out of the library.

Once they arrived at the royal chambers, a servant opened the door for them. Keir led Lysandra in. In the main room roared an enormous fireplace, two chairs before it. Beside the fireplace, a small table sat between two windows. Two different chairs were behind it, and a fruit bowl filled with seasonal fruit rested in the center. The two windows in the room provided a magnificent view of the garden down below and the valley beyond.

"I hope you like it. If there is anything you need to add or change to the room, don't hesitate to ask a servant to help. I wasn't sure what color the drapes should be," said Keir.

"The drapes are lovely. I don't think there are any changes I would want or need. I'm still getting used to having a room this size," said Lysandra with a laugh.

"Before I go, may I ask for your company at breakfast in the morning again?"

Lysandra gave him a sweet smile. "Of course. I would love that."

Keir smiled and bowed his head before leaving the room, with Richard following. Thallan shut the door, leaving just him and Lysandra alone for the first time all day.

"I thought you said that he isn't nice? He has been nothing but extraordinarily kind to me since we met," said Lysandra.

"Do not be fooled. He is only pretending to be nice because you are someone new and beautiful. He may want to have you as a blind follower for a wife versus his previous wife, who was always questioning his every move," said Thallan.

"I know. I was only joking. And just so you know, I am only acting sweet and kind to him so I can build his trust and get close to him. He may not notice, but I can tell you were not happy with how close I have been to him today. I'm thinking it is best to get him to really like me in case Vaxar ends up complicating things somehow. He rules over Vaxar. Doesn't hurt to get a little close to the king, since I am to be his wife," said Lysandra.

"I still dislike it, but I had my suspicions that you were up to something," said Thallan.

He paused for a moment to listen with his heightened

hearing. He wanted to make sure no one was outside the door who could overhear what he had to say next.

"On the topic of Vaxar, Richard and I spoke earlier about a plan that could make him leave early during the wedding festivities, but we need your help," said Thallan.

"What's your plan?"

"We want to cause an attack somewhere within the kingdom. Knowing Vaxar, he will want to take care of it personally. The problem is, it's too dangerous to use the few men we have loyal to us. Vaxar would identify them and discover us."

"I agree, it's too dangerous for your men. So, what do you need me to do?"

"I was wondering if there was a way you could magically contact any of our allies? Maybe Valda, since she may still be the closest. I also have another idea if you cannot. Could you magically disguise my men to prevent recognition, if possible?"

"Disguising spells have their limits and don't last very long. And it wouldn't fool somebody like Vaxar if he were the one who captured them. But..." said Lysandra before going silent.

Lysandra thought to herself.

I have Valda's pendant. She should still be near the Cinder Outpost. Richard said that the assassination halted her plans to destroy it. She has been lying low with her plans delayed. I can use the spell to contact her, letting her know when to proceed with her plan and to return safely to the bakery. Vaxar would expect her to retreat, not enter the kingdom. It just might work, thought Lysandra.

"I can contact Valda. She gave me a letter from my father, detailing a spell that I can use to contact others through personal objects. She gave me a pendant, which I have here, with my things hidden in the small chest at the back of the wardrobe. Valda planned to take out an outpost, but recent events delayed her. With tensions dying down from the news of the wedding, it should help her sneak into the outpost to destroy it. We know Vaxar is on his way, and by the time he arrives tomorrow, she can attack the outpost. Word will be here before the wedding, or at least before Vaxar can get the chance to be near me without you or Gwyneth beside me. He still uses those shadow ink journals to communicate with the outposts, right? Therefore, someone at the outpost will inform him almost immediately," said Lysandra.

Thallan's eyes widened, surprised at how quickly she came up with the plan.

"Sounds perfect. How soon can you perform the spell?"

"Right now. You just need to make sure no one comes in and catches me doing magic," said Lysandra, as she walked over to her dresser to retrieve the pendant.

Thallan went to the door and locked it. If someone should try to enter, they would need to knock, which could help buy some time for Lysandra to end the spell and hide what she was doing. He stayed standing beside the door to stay out of Lysandra's way. Thallan felt both nervous and excited to see her use her magic, other than what he had seen when they last trained in the forest. He knew she preferred to practice alone and had never really shown anyone how powerful she was. He wished she did not hide her use of magic from him so much and would show more confidence in her skills. But with the latest events, he noticed she was finally showing some of her true self and hoped to see more.

Lysandra fetched the small chest from the wardrobe and brought it to the table. She opened the chest and found the letter, along with a piece of paper and a quill, before closing the chest.

Lysandra then grabbed the candle from the table, setting it closer to her. Her eyes glowed blue as she muttered, "Pestium infinetus," and pressed the tip of the quill to her finger. The magic drew blood to the quill. Once the tip of the quill was red, she wrote the plan out for Valda, as well as explaining what happened and why they needed her help so soon with such a dangerous mission. As she used the quill, her eyes stayed glowing blue from her magic. Thallan marveled at the vibrant blue of her eyes.

Once everything was written, Lysandra muttered, "Transiego anametus illumius," holding the necklace high above the unlit candle with its pendant dangling. After she spoke the words, the candle magically ignited. She then began incanting the second portion of the spell, transiego anametus, while dangling the pendant above the candle. The flame turned blue and emitted a small puff of dark smoke. She let go of the pendant. Instead of it falling, it floated without the use of a levitation spell.

She then grabbed the parchment and, as she moved it into the flame, bit by bit, it disappeared into thin air. Once the parchment was gone, the candle extinguished in an instant, and the pendant dropped onto the table as her eyes returned to their normal color.

"There, Valda just received instructions on what to do, as well as all that has happened. I also informed her why plans have changed and the urgency behind them," said Lysandra.

Thallan stood, staring at her.

"Did I just see you do multiple spells at the same time? Both needing concentration, especially the spell to send the letter to Valda."

"It was simple magic to me, as it doesn't take too much concentration. Being able to perform magic while fighting requires much more concentration than what I just did here."

They talked for some time before they went to bed for the night. Thallan slept beside the fireplace to stay close to Lysandra, as he was secretly worried that Vaxar may arrive earlier than expected. He gave her a light smile, though, to hide his worries from her. He instructed a servant to bring a cot, spare blankets, and a pillow for him. The door between the bedchamber and the main room remained propped open for the night, so if something were to happen, Thallan could get to Lysandra quickly. Before going to bed, they talked some more, making sure they were prepared for Vaxar's arrival to meet with the new future queen.

12

BLENDING IN

It was far too early in the morning in Lysandra's opinion when a servant woke her up to prepare her to have breakfast with Keir. The servant followed Lysandra behind the screen to help her with the laces on the back of her newest gown. It was nothing too fancy in design except for the vibrant midnight blue color.

Lysandra was trying her best to hide any signs of fear or worry. Her anxieties about Vaxar's expected arrival gave her a trembling feeling. Lysandra hoped she could hide her trembling and for no one to notice. After dressing, she stood in front of the mirror. She was about to braid her hair when the servant unexpectedly stepped in and started working on her hair.

"Oh, I can do that. Thank you though," said Lysandra.

"Yes, my lady," said the servant as she bowed and took a few steps back.

"Thank you, though. I prefer Elvish braids over other styles. They are more comfortable to me," said Lysandra.

"I am afraid I do not know their style, my lady," said the servant woman.

"That is all right. Maybe I can show you someday. Thallan's mother taught me," said Lysandra.

The servant woman smiled at Lysandra's kindness and bowed her head.

Lysandra braided her hair, this time trying her best to keep it tidy. As she struggled, the servant woman watched from afar, waiting for Lysandra to ask for help. Lysandra was trying to work the two small single braids on either side of her wavy hair that was not braided, to meet in the back of her head and then braid the two strands together. The servant woman realized that she may need her help.

"My lady, would you like some assistance?"

"Yes, please. Please braid these two together, leaving the rest free underneath. Usually, I don't worry about a messy result, but given the circumstances, I should have it braided neatly," said Lysandra with her cheeks blushing.

The woman nodded and then helped Lysandra with her hair.

"You'll have to be patient with me. I am not used to having people help me with things," said Lysandra.

"I understand, my lady. Perhaps I can teach you how things work, as you teach me to braid to your liking."

"I would like that. What is your name?" asked Lysandra.

"I am Celia, my lady."

"Nice to meet you, Celia. I'm Lysandra, although you probably already knew that."

Celia finished braiding Lysandra's hair and noticed that she appeared cold by the slight shivers she was trying to hide. She made her way towards Lysandra's wardrobe for a shawl that would look nice with her gown.

As Celia looked, Lysandra's heart skipped a beat with fear at the chance that Celia may find the chest. Then she would find the spellbook alongside the letter from her father, hidden beneath old clothes. Both would surely give away to who she is.

"Celia, may I ask what you're looking for?"

"I am looking for a shawl that would look nice with your dress, my lady. I noticed you are cold."

Lysandra quickly thought of what she owned that would look good with her dress to prevent Celia from stumbling onto the hidden secrets within the wardrobe.

"I believe there is a black one on the far right. That one would look better than my worn brown cloak. I have little, as you can see," said Lysandra.

Celia nodded and searched for the black cloak. She removed it to examine it. Slight wear showed on the sleeves and bottom of the cloak. The faded color made it look quite dirty, even though it was clean.

"If you do not mind, my lady, I am sure we still have some of the previous queen's cloaks. I could get one that would look nice on you today until the seamstresses make new ones."

"That sounds like a good idea. Maybe when you get the chance today, ask the seamstresses to make some new ones or to purchase some from Holbrook even? I'm sure they are busy with wedding preparations."

"Yes, my lady."

Celia bowed, then left to fetch the cloaks.

Though Celia was nice, Lysandra was happy to have a moment to herself. She was not used to having someone always there by her side, ready to help with anything. She preferred solitude over being around people, as it felt safer and more comfortable for her. As she was enjoying her moment alone, there was a knock on the door.

"Yes?"

The door opened, revealing Thallan.

"Good morning. Are you getting used to being up early?"

"For a while before moving here, I have been getting up before the sunrise."

"I know. Sometimes you think you're stealthy when leaving in the mornings, but Gwyneth hears you every time," said Thallan as he laughed.

"Wait. Every time? I thought I was being so quiet. I even learned where not to step to prevent the floor from creaking! Damn your Elvish hearing," said Lysandra as she laughed.

"It is nearly impossible to be quiet with our hearing," said Thallan, as he also laughed.

They left the royal chambers and walked down the hallways and staircases towards the dining hall. Servants filled the hallways, preparing for tomorrow's big day, but all paused and bowed their heads or curtsied out of respect when Lysandra passed. Another thing she would have to get used to. They entered the dining hall to find that Keir was already there. He pulled out her chair for her to sit and then sat next to her.

"Good morning, my dear. I hope you slept well," said Keir.

"Good morning. I slept well, thank you. I hope you did as well," said Lysandra.

"I did," said Keir.

The servants entered carrying plates of food. The food was nothing special to Lysandra because she had grown up at her family's bakery. As far as she was concerned, nothing could beat Gwyneth's cooking.

"I am sorry, but we cannot spend as much time together today as we did yesterday. I have meetings today with guests arriving from Bullmaren," said Keir.

"That is all right. Are there any royal duties that I can help with today?" asked Lysandra.

"There are some final decisions to be made for the wedding tomorrow, if you would like to handle those? The servants will help you with anything you need, of course. I believe the only things left are the food and flower arrangements," said Keir.

"Sounds simple enough. Do you have any preferences?" asked Lysandra.

"No, I trust your judgement. Oh! Before I forget, can you have a servant go to your family's bakery today? I would like to pay them to bake us a wedding cake. I meant to send a servant yesterday. If we ask them today, will they have enough time to bake a cake for at least two of us? My cooks can have some made for the guests," said Keir.

"It should be enough time. Gwyneth and my mother are exceptionally skilled bakers. They will be honored to bake our wedding cake," said Lysandra.

She had a rush of anxiety when she spoke the words. The thought of marrying Keir had finally become real at the mention of her mother making the cake.

"Excellent. We shall have a servant leave to inform your family first thing this morning."

The doors to the dining hall opened without warning. Erebus briskly walked to the table and sat across from Lysandra, and a servant quickly brought a plate of food to him. Keir stiffened in his chair as he ate, avoiding eye contact with his father. Lysandra remained quiet and avoided eye contact with Erebus, too, following Keir's example. Erebus remained quiet as he promptly began eating his breakfast.

"Did you at least check with either Bellehaven or those representatives from the old kingdom of Gragon if they had a woman for you to take as a bride, Keiran? Those peasants there are still giving us issues. In denial of their rulers being vanquished and being a part of our empire," said Erebus.

"No, I did not, Father. I did not think to do that," said Keir.

"That seems to be all that you are good for. Never thinking. I am amazed you have lasted this long as the king and have not handed the crown back to me," said Erebus.

"You know the laws that our ancestor created when he built our kingdom. I cannot hand the crown back to you since I came of age," said Keir.

"I should have overthrown that law. My empire would have been built by now," said Erebus, scoffing.

Keir gulped his breakfast to get started on his tasks for the day and to further avoid Erebus. When he finished eating, he excused himself and left, with Richard following close behind him. Thallan remained in the dining hall with Lysandra and Erebus. Once Lysandra was done, she excused herself and was leaving the dining hall when she bumped into Celia carrying a beautiful hunter green cloak for her.

"Pardon me, my lady. I have a cloak for you. Our seamstresses had this completed for you yesterday evening," said Celia as she offered to help put it on her.

"Please give them my thanks. Those ladies are busy working on making such fine clothes for me. They are quite fast with their jobs," said Lysandra.

"Of course, my lady."

"Thank you. Thallan, can you show me the way to the garden? I still don't know my way around."

"Of course. Right this way."

Thallan led her down two hallways until they arrived at the doors to the garden. The air outside was crisp with an icy breeze, and snow flurries melted upon the ground. A snowstorm would be upon the valley any day now, covering the land in a fresh white blanket. Of all the seasons, Lysandra loved winter the most because of the cooler temperature and how beautiful the land looked with fresh snow.

"The view is gorgeous from here," said Lysandra.

"Yes, it is. I guess I always seem to forget the beauty this place offers," said Thallan.

They took in the view for a little while longer before returning inside where it was warmer. Lysandra asked Thallan to take her on another tour of the castle to help her learn where things were as she found the castle quite large and hard to remember where certain rooms are located. Thallan showed her where the kitchen and other bedrooms were as they walked through the castle halls. He pointed in the direction of the dungeons, but clarified they were not going down there. Then he took her by Keir's study down the hallway from the library.

Lysandra let her curiosity get the best of her. She stopped to open the door, wanting to peek inside as she sensed something strong with magic from inside. To her surprise, Keir was with two men. One of them she did not recognize until he turned around at the intrusion. Vaxar stared right at her with a look of abject annoyance.

"For-forgive the interruption. I was taking a tour of the castle and didn't know someone would be in here," said Lysandra.

"This is the king's study. You may not enter this room! Attend to your duties as the future queen! No surprise that you chose a poor excuse of a woman to be the next queen, Keir," said Erebus.

Keir looked between her and his father with surprise before a hint of worry appeared on his face.

"She is new to the castle father. She is still learning where things are," said Keir.

"That is no excuse, Keiran. Master General, take her elsewhere. This is an important meeting," said Erebus.

Lysandra quickly bowed her head and shut the door. A mixture of worry, fear, and embarrassment filled her mind.

Vaxar was not supposed to arrive till this evening or tonight. How did he get here so quickly? And when did he arrive? Does Thallan know and just chose not to tell me? The scar on Vaxar's face has healed some since that day I saw him in Holbrook. He looks so frightful. This place is already scary enough. How will I ever do this? thought Lysandra.

Lysandra asked Thallan to lead her to the library to find more books to read to pass the time. Thallan watched her closely as she remained quiet after the harsh encounter with Erebus. He chose to give her space until she was ready to talk. He was not sure how to best help her with everything that she is now facing. Thallan gathered logs from the stack beside the fireplace and started a fire to warm the room.

Celia entered the library with refreshments for both Lysandra and Thallan. She placed the plate of food, bottle of wine, and goblets on the table in front of the fireplace. Lysandra informed Celia that she would have her lunch in the library and to send anyone needing wedding decisions here. Once Celia left, Lysandra motioned for Thallan to shut the door.

"Did you know Vaxar is already here?" asked Lysandra.

"Vaxar is here? Was that who was in the study with Keir? I could not see, but I heard Erebus. I did not know he had arrived. No one has told me yet. He must have recently arrived and none of my men have had the chance to tell me. They are to alert me when anyone arrives at the castle. I know that there is a representative from Bullmaren who arrived this morning," said Thallan.

Thallan looked at Lysandra. She stared at the floor, her hands fidgeting with the ends of her shawl. He could see her anxiety rising. Thallan tried to think of something that could help ease her mind until he remembered about Keir's medicine. It was not the best time to tell her, but given the circumstances, she needed to know.

"Lys, there is something that you should know about Keir. Vaxar informed me at the Cinder Outpost that Keir must take a special potion to help keep his anger and mind in check. It is a potion he must take daily. When he does not take it or is getting close to needing to take it, he won't be his calmer self. Although he remains an awful person while on the potion, I would hate to find out what he is like without it," said Thallan.

"What do you mean? That Vaxar is actually trying to keep Keir from being even more evil?"

"That is my guess."

"When I get the chance, I'd like to inspect this potion to determine what it is myself. I don't trust Vaxar's word... But for now, I need you to stay beside me, since Vaxar has arrived early. Now is not the time to take either of them out. I think we would have a better chance defeating the king once Vaxar is away."

"Do not worry. I will never leave your side with him here."

They spent the rest of the day in the library, as Lysandra looked through the books, scanning all the covers and inner pages, looking for a book or two that would catch her interest. They ate lunch beside the roaring fire. Lysandra felt relaxed with Thallan, who, to her surprise, helped here and there looking for books she might like. Sadly, he was not an excellent judge of books as he kept grabbing romance or dramatic tales and plays. Lysandra was not very interested in such things. She preferred tales of adventure or history. After he failed to find a good book for her, he sat beside the fire and watched her have fun in the library instead. He struck occasional conversations about life at the castle and asked about the stories that she read from home or borrowed from neighbors and friends, trying to keep himself from boredom.

Finally, Lysandra stumbled upon a book about Lamorra. She had just taken the book from the shelf when the door to the library opened with a light knock. Keir entered with two servants carrying covered plates. She realized it was dark outside, night having closed in on the castle through the window.

"I hope I am not being premature in trying to make amends over the way my father reacted earlier. There is no excuse for his behavior. I do not wish for our relationship to turn into my last one," said Keir.

Servants placed the dishes on the table, then tended to the fireplace.

"It's all right. I'm sorry for interrupting. I let my curiosity get the best of me and forgot that you may be in there," said Lysandra.

"That's all right. My father and Vaxar were more annoyed than I was at the interruption, but I simply don't care how they feel. They both can be asses, and think too highly of themselves and often forget that neither of them is the ruler of the kingdom."

Keir sat down in one of the chairs before the fireplace. Lysandra smiled at him as she sat in the other chair. Thallan sat beside the open door, watching over Lysandra as anxiety filled him anytime she was near Keir. They both ate their baked chicken dinner with a roll of bread and vegetables. While they ate, Keir noticed the book sitting on the table beside Lysandra's plate.

"Have you started reading it yet?" asked Keir.

"Not yet. I found it just before you arrived. Is it any good?" said Lysandra.

"I read it some years ago. It's rather old, and much of it is missing," said Keir.

Lysandra delicately opened the book as she continued eating. The candlelight and the fire were enough for her to read the book with ease. Keir continued eating as he watched her read the book. He felt happiness for the first time with seeing someone he was fond of enjoy reading as much as himself.

An abrupt knock jolted their attention to the door.

"There you two are. Been looking for this soon to be bride of yours, Keir. I wanted to ask her a few things to check where her loyalties lie and who she is," said Erebus.

"I answered your questions earlier, Father," said Keir.

"Yes. I am well aware. I want to hear what she has to say," said Erebus.

"It's all right, Keir. Lord Erebus, I am loyal to the king of Nathair. I was born in Holbrook and have lived here all my life," said Lysandra.

"Good. Where is your father? All I know of him from what Keiran has told me is that Thallan and his mother took you and your mother in and lived with them, helping in the bakery," said Erebus.

"My father died when I was a baby. Drunk men in Bellehaven killed him," said Lysandra.

"My condolences. I hope our soldiers apprehended those drunkards and dealt them their punishment for distasteful actions. If you stick to your duties as queen, then Keir may have chosen wisely. We shall see in time. I have my own duties to return to," said Erebus, as he promptly left.

"Thank you, Lysandra. I apologize for his interruption and rude attitude, tone, all of it," said Keir.

"Of course. I'm sure he's focused on ensuring the kingdom remains in good hands," said Lysandra.

"He is," said Keir.

She returned to reading what little the old book offered. Many of the pages were so worn that it was hard to read the words, and many pages were missing, like he said. She read through a few pages until she finished with her dinner. When she looked at Keir, she could not help but silently chuckle at seeing the book he was reading: a romance novel. She found it surprising how much she liked the simplicity of his company, both reading their own books in comfort. She continued with her reading.

In the book of Lamorra, she learned that the current realm she knew of had only existed for a little over a thousand years after something to do with the Ancient Hollowed Lands. She believed the worn pages mentioned some sort of devastating war that destroyed the old lands, causing many of the people who lived there to travel to what was now Lamorra and formed the known kingdoms some years later. On another page, it mentioned the war was started by the dark sorcerers attempting to do something that she couldn't make out. Should she ever meet her father, she would certainly ask about Lamorra's history. Surely he must know something, as he taught in the sorcery temples when they were still around.

Once she finished reading, Keir noticed and placed his book on the table. He stood up and shifted the logs on the fire before returning to his seat.

"It is an interesting read, isn't it?" asked Keir.

"Yes. However, I wish the book was in better condition. Much of it depends on guessing what happened long ago," said Lysandra.

Keir nodded in agreement before yawning.

"Shall we call it a night? I'm sure it is late by now. I began reading as well and didn't notice that the servants had cleaned up our dishes at some point," said Keir.

He looked off to the far corner of the room, seeing Thallan sitting in a chair, trying to stay awake.

"I think we should head to our rooms and allow someone over there a good night's rest," said Keir with a chuckle.

Lysandra let out a quiet giggle. She stood up and tip-toed quietly towards him. He must have been quite tired if he had not heard or noticed her approaching. She placed a hand on his shoulder to get his attention. His head shot up quickly.

Both Lysandra and even Keir laughed.

"Thallan, it is time for us to make our way to our chambers and get some rest," said Lysandra, trying to hide her laughter.

"My friend, you need some rest. I don't believe I have ever seen an Elf get startled like that, given your hearing," said Keir, chuckling.

Thallan nodded without saying a word and stood up. They left the library side by side, Lysandra's hand tucked in the crook of Keir's elbow, as Thallan followed more closely behind than before. They walked through the hallways and up the stairway, all lit by candlelight, until they made it to the hallway that led to the royal chambers. Keir walked her to the main royal chambers and opened the door for her before he followed her in. She noticed that Keir's things had been moved into the room while she was away.

"Well, it looks like my father decided for us to not sleep separately anymore. I'm sorry. Old man does not understand boundaries. I argued with him and Vaxar about it earlier today, but to no avail. I may be king, but somehow, they both have control over things with what I do or even say sometimes," said Keir.

"I understand. It's probably best to stay on their good side and avoid further confrontation," said Lysandra.

Lysandra felt emotions rushing from him of a mix of sadness, hopelessness, and anger.

"I can sleep in the main chambers on the floor with some blankets and a pillow. You can have the bed," said Keir as he stared at the floor.

"No. You should sleep in your own bed. I know it's a bit nerve-wracking to share a bed when we have only just met, but we both need a good night's rest. After all, tomorrow is going to be a very busy day for us both. I'm fine with sharing the bed. We will need to do it eventually, since we are to be married. Might as well start tonight," said Lysandra.

"Only if you are sure, my dear. But thank you," said Keir, giving her a sincere smile as he looked at her softly.

Lysandra felt a slight uneasiness at sharing a bed with Keir. She had been hoping it wouldn't happen until after the wedding, at least. She felt more scared of Erebus and Vaxar, however, and found an unusual comfort with Keir's presence. Still, sharing a bed with someone still felt daunting.

"Your Majesty, I will be in the main chambers. Two soldiers will be outside in the hallway guarding the main entrance to the royal chambers," said Thallan.

Thallan bowed, then shut the door behind him, leaving Lysandra alone with Keir for the first time. Her hands grew fidgety again, and she tried her hardest to contain it. Her breathing also quickened, which meant another thing for her to hide. She did not want Keir to notice her anxieties and question what was wrong or anything of the sort.

Lysandra made her way towards her wardrobe and found a nightgown. She did not own any nightgowns and knew it must be a new one from the hardworking seamstresses. She ducked behind the changing screen to dress as Keir changed into his nightly attire behind his screen as well.

Once she changed, she walked towards the bed when she heard something growling. She took another step closer and saw that it was a riker. Its fur was pitch black, with brown streaks of hair along its back, and its glowing green eyes stared intently at Lysandra. Rikers may be small, but they were strong, fierce little creatures that moved incredibly fast and were quite territorial.

"Oh! I'm sorry. I forgot to tell you about Astra. I found her a few years ago on one of my walks in the forest. She was just a baby, and I couldn't leave her because she looked abandoned and needed help. I have always been fond of rikers," said Keir.

"I am surprised you have one. Thallan never told me you had a companion," said Lysandra.

"I keep her a secret. If Vaxar or my father found her, they would both call for this little one to be killed immediately. I rescued a cat when I was younger. My father and Vaxar ordered me to kill it myself. I refused until forced," said Keir.

He approached Astra and petted her little head.

"Can you please keep her a secret? I feel like I can trust you and that is why I thought it would be all right to have her in here instead of the other room. I had her hidden, but she clearly didn't stay put," said Keir, chuckling.

"Your secret is safe with me. Although, you might want to let Astra know I am a friend and not a foe. She looks like she is ready to attack, even with you petting her," said Lysandra.

Keir picked up Astra and held her dearly as if she were a child. After he held her for a minute, petting her head to calm her down, he walked towards Lysandra.

"It's all right. No need to growl. She is our new family member, Astra. She'll help me take care of you, darling," said Keir softly.

Astra listened intently. Lysandra held out her hand for Astra to smell, hoping she would not bite. Astra sniffed her hand for a moment before rubbing her head against Lysandra's hand and letting out a small little squeaky noise.

"There, she likes you. It seems I am an excellent judge of character. She tends to know whenever Vaxar is approaching the door, or my late wife. Astra would growl and then try to get to the door to attack. I'd have to stop her and place her in the makeshift cage hidden under the bed," said Keir.

"She seems like a handful. Strong like her companion but feisty enough to pick a fight with someone she doesn't like... Astra, I think you and I are going to be good friends," said Lysandra as she petted Astra on her head.

Keir smiled in response before setting Astra down on the bed. Both he and Lysandra climbed into bed, Astra between them. There was an awkwardness between Keir and Lysandra as they both faced opposite directions. Having Astra in the middle helped with diffusing some of the awkward tension as there was enough room on the bed for them to be comfortably away from each other.

Astra curled up against Keir's back and quickly fell asleep. Keir leaned over to his nightstand and blew out the candle, leaving only two candles across the room lit for a small bit of light.

Lysandra remained awake for some time after Keir had fallen asleep.

Tomorrow is the big day. I hope Valda succeeds in getting Vaxar out of the castle long enough for me to take care of Keir. But there is something off about him. He doesn't seem like some Dark King the way Thallan and others have described him... It must have something to do with that potion from Vaxar. I need to find out what it really is. Keir has too much good in him to be the infamous Dark King. His father, on the other hand, no doubt about it, thought Lysandra.

13

THE WEDDING DAY

Lysandra woke up to Keir opening the curtains to one of the two windows in the room, letting in the morning sun. She rubbed her eyes to adjust to the bright light as she sat up in bed. Keir stood in front of the window, looking out to the valley below.

"Good morning," said Lysandra.

"Oh, good morning. My apologies if I woke you. I forgot for a moment we shared the bed last night. I must still be groggy," said Keir.

"It's all right. This is usually the time I wake up in the morning anyway," said Lysandra.

He gave her a sweet smile.

"You should see the view. The snow is finally sticking to the ground," said Keir.

Lysandra got out of bed and joined him at the window. The clouds hung low across the entire valley, hiding the mountaintops, while light snow flurries glittered in the sunlight. At least a couple inches had piled atop the castle walls. The sun, shining through the clouds, shone against the fresh powdery snow, lighting up the rooms brighter than ever.

Out of the corner of her eye, Lysandra noticed Keir's hand reach for hers, but he dropped it to his side before he could make contact. Lysandra wondered why he was so hesitant to show affection since he had been so kind to her.

"I was thinking, maybe sometime soon before the snowfall gets too deep, I could show you a secret place of mine in the mountains. It has the most enchanting view," said Keir.

"I would love to see it. Let's hope the snow doesn't prevent us from traveling," said Lysandra.

They were both startled by a sudden knock on the bedroom chamber doors.

"Enter," said Keir.

The doors opened, revealing Celia with another servant.

"Pardon the interruption, Your Majesty, but Vaxar is requesting your presence before you begin your preparations for the ceremony today," said the servant.

"Of course. Tell him I shall meet with him in the study shortly," said Keir.

The servant left. Celia gently set the wedding dress wrapped in paper on the bed to help Lysandra change into. Keir grabbed some simple clothes from his wardrobe and went to his changing screen after deciding to change into the clothes for the ceremony once he is done meeting with Vaxar. Lysandra couldn't help but stare at Keir's back, which was much more muscular than expected, and she felt even more shocked at the sight of his biceps. They might have been slightly larger than Thallan's, and he had a toned abdomen and chest. She hadn't seen Keir work out or train once since moving here, but then again, he had been busy with the wedding preparations, and with Vaxar or his father.

Lysandra realized she was staring and quickly looked away to join Celia at her wardrobe.

By the time she'd changed, Keir had already finished and was heading out the door. She quickly made her way to the dining hall, where breakfast was just being set on the table.

She ate her breakfast alone, aside from Richard standing beside the main doors across the dining hall. As she finished eating, Thallan entered with Eleanora and Gwyneth behind him. Lysandra leaped up and ran to her mother and Gwyneth to hug them tight. It had been strange living without them these past few days. She was so happy to see them again as she was missing them dearly.

"I wasn't expecting you both so early today. I am so happy to see you," said Lysandra.

"We couldn't wait to see you, my dear. It's not the same without you at home," said Eleanora.

"It is sadly quiet in the bakery without you. Could we get something warm to drink? It was a cold ride in the carriage," said Gwyneth.

Lysandra turned towards Celia, but before she could say a word, Celia was already giving orders to another servant to fetch drinks.

"So, how is it having a servant follow you everywhere? It seems you are still learning, as she was already a step ahead of you just now," said Gwyneth.

"It's taking some getting used to. Though Celia is sweet and very helpful, but I still like doing things myself," Lysandra admitted.

"Is that so? From what I remember, it would take you ages to do the dishes or laundry around the house," said Thallan, chuckling.

Lysandra looked at him, annoyed.

"I don't remember that. You must have me mistaken for someone else," said Lysandra, laughing.

"I am fairly certain that it was you. After all, you have that particular facial structure belonging to an adoptive sister of mine," said Thallan.

Lysandra playfully punched Thallan in the arm, just hard enough to surprise him but not enough to leave a bruise as they all laughed at his remark.

"So, who has been doing the deliveries since I am here now?" asked Lysandra.

"Deliveries? No one. Everyone has been coming by the bakery to gossip about you becoming the new Queen. Whole town is buzzing about the news. We haven't needed to do deliveries since you moved here," said Eleanora.

"Well, I guess that's good that you don't need to worry about delivering orders. But if you need someone, I have a person in mind," said Lysandra.

"We will let you know when that day comes. For now, I think the whole town will keep piling up at our door long after the wedding," said Gwyneth.

A servant returned with a tray bearing four mugs of hot cider. The sweet aroma of the cider filled the air as they waited impatiently for it to cool enough to drink. As they drank their hot cider, they made their way to the royal chambers passing by the Spirit Priest to prepare for the ceremony at noon.

The Spirit Priest gave a low bow with a smile before making his way to throne room for the ceremony. Spirit Priests are people that preside over temples to creator Meridia and her Dusan Spirits. They help with those needing spiritual help and guidance, giving blessings to all, and officiants to weddings to spread Meridia's love and prosperity to their marriage.

Thallan stood guard outside the royal chambers while Gwyneth, Celia, and Eleanora helped Lysandra prepare. Gwyneth styled Lysandra's hair, creating an authentic Elvish braided bun adorned with a vine from the forest. It seemed to take forever, and yet not nearly long enough, as the seamstresses arrived with the gown, for which they only had to make a few minor adjustments. The seamstresses waited outside as Celia and Eleanora helped Lysandra carefully lace the dress on. Then the seamstresses made their few alterations, which only took a short while before they shuffled quickly out of the room, as the gentlemen of privy entered and grabbed Keir's royal clothes to take to the smaller royal chambers for him to change into.

Lysandra stood in the middle of the room, feeling far too on display. The dress was pretty but felt uncomfortable compared to her usual wear of pants and shirt. She also did not like feeling like all eyes were on her as her family looked at her in her bridal gown in awe. The gown was an elegant emerald green with midnight blue flowers and vine designs sewn down her chest to the hem, the train draped to the floor. Her shoulders were left bare, with the sleeves draping to her wrists with a strand on each to hook the cuffs to her middle finger.

Celia helped Lysandra into elegant shoes that almost resembled her boots, but much more formal and matching the color of her gown. They were most certainly not as comfortable. Once she was ready, Lysandra noticed her mother and Gwyneth with tears in their eyes. She knew they hoped someday this would happen, although to someone better than the Dark King. Then again, she had yet to witness anything sinister about him. Perhaps that would come with time.

The moment she was ready, it was time for her to make her way to the throne room where the ceremony was to take place. Eleanora and Gwyneth made their way inside to find their seats in the pews that were set up in rows throughout the large room leading up to the raised floor where two thrones sat. Thallan stood beside Lysandra outside the doors while they waited for the ceremony to begin.

Music from the musicians filtered out of the throne room. She could hear the duduk, violin, wooden flute, and a wooden double flute. Lysandra rarely ever heard music playing in Holbrook, so naturally when the doors opened, allowing her and Thallan to walk down the aisle towards the throne, she glanced at the musicians playing the beautiful song for them to walk to.

Lysandra then looked towards the front of the room, first seeing her mother and Gwyneth standing side by side to the left of the Spirit Priest. Then her eyes shifted to Keir, to the right of the priest, dressed in his emerald green royal clothes and the silver crown upon his head for the first time.

Thallan gave a reassuring squeeze on her upper arm before he offered her hand to Keir. He took it, his touch soft, and smiled at her when Thallan moved to stand behind Keir. Keir guided her up to stand across from him, standing face to face.

Vaxar arrived in the throne room from the side entrance. He walked over to stand a few feet behind Thallan, almost leaning against the wall like a child being forced to attend the ceremony.

She returned her attention to Keir, who gave her a smile as he took her other hand. They stood facing each other as the Spirit Priest, in his brown and white robes, grabbed a vine from the small table beside him. He wrapped the vine around their hands. He then handed the royal staff to them to hold together in one hand and a lit candle in the other. The room fell silent.

"Ladies and gentlemen, let us join these two in matrimony before the Dusan," said the Spirit Priest.

The Spirit Priest took out a small, rolled bundle of what smelled like sage. She tried to contain her worry and fear at being so close to Vaxar and for marrying the Dark King. She was more worried than ever about containing her secret that could very well lead to her death. She got so lost in her fearful thoughts that she almost missed what the priest was saying. She brought her focus back to reality just in the nick of time.

"King Keiran Nathair, do you pledge your life, in the name of the good spirits, to be one with Lysandra? To spend your lives together until death?" asked the Spirit Priest.

"In the name of the good spirits, I do," said Keir, his gaze on Lysandra.

The Spirit Priest took one end of the sage and lit it. He then waved it from Keir's face down to his hands where he paused.

"Lysandra Stormlow, do you pledge your life, in the name of the good spirits, to be one with Keiran? To spend your lives together until death?" asked the Spirit Priest.

Lysandra felt a brief relief hearing her fake last name as it helped provide some safety. She knows Vaxar would recognize her true last name in an instant.

"In the name of the good spirits, I do," said Lysandra, as firmly as she could, trying to hide her nerves.

The Spirit Priest then moved the lit sage from their hands towards her face before he circled around them, smoke trailing in his wake. He then returned to where he was originally standing and moved the sage over the rings, laying on a square of cloth on the table to bless them before placing the sage in a dish. He placed the smaller ring upon Lysandra's ring finger, on the hand loosely wrapped in the vine, then the priest placed the larger ring upon Keir's ring finger. Lysandra admired the ring's simple beauty: fine silver with engraved vines bearing tiny silver leaves, all encircling a small, deep blue gemstone. Atop the gemstone were thinner, smaller vines forming what looked like the point of a crown.

Keir's ring was much larger, with a large, flat, deep blue gemstone held by a solid flat, silver design. Along the sides, thin vines intertwined.

"In the name of the Meridia, the creator and protector of the spirit realm and the Dusan, I now join these two people in matrimony and, in so doing, crown the new royal queen of the Nathair Kingdom. You may now kiss the bride, Your Majesty," said the Spirit Priest.

Lysandra's heart pounded as she and Keir leaned into one another. She never expected that the person she was fated to destroy would be her first kiss. She focused on maintaining her composure, not allowing her hands to shake. The tenderness and softness of Keir's kiss surprised her. And what shocked her even more was the feelings rising from the kiss that seemed to last forever but in reality only lasted for a few seconds.

The Spirit Priest retrieved the vine and staff before placing the royal crown upon Lysandra. Her crown was gold with vines and branches intertwining forming the base of the crown with a small engraved symbol of the head of the grimog on the front matching Keir's crown. They both turned towards the audience, holding each other's hands as the room bowed.

"Long live King Keiran and Queen Lysandra Nathair!" cheered everyone in the room.

The musicians played lively music as Keir and Lysandra walked down the steps toward the thrones behind them all.

Thallan stuck close behind her, more so than Keir, to help mask her aura from Vaxar, not far behind him.

They approached Lysandra's mother as she curtsied to them. She didn't like seeing them curtsy to her and Keir. It felt odd to her seeing family do something so formal to her like how others in the castle had been doing since she moved in. Eleanora gave Lysandra a big hug. To both Eleanora and Lysandra's surprise, Keir hugged Eleanora as well. Behind them stood Vaxar, disapproving of Keir's kindness with a scornful look on his face. Keir and Lysandra exchanged pleasantries with any guests who approached as they walked towards the ballroom. Many of the people attending the ceremony had already headed in the same direction.

As they walked, Lysandra quicky looked behind her to make sure that either Thallan or Gwyneth remained nearby. Now that one of her worries has passed of marrying and kissing Keir, the other worry rose as the rest of the ceremony was to continue and Vaxar still hadn't left.

Valda better have attacked the outpost by now. And I wish Vaxar wouldn't stay so close by us. I just hope he doesn't grow suspicious with Thallan or Gwyneth remaining so close to me, thought Lysandra.

Outside the ballroom, they waited for everyone to arrive and for the master of ceremonies to announce their entrance. As they waited, Vaxar approached Keir and Lysandra. Thallan stepped closer to Lysandra's side, only a few inches away. With Vaxar now standing in front of her, Lysandra's worry heightened. She focused intently on not squeezing Keir's hand or trembling in fear.

"Congratulations, Your Majesties," said Vaxar as he bowed his head. When he raised his head, he added, "Keir, I must admit, your quick discovery of your new bride surprised me. It seems you made a wise choice. I have learned that she is closely related to our most trusted general."

"Thank you, Vaxar," said Keir.

"My queen, I have only a few words of advice, knowing that you are new to royal duties. In order to keep this kingdom strong with its lineage, I urge you to provide the king with an heir soon. Also, I am unsure if you have noticed, Keir can be quite forgetful at times as I have reminded him for years to take his medicine on time. So, I ask you to help me ensure he continues taking the special potion I make for him, as it is medicinal magic.," said Vaxar.

Keir rolls his eyes at Vaxar in annoyance.

"Thank you, sorcerer. I shall take your advice under consideration," said Lysandra.

For an infinitesimal moment, they stood there in an awkward, tense silence until a soldier with a small piece of parchment rushed towards them, finally pulling Vaxar's gaze away from Lysandra. Vaxar and Thallan both stuck out a hand to urge the soldier to slow down.

"What is the meaning of your intrusion, soldier?" demanded Vaxar.

"Apologies, sorcerer. I have just received this missive from the soldier in charge of your shadow journals. Cinder Outpost is under attack by General Valda Nilsine of the Krogodo Kingdom," blurted the soldier as he gasped for air.

"Vaxar, you will be the quickest. Leave now and stop this attack. Thallan, increase the defenses around the castle. This may be their way of trying to weaken us to attack here," said Keir.

Vaxar and Thallan both bowed and set off, walking at a rapid clip down the hallway until Vaxar turned down a separate hallway from Thallan. Once Vaxar was far enough away,

Lysandra let out a silent sigh of relief. She wished the plan had worked sooner.

She had noticed how Vaxar looked at her oddly, as if she seemed familiar in a way he couldn't place. But he did not seem alarmed, to her relief. If he returned sooner than expected, before she could do anything about the current situation with the king, she knew she would need to be even more careful than before. She hoped he did not have any suspicions from their first meeting that day in her family's bakery.

Not a moment later, the ballroom doors opened for Keir and Lysandra to enter as the master of ceremonies announced their entrance, with the royal tune of music soaring out of the musicians' instruments. Keir and Lysandra walked towards the center of the ballroom hand in hand and waited a few seconds for the music to signal the start of the dance. The musicians played a soft, beautiful song, and one by one, pairs of people joined in until soon many of the attendees danced around them.

For the rest of the evening, Lysandra found herself enjoying the festivities and nearly forgot her worries about Valda needing to escape before Vaxar arrived. She silently hoped and prayed for Valda's safety, and then the ball captivated her once more. Keir was ever so kind and generous, and to her surprise, even offered her mother a quick dance, which she kindly accepted. Lysandra, for a moment, felt happy until her mind once again wandered.

Thallan mentioned the potion that Keir must take, and now so has Vaxar. I don't know why, but I believe there's more to that potion than what Vaxar revealed. I just have this feeling that it holds a much darker purpose. Surely someone with so much kindness in his heart, in his actions, cannot contain such evil. I am almost certain it's the potion that makes him the Dark King for Vaxar and Erebus to control. Erebus is more the Dark King than

Keir. *And just being near Vaxar, I can tell there is more to him than anyone sees. He's smart. Nothing he does is random. It must have a deeper meaning. A well thought-out plan he has calculated and makes sure it does not fail. In the morning, I will learn the true purpose behind that potion,* thought Lysandra.

The rest of the night, she focused on enjoying the ball, the food, and the drinks with such splendid company. Everyone was so cheerful and happy and, not to mention, the food was surprisingly good compared to the previous meals and desserts she had eaten at the castle all thanks to her mother and Gwyneth for making the desserts for the ceremony. As it got late, the ball came to an official close. Lysandra said her goodbyes to her mother and Gwyneth before returning to the royal chambers with Keir.

As they both changed into their sleepwear behind their screens, Keir remembered something that Vaxar had mentioned earlier. He thought he should bring it up to ease Lysandra's mind on the matter, in case she had been worried or nervous about what the sorcerer instructed.

"Lysandra, just so you know, what Vaxar said about providing an heir does not need to happen anytime soon. Both Vaxar and my father treat it as an urgent matter when it really isn't, not to me. There is plenty of time still before that is to be considered. Afterall we just got married and I want to enjoy the time of it being just us. I'm personally not ready for children yet," said Keir.

"Thank you. I have, well, noticed their focus on that," said Lysandra.

"My apologies for their behavior. Vaxar and my father have always been eager to plan for the future and ensure nothing goes wrong. They have always been prudent about such things, having a set of alternate plans if the primary plan doesn't succeed," said Keir.

"Yes, Thallan is like that, although not quite as intense," said Lysandra.

"Tomorrow, I have some royal duties to attend to. Normally we would whisk ourselves away for a honeymoon, but Vaxar and my father have explicitly told me that now is not the time after latest events and with the Krogodo general rumored to be somewhere in the kingdom. So, due to safety reasons, we shall remain at the castle. Later in the day, I would like to spend some time together in the library to continue to get to know one another, if that is all right?" asked Keir.

She gave him a smile. "I would love that. Of course," said Lysandra.

Keir moved in to share a tender kiss before they made their way to the bed. The minute they climbed under the covers, Astra jumped onto the foot of the bed and made her way to snuggle between them. They both caressed her soft fur before Keir blew out the candle and they fell quickly asleep.

14

THE POTION

Lysandra woke to Keir quietly dressing in the candlelight, unwilling to open the curtains and wake her. She was about to sit up when she noticed Astra curled up into a tight ball against her stomach. Lysandra could not help but smile at the little creature. She looked over to the top of the small dresser against the wall to see if Keir had taken his morning dose of medicine and noticed he had not.

Lysandra slowly sat up, trying not to disturb Astra. Keir noticed and walked towards her before putting on his shirt.

"Good morning, my dear. I see little Astra has grown to like you."

Her answer was delayed: "Good morning." She had almost forgotten how muscular he was. Seeing his physique made her wonder if Keir was skilled as a fighter. She'd heard nothing from Thallan about whether Keir was a fine swordsman. When she realized she'd been staring at him, embarrassment warmed her cheeks.

Lysandra turned her attention to Astra as she tried to slide away to stand. Keir offered his hand to help her out of bed. Once she was on her feet, Keir surprised her by pulling her in for a kiss full of passion. Lysandra didn't know whether to kiss him again or let it end when he slowly pulled away. She decided on sharing a sweet smile. He smiled back.

The more time she spent with Keir, the more Lysandra was developing feelings towards him. She found it very hard to believe what Vaxar and Thallan had said about him, as there was too much good in him. Keir had instructed the servants the night before to give them time alone in the morning and to meet them in the dining hall.

Keir returned to his changing screen to grab his shirt draped over it. Lysandra followed, to go to her wardrobe to grab her clothes to get dressed for the day. As she moved things around, she tried to be careful to keep her chest containing her spellbook hidden.

"Why don't you move that small chest out of the dresser? You would have more room for your boots without it in there," said Keir.

Lysandra quickly tried to think of some excuse to have kept it in the wardrobe.

"It's been in my family for generations. I feel safer with it in here since it is so old, and I don't want it to get damaged by accident."

"I understand. In that case, I wouldn't want to risk little Astra or the servants accidentally damaging it."

Relief flooded her, that her excuse worked. She found her clothes and ducked behind the screen to change. She expected Keir to leave, to attend to the royal duties he'd mentioned, but he remained in the room.

An awkward silence stretched between them. Once she buttoned her pants, she reached for her shirt. She wanted a break from dresses today, since there were no royal duties to attend to. Keir wanted to handle all the royal duties to give her time to adjust to the change in life from bakery to castle. Lysandra felt more comfortable in clothes clearly meant for travel or fighting. Certainly not what a queen would typically wear.

As she tied the strings on the side of her shirt to help make it fit a little snugger, Keir knocked on her changing screen and peeked his head around the side, surprising her.

"Do you need any help?"

"Oh, no, thank you. I think I've got it. I hope you don't mind me wearing one of my more usual outfits. I'll be honest with you, I am most certainly not one of those women who loves to wear dresses. They can be quite uncomfortable."

Keir gave her a smile. "That is all right, my dear. If you like, you can ask the seamstresses to make clothes more to your liking. There is no rule saying you must wear dresses. You can dress however you like."

"Thank you. I just might visit them after breakfast then."

"The servants can bring them to you if you like," said Keir.

"I know. I want the excuse to go to them to still learn the layout of the castle. It's big and confusing compared to the bakery," said Lysandra.

"Hmm. It is big. I had not thought of how confusing it could be changing from a smaller home to a far bigger one. Take all the time you need to adjust and learn the place," said Keir.

Lysandra walked to sit on the edge of the bed to put her boots on. Keir followed, keeping his gaze on her. She could tell he was thinking, even though his expression didn't show it. She let him believe she didn't notice him staring, keeping her face down as she laced up her boots.

"I wonder if I'll ever get used to having a woman around who isn't all about looking like royalty and expects everything done for her. Also, the sweet kindness."

Lysandra peeked up at him with a smile. "Or a woman who is skilled with a blade and bow."

"That is true. I will have to thank Thallan for teaching you how to be the strongest woman I know. I will also need to thank your mother for raising such a kind and gentle person I am grateful to have in my life," said Keir.

Then he offered his arm to her to lead her to the dining hall for breakfast. As they ate, Keir was ever so curious about her skillsets as a fighter and asked her questions about training with Thallan. He expressed his opinion on why Thallan was the greatest warrior he knew, leading to his decision to make him the Master General Knight of the kingdom.

Once they finished breakfast, Keir bid her goodbye, leaving Lysandra alone in the dining hall with Celia. She sat there for a moment, trying to plan out her day of things that she could do. All she could think of was going to the seamstresses to request new clothes similar to the ones she was wearing, and that wouldn't take long at all.

Lysandra quickly realized how much time she had spent training, practicing magic, and working in the bakery before moving to the castle. She was now facing a problem of what to do for the day while Keir was away to keep herself from being bored. She was far too afraid to attempt practicing magic, as she did not know where Celia's loyalty lay and if someone else might catch her. Lysandra reluctantly knew that her identity must remain a secret in order for her to take down Vaxar.

She thought for a moment and realized now might be a good time to investigate Keir's medicine. Lysandra was about to head towards the room before she decided she needed something to cover for her, wanting to be alone. She changed course and headed to the library to grab a couple of books. Therefore, she could have a believable excuse for Celia to leave her alone in the room just long enough to do a quick potion test on Keir's medicine. She knew she could have servants get books for her, but she wanted to peruse what the library has to offer some more.

In the library, she looked around to find a couple books. She found one on the kingdom's history and another about the creatures native to the kingdom. Lysandra figured the testing of the medicine shouldn't take too long and these books sounded interesting to her to read to fill up the rest of her day.

With her books in hand, she returned to the royal chambers as Celia followed at a distance. Once she made it to the room, she placed the books on the table as Celia was having a servant stoke the fireplace back to life. When the fire was crackling once more, Lysandra asked Celia to bring her something warm to drink and a snack for her day of reading. Lysandra promptly sat in the chair beside the fireplace and read the book about the creatures in the Nathair Kingdom as she waited for the servant Celia sent to the kitchen to return.

I wonder if Keir trained Astra to hide from servants during the day. Hopefully she comes out later once she realizes the servants won't be in here much of the day. I have grown fond of her, thought Lysandra.

She skipped to the next creature mentioned in the book, the Kamari. She had seen them often in the forest on her walks to the waterfall where she trained. They were equally beautiful and intimidating with their large size and sharp talons compared to their wooded owl cousins, so she could never get too close.

The next creature was one she was very grateful to have never come across: a Grimog. They were large, deadly creatures that have killed many people, including some of the most skilled soldiers of the Nathair Kingdom. A few months ago, Thallan had warned her of one venturing too close to Holbrook and advised her to be careful if she ever went into the forest. Soldiers had tried capturing and killing the creature but failed every time. However, the beast was injured and killed many soldiers and hunters that went after it. Because of their speed and ability to blend into the shadows, they were a formidable foe.

She was reading about the Grimog when the servant returned with hot cider and a plate with a grugalberry muffin, grugalberries in a delicate glass dish, and a sliced apple. She thanked Celia and dismissed her for the day, as she wished to be alone to read. Lysandra returned to reading the book as she wanted to learn what she could about the Grimog before testing the medicine.

As she read, Lysandra began to understand the Grimogs' terrifying reputation. They remained extremely quiet as they hid in shadows, and you only knew when one was nearby when their eyes and streaks of their fur and tail glowed a dark blue from the magic that flows through them. The book says nothing about any magical abilities they possess other than their glow. Lysandra wondered if their magic deals with elements since they are incredibly stealthy and hide well in the shadows, something to help with their hunting capabilities. On all fours, they would stand at the height of the average man's hips. At the end of the passage was a terrifying sketch of a Grimog. Its face was a perfect mixture of a bear and wolf, with the tall pointy ears, the long snout of a bear, and the large canine teeth of a wolf. Below the description and picture at the bottom of the page, a handwritten label classified the creature as magical.

What makes this creature magical, other than its glowing eyes and fur? Wish there was more written about it... I wonder if even Vaxar is afraid of the Grimog, thought Lysandra.

She put down the book and went to the door to listen carefully for anyone besides her guards outside that Thallan placed to add more protection after what happened to Seraphina. She contemplated telling the guards to not let anyone enter, but worried if they would ask for a reason. She decided against it and, as quietly as she could, locked the door instead.

Lysandra made her way to Keir's dresser and opened the middle drawer to steal one of the medicine bottles. A couple of drops were all she needed. The small amount shouldn't be noticeable if Vaxar was being truthful of the purpose. She then went to her small chest to grab her spellbook and the belt with herbs and other magical ingredients in small vials that she hid underneath the clothes in the chest.

Lysandra sat at the table and flipped to the part of the spellbook covering potions. She grabbed the spoon from the plate with the drink and snacks. Then she poured three drops of the medicine onto the spoon, holding it above one of the lit candles. She grabbed a small vial with a powdery blue substance and sprinkled a little onto the spoon. Then she grabbed finely crushed red maple leaves and brown pine needles from a pouch and placed three small pieces onto the spoon while she kept it over the flame.

The medicine changed color. She held the spoon over the flame until the color change and solidification was complete. Then she opened her book to the medicinal potions, looking for the potion color and smell description that matched what was in the spoon. None matched, as she suspected, so she moved on to the rest of the potion sections and searched through them one by one until she found it.

It was a potion designed to make someone more susceptible to the brewer's orders. She remembered when she was younger, and Eleanora attempted teaching her some things that she knew from Krarick. She had told her that this potion, along with some spells, could give the spellcaster the power to bend someone to their will, to control them, depending on the potency.

Thallan said that Keir has been taking this for as long as he can remember, Lysandra thought. *If he's been taking this for years, that means he isn't the Dark King. Erebus is. It means Vaxar and Erebus are, and Seraphina must have known the truth, or at least some of it. I have a feeling that Keir wasn't turning out the way Erebus wanted, so he and Vaxar lied about the medicine and its purpose. That's why Keir is always so different when the potion wears off and he needs another dose. But the potency that Vaxar is making is no longer strong enough to fully control him. That's why he's always late or forgetful. It's the good side of him trying to fight the evil being forced upon him...*

This must be how I fulfill the prophecy. I need to switch out his medicine with something that looks and tastes like Vaxar's potion but will only have the effect of removing their control. If I remove that, then hopefully I can speak freely with Keir, and he'll see the truth and join forces against Vaxar, thought Lysandra.

Lysandra quickly dumped Vaxar's potions from the remaining three bottles hidden in the drawer into the fire. She at once brewed a new potion to take away the effects and help Keir regain control over himself.

She made the potions and bottled them after about twenty minutes. They looked identical to the original potions from Vaxar. She placed them in Keir's dresser drawer and knew he would never suspect a thing—not even based on their flavor. Now, all Lysandra could do was hope that this plan would work, and she could gain Keir as her ally. After all, he would be a powerful one, as he knew Vaxar better than anyone.

A knock on the door interrupted Lysandra as she was

cleaning the table. Terror struck her at her core, and she worried who it might be.

"Who is it?"

"Thallan. Is it all right if I come in? The guards said Celia told them you wished to not be disturbed," said Thallan.

She sighed in relief. She felt ever so grateful for Celia. Lysandra went and unlocked the door, opening it to let Thallan in and quickly shutting it behind him.

Thallan's eyes fell on the table, and widened. "You should not be doing that in here. It is not safe! You are lucky it was me and not someone else."

"That's why the door was locked and Celia and the guards were told not to disturb me. They think I wanted time to read some books. Also, Keir is busy and will be away until lunchtime."

"He may be away longer than that. He cannot reach Vaxar through the shadow journal. We sent a bird out this morning. It's unusual for Vaxar to not respond to either myself or the Dark King."

"Where was he last known to be?"

"At the Cinder Outpost. I doubt Valda stayed there long enough to meet him. Something must have distracted him or he caught Valda's trail. Or better yet, maybe that notorious grimog we've been having trouble with got to him."

"Let's hope."

Thallan took a moment to consider his next words. "What, exactly, were you doing? I doubt you were practicing magic. You would only do this here if you had to."

"I was testing Keir's medicine to see if what Vaxar said was true."

Fear gripped her throat. She worried if Thallan would listen and believe her.

"Well, is Vaxar telling the truth?"

"He lied. It's a potion used to control and manipulate someone. Vaxar is likely only using this because Keir doesn't hold up to the standards that he and Erebus demand of him."

Lysandra could see in Thallan's face that he was not believing her.

"Keir is under their control, Thallan. Even you agree Keir has been showing far more kindness since we met. The potency that Vaxar makes the potion is not strong enough to make Keir do their dark bidding. The good in him is fighting to get out. Erebus is the true Dark King, not Keir. There is good in Keir."

"Are you sure you did the testing of the potion correctly? I have been around the Dark King for years. I have seen the aftermath of the terrible things he has done or has ordered others to do. I just do not think that a simple potion can control someone enough for them to do the things I have seen him do without Vaxar telling him to do them. I am also worried about what could happen if Vaxar learns or notices Keir not on his potion. If what you say is true, he could start to act differently and it may be noticeable."

"It doesn't have to be Vaxar pulling the strings. Erebus is constantly by his side, telling him what he should do. The potion only lasts for a certain length of time. That is why he must continue taking it every few hours during the day, from the moment he wakes until he goes to bed."

"I am sorry. I am not sure if I believe it. I have seen so much darkness from him. But as you said his father is always hovering around him. I am not sure what is the safe way to go about the information though."

There was an awkward moment of silence as Lysandra chose not to continue arguing with him. She knew he would not listen to her. He always struggled, listening and trusting her.

I know I wasn't trained in a temple like my father but I know I am right about this, thought Lysandra.

"Lysandra, I hope you are not reaching for something that is not there with him. Keir may act sweet with you, but that would quickly change if he knew your true identity. He would try to kill you. He does not love you. Keir is just looking for an heir and someone to look pretty by his side. There are plenty of other people out there that would be better to fall in love with than him."

Lysandra remained silent as she resumed cleaning the table.

"I just do not want you to get yourself hurt because you are falling for a man incapable of love. Just be careful, please. Remember the prophecy. Your destiny is to defeat the Dark King and the Dark Sorcerer. Not fall in love with the Dark King who has terrorized the lands for years, continuing his father's legacy."

She sighed. "I know. I just think that if there is a chance that I could save him and bring him back to the path of good, then it is something that I should try. For all we know, this might be how I fulfill that part of the prophecy. Those things aren't exactly word for word most of the time anyway. But don't worry, I will be careful. I won't do anything foolish and reckless. And for your information, I am not falling in love with him."

"I hope so."

"Can I be alone for a while? I am sure you have some kind of royal general duties to attend to. I'd rather be alone and actually read these books."

Thallan nodded and left the room in silence, shutting the door behind him. Lysandra sat down and drank some of her cider. She picked up the book she was reading earlier.

When will he ever listen and trust me? thought Lysandra as she fought back tears.

She continued to read the book on the creatures to help distract her mind from Thallan, Keir, Vaxar, and the prophecy. She focused intently on the rest of the book, learning about the fairies' extinction years earlier. Then she read about the Phoenix before she grew tired of reading and went for a walk in the garden to get some fresh air, hoping to spend the rest of the day avoiding her thoughts, her feelings.

Sadly, later that day, Thallan attempted to talk to her again, wanting to plan their next moves to take down Keir and Vaxar. Lysandra, once again, told him to go away. He tried to argue the importance of needing to set up a plan, but she simply ignored him. If he would not listen to her, she would extend him the same courtesy. For now, at least.

Then, not long after Thallan bothered her, Keir was back at her side in the late afternoon and evening. She found it hard to fake a smile of happiness and be kind to him when all she wanted was to be far away from the castle, alone, without a prophecy to fulfill or some evil person needing to be killed.

15

SPARKLING WINTER TEA AND LEAF BISCUITS

Keir gently woke up Lysandra and had Celia help her get dressed in warm travel clothes before they ate a quick breakfast in the dining hall. Lysandra was curious about his excitement. She could tell that he was attempting to hide it, but he was not good enough to keep it from her.

After breakfast, they went outside to the castle's stables and mounted their horses. Lysandra's curiosity grew too much to bear.

"So, am I to continue wondering where it is you are taking me today, or will you finally tell me?" asked Lysandra.

"It is a surprise. You will see soon enough."

He wore a smile she hadn't seen on him before. It was a smile of happiness like that of a child giving a gift they were ever so proud to give.

They began their journey, leaving through the side gates of the castle and into the woods. Even though it had only begun snowing a few days ago, much had fallen in the woods in the higher elevation compared to the valley. The snow was at least a foot thick beneath them as they rode through the forest. Not long after they began their journey, the snowfall began again. But to their luck, it remained light. Knowing the weather in the mountains, though, by the afternoon the snowfall would be much heavier and more dangerous to travel in.

For a good portion of the journey, there was silence between Keir and Lysandra. Even the four guards and Thallan were silent. They could only hear the horses' hooves crunching on the snow.

"I am unsure if what I am about to say is true, but the last half of the day yesterday, you seemed distant. I guess what I am trying to say is that you seemed unhappy over something. I was afraid to ask then, as I figured you wanted some privacy or space. That is why I'm hoping what I show you today may brighten your spirits," said Keir.

Lysandra gave him a sweet smile.

"Thank you, Keir. I was having a rough afternoon. It was only because I was a little homesick and still feeling new to the castle."

"If you ever want to visit your mother, you are more than welcome to do so. You don't have to spend all your time in the castle."

Keir reached over and rested his hand on her shoulder and gave her a caring smile. Lysandra felt comfort from his gentle reassurance.

They rode for another half hour before stopping. Before continuing, Lysandra was about to remind him of his medicine when she turned and noticed he was already taking it. When he was taking Vaxar's potion, he often forgot to take it or was always late. Now that he was taking hers, he had remembered to take it on time. By tonight, when he finishes the last bottle, he would have eliminated Vaxar's potion and its effects. They had not received a package from Vaxar containing more, though, which made her worry.

"Thallan, you come with us. The quad can stay here and guard the horses. We won't be too far up ahead. They will hear us if something happens," said Keir.

Thallan nodded and relayed the orders to the captain of the quad. Keir led them onward. They trekked through the snow, ducking beneath low branches weighted down with the snow as their feet sank into the fresh powder.

While walking underneath some tree branches, Lysandra slipped and instinctively grabbed a tree branch, knocking snow onto her face as she fell onto her back. Filled with embarrassment, she avoided eye contact while looking down to hide her blushed cheeks. Keir let out a slight giggle.

"Are you all right?" asked Keir.

"Yeah. I'm fine, other than my pride. That branch did not help stop me from falling," said Lysandra as she laughed.

Keir helped her up and caringly wiped the snow from her back and hair. He took her hand and walked beside her to help prevent her from falling again. Thallan, who was walking behind them, did not like how close and comfortable Lysandra was to Keir. He realized then she had developed feelings for him. They walked for another few more minutes before Keir stopped.

"Thallan, stay here. This area is so beautiful. I know you have given me many reasons to trust you, my friend. I want to first share this with Lysandra. Don't worry, we will only be on the other side of these large bushes here in front of us. There is no danger here," said Keir.

Keir looked at Lysandra with eyes filled with excitement. Thallan did not trust him. He didn't like the idea of leaving her alone with him out here.

Keir lifted a branch from the bush, revealing a hidden

passageway. He motioned for her to follow as they walked through. Keir quietly told her where to duck and where to watch her footing to avoid tripping on the roots sticking out of the ground. She struggled as they walked through the bushes, holding her cloak to prevent it from snagging on the branches while the other hand moved some branches out of her way.

While they meandered through the narrow passageway, Lysandra looked around her and noticed a few other paths through the bushes leading off in different directions. It felt as if they had been walking for a long time, moving through the thick snow-covered brush. Then a bright, warm light peered through branches in front of them.

"Try to be quiet. I have never brought anyone here, so they are not used to me being with others."

Lysandra could feel something as they moved closer. It felt like magic, but stronger. She wasn't sure what it was. All she knew was that it felt like a strong connection to the land spirit Dhara. Gwyneth once spoke of Elves slight elemental magic giving them a sense of connection to Dhara. She wondered if this is the connection she was feeling now.

Keir turned around with wide eyes and a big smile and placed a finger on his lips, reminding her to be quiet. As soon as she made it out of the bushes, she saw what was creating the light. Lysandra knew immediately what magic she felt now that she could see them flying around their hidden grove in the forest.

Fairies! thought Lysandra.

Her eyes grew wide in amazement. Their warm light emitted from them as they so elegantly flew around and the light from their wooden houses built against the trees all reflected off the fresh white powder upon the ground and in the trees. Some fairies stopped for a moment, noticing their presence, but then simply resumed flying and going about their business.

As the fairies flew around their hidden paradise, she noticed their attire blended with their surroundings. Their clothes looked to resemble leaves from the trees of the forest, mixed of greens and browns with designs similar to Elven attire. Some even seemed to have small swords and wore armor of the same shades of greens and browns. Lysandra assumed, given their size, they would be difficult to fight against. She wondered if they had their own magical abilities. The book she read the day before lacked information on fairies.

Their beauty amazed her, and she couldn't stop admiring the sight. Keir had broken his gaze on the fairies and was watching Lysandra's reaction to them. He watched her for a moment before looking back at the fairy village. He noticed a few of the fairy guards watching and then one of them flew up to them, a trail of sparkling light trailed behind them until they stopped, and the fairy dust danced around them. Their wings were nearly transparent with a soft vibrant glow of yellow-orange fairy dust. They wore a mix of chocolate brown and dark green shades of clothes with glistening silver armor over them, with the tiniest swords that Lysandra has ever seen.

"Hello, Keir. We haven't seen you in a long time. You look like you are doing much better since the last time we saw you. Who is this that you have brought with you?" said the fairy guard.

"Yes, lately I have been feeling better, and it may have something to do with my lovely new wife. This is Lysandra."

The fairy flew closer and gave Lysandra a bow. He then gave her a look as if he saw right through her and knew immediately who she was.

"It is an honor to meet you, Lysandra. I can tell you are a very special person. We will see great things from you, I am sure of it. Come now. Our Queen and King would love to see you both," said the fairy guard.

"We cannot stay for long. The weather has already made it tricky to get here, and I worry if the snowfall continues it may get dangerous going home," said Keir.

"Of course, Your Majesty. Would you be able to stay long enough for a cup of tea?" asked the fairy guard.

"Yes. That would be splendid."

"Fantastic! Follow me," said the fairy guard.

The fairy flew ahead of them and at one point stopped another fairy, passing along orders. They walked through the center of the large fairy village. The fairies were all intrigued and interested in their arrival.

Lysandra was in awe of how beautiful their village was. There were little structures built against the trees, from the ground to nearly the tops of the trees. Some of them provided a porch and an entryway to each home inside the trees. Others had everything built on the outside, with stairs encircling the center of the tree leading to other beautiful establishments. Their village resembled much of the Elvish kingdom from the descriptions and stories Gwyneth and Thallan told her.

The fairy led them to the largest tree in the village. In front of it, there were at least a dozen fairies with two of the brightest flying in front. Lysandra assumed they were the Queen and King. The Queen was wearing the most beautiful shade of violet and blue-green colored dress with gold beaded lace over the middle and bottom. The King wore a suit matching the Queen's outfit with lace on the cuffs of his sleeves, shoulders, and chest.

As they approached, Keir bowed to the fairies. Lysandra

quickly curtsied, wanting to make sure she made a good first impression. The fairies bowed in return. They were around half a foot tall with translucent glowing wings fluttering behind them just slightly longer than the length of their arms.

"Oh, we are so happy to see you again Keir, my dear!" said the Queen.

"It is good to see you both again. It has been too long since I visited," said Keir.

"Indeed, it has. The others have tea and cookies prepared for us," said the King.

They led Keir and Lysandra to the back of the large tree where there was a round table with two chairs made of wood. A far smaller table and chairs for the fairies were on top of the table. On both tables sat a teapot, cups, and a plate of leaf biscuits.

They all sat down at the table. Keir poured Lysandra and himself a cup of tea as the fairies did the same. Keir then handed one of the leaf biscuits to Lysandra. The cookies were leaf-shaped, but thicker and brown.

"You must try these. They are delicious! They use their magic to make the tea and biscuits larger for us. Don't worry. It is perfectly safe," said Keir.

Lysandra took a bite of one. It had the softest texture and it practically melted in her mouth. It was sweet, like a molasses sugar biscuit with a hint of a grugalberry taste.

"This is the best biscuit I have ever had. It is so delicious," said Lysandra.

Keir smiled at her as he sipped his cup of tea.

"Queen Meira and King Silas, it is my honor to introduce you to my new wife, Lysandra."

Lysandra bowed her head to the fairies as she smiled.

"It is so nice to meet you, Lysandra. I am glad Keir has someone that he can trust and who loves him. We heard about how cruel his previous wife was. I am glad that you are now with someone better for you, my dear," said Meira.

"I am grateful to have him in my life. I am also honored to be someone that he can comfortably confide in. It is a great honor to meet you both," said Lysandra.

There was a moment of silence as they drank the warm, sweet tea and ate their biscuits. The cold weather seemed to have disappeared despite snow still being all around them. Lysandra wondered if it had something to do with the magic of the fairies.

"Keir here saved us from that evil sorcerer and his father many years ago when he was just a young teenager. They wanted us dead simply because of our magic," said Silas.

"We helped with what we could during the Nightshadow War between the sorcerers when a large number of Dark Sorcerers rose up, spreading darkness and killing other sorcerers that were against Keres, lord of death. We fought alongside those that were against them," said Meira.

"Vaxar wanted to finish off his enemies from that war, and my father obliged. I didn't agree with it. All you have ever been is kind and generous to me. I could not bring myself to do what they ordered me to do. You have raised me more so than my father," said Keir.

"You have a good heart, Keir. I am glad that you saved them. I am also grateful for them raising such a kind and gentle soul," said Lysandra.

"He does. I wish, as he grew up, he could have lived here, away from that darkness of his father and that wretched sorcerer. We offered to provide him with a home and safety here," said Meira.

"I wanted to, but I knew my father would have Vaxar hunt me down. Then Vaxar would have discovered you. I couldn't put you all in any danger," said Keir.

"Enough talk of the past. Tell us about you, Lysandra. How did you come to meet our Keir?" asked Silas.

"He wandered into my family's bakery after seeing me walking through Holbrook," said Lysandra.

"I'm sure you must have been nervous about meeting him for the first time," said Meira.

"I know I was nervous. In fact, I still get nervous around her sometimes," said Keir.

"Ah, that classic butterflies in stomach feeling. Honey, our little boy is in love," said Silas with a chuckle.

Keir blushed as he glanced down at his cup. Lysandra gave him a loving smile. It was becoming clearer to her that the potion was working and that he was becoming more himself. Little did she know that Meira also was noticing the change in behavior and could feel the darkness leaving him.

They drank the last of the tea and Meira had a fairy bring a cloth to wrap the last of the biscuits in for Keir and Lysandra to take on their journey back home. Meira held the cloth in her hand and with her other hand, she waved it over the fabric. A yellowy-orange aura left her hands and touched the fabric, making it glow the color of her magic. She placed the fabric down and backed away from it as it grew until it was big enough to carry the rest of the leaf biscuits. Lysandra was in awe of the magic and its beauty. She hoped that one day she could learn from Meira about their magic and their culture.

"I hope we will get to see each other again soon. Safe travels, my dears," said Meira.

Keir took Lysandra's hand as they headed back towards the bushes. Before they entered the bushes, Lysandra stopped, turning to Keir.

"How did you convince your father and Vaxar that they were dead?" asked Lysandra.

"When my father and Vaxar ordered me to kill them, Vaxar gave me a special powder in a jar that I was to light. He said that it would magically engulf all the fairies and their homes in a fire. They told me they were a threat to the kingdom. I couldn't do it. I told Queen Meira and King Silas, and we devised a plan to fake their deaths to Vaxar. We were so grateful that it worked. Since then, I have kept their new home a secret from everyone...until now, of course," said Keir.

"Why did you decide to trust me?" asked Lysandra.

"You have a caring heart... Also, I noticed how uncomfortable you were around Vaxar during the wedding. That was when I knew for sure you wouldn't tell him. Not to mention, you continue to help keep Astra a secret from everyone, even Thallan."

"Thank you for trusting me, Keir. I will keep this as our secret."

Keir smiled and gave her a hug, and she hugged him in return. For the short time they hugged Lysandra felt some sort of feeling, as if it was comforting. Before she could think more of what the feeling could be, the hug had ended. They began their brief journey through the passageway and through the bushes.

Thallan was relieved to see Lysandra back, safe and sound. They walked together side by side towards the horses, with Thallan following closely behind them. Not long later, they were back at their horses and promptly began riding back towards the castle.

They rode in silence as the snow continued to fall, soaking and covering their cloaks. Lysandra was looking forward to getting back to the castle as she was getting cold from their journey to the fairies.

What threat could the fairies hold to Vaxar? There must be more of a reason than simple revenge. I need to find out what I can about the fairies soon. Maybe once I get Keir on my side, I can visit them again and he can help me learn more about them. They may know of a way to kill Vaxar, thought Lysandra.

Her mind continued to wonder about the fairies and her next steps, all comprising ways of having Keir beside her in the fight against Vaxar.

16

A DEADLY ENCOUNTER

After some time had passed on their journey back to the castle, the horses suddenly got startled and refused to calm down. Then a guard screamed from behind. By the time they turned, the guard was nowhere to be seen, and his screams silenced instantly.

"We need to go now! Ride out! Hurry!" yelled Thallan.

They all forced their horses to run as fast as they could in the snow. Lysandra's heart was racing as she looked around her while making the horse maintain its speed. She kept looking slightly behind her, making sure that Thallan and Keir were still there.

Then, once again, with no warning, something attacked another soldier. This time, whatever was hunting them went for the guard and his horse, causing them both to land in a bloody, sprawled out mess. Lysandra almost lost her focus on making her horse keep running, seeing the sight of the guard's guts completely sprawled on the ground, tangled with the horse's gutted body as it landed partially on top of the guard.

"Keep going!" yelled Thallan.

They pushed their horses even harder. Lysandra kept checking the forest surrounding them for signs of what or who their attacker was. She wondered how far away they were from the castle and hoped they would get there before the attacker could get them again.

Then out of the corner of her eye to her left she saw it, the glow of the eyes. Before she could react, it was already lunging towards her. It slashed into her horse, digging its claws deep into its flesh, slinging blood into the air, some of it hitting Lysandra's face as she fell to the ground. The creature got its claws stuck into the horse's ribs and fell with it, landing on top of the horse just mere inches in front of her.

She looked up and saw its glowing deep blue eyes and the streaks of glowing fur. She was inches away from a grimog. Lysandra panicked. She was trying to crawl backwards away from the creature as it ripped its claws out of the horse's ribs, cracking them open and throwing them up into the air as the grimog kept its eyes on Lysandra.

Panicking, she began wondering what she could do. If she did magic, that would surely give her identity away to Keir and if she survived against the grimog, then she would have to face that problem. Normally, she would also have her weapons with her when traveling in the woods. She hated herself now for forgetting them.

The creature slowly stalked her, watching her, with its head tilting from side to side as if analyzing her. Lysandra kept sliding backwards as the grimog continued moving towards her slowly until she backed into a tree. As it was sniffing, a knife flew through the air and grazed the creature's thick muscular, black furry forearm, causing it to let out a howl.

The grimog turned its attention to Thallan as his face grew pale white.

"Lysandra, go! Run!" yelled Thallan.

"No! I am not leaving you behind!" yelled Lysandra.

The grimog froze, then turned back to Lysandra and began walking towards her again. She immediately wondered what the creature was doing. If it wanted her dead, it would have already done so. It could have easily attacked them all, but it was cautiously approaching her. It stopped a foot away with its eyes fixed on her.

Then the ring of a sword being pulled from its sheath caught both Lysandra's attention and the creature's. She glanced behind the grimog to see Thallan, with his sword in hand, slowly making his way to the creature. Without thinking, she slightly lifted her hand up.

"Thallan, no! Wait! If it wanted me dead, it would have already done so. Trust me, please. Back up," said Lysandra.

"Are you crazy?" asked Thallan.

"Thallan, listen to her. She's right. Stand down but be ready just in case. Give me your other sword. Lysandra, please be careful," said Keir.

Lysandra then returned her gaze to the creature. The glow in its fur faded as Thallan backed away, and soon its eyes stopped glowing as well. Its eyes were a deep brown, almost black, as if she was looking into the night sky. The grimog moved a little closer before sitting down in front of Lysandra. They stared at each other for a moment before Lysandra thought of trying something that could be very foolish and dangerous to do.

She extended her hand out to the grimog. The creature leaned out and sniffed her hand as she tried to prevent herself from shaking in fear. Then the creature nudged its head into the palm of her hand. The grimog's fur caught her by surprise. It was the softest thing she had ever felt. It was as if she was petting the soft clouds in the sky.

The grimog seemed to enjoy Lysandra petting it. She was in shock that this vicious creature who, moments before, killed two guards and their horses was now letting her pet it. She wondered why such a fearful creature could be acting in such a way.

"It seems you have made a friend," said Keir.

"I would not say that thing is a friend. It may change its mind and attack you. It needs to be dealt with. That creature is too dangerous," said Thallan, as he took a step forward.

The grimog sensed Thallan and stood back up on all fours, staring at him. Its eyes and fur once again were glowing. This time, though, Lysandra noticed the creature's stance. It looked like it was protecting her from Thallan.

"Thallan, stop! Look at the way it is standing. It's guarding me from you! Put your swords away!"

Thallan stopped but didn't put his sword away as instructed. The remaining guard followed Thallan's lead.

"I said put your swords away! It is no threat. Stand down! That is an order, General Thallan," said Lysandra.

Thallan, shocked at how Lysandra had just addressed him, reluctantly sheathed his sword and stood back. Lysandra then stood up and pet the top of the grimog's head.

"It's all right. They're friendly, not a threat," said Lysandra.

It looked up at her and, as if it understood what she said, its glow faded away. Lysandra walked towards Thallan and the grimog followed behind her, to her surprise. She wondered why the grimog was acting this way towards her. Then she thought perhaps it sensed her magic, since it was a magical creature. She questioned what made her so special for a vicious creature not to attack her.

"I wonder why this creature was drawn to you. It seems to listen to you," said Keir.

"I am not sure why, either. I know little about them. Has this ever happened before?" said Lysandra.

"Not to my knowledge. I have only known them to be dangerous monsters. And it has very clearly demonstrated that with the men it just killed moments ago," said Thallan.

The grimog gave a low, deep growl in response to Thallan as if it understood his words. Thallan took a step back and placed a hand on his sword, unsure of what the creature may do next. Keir and Lysandra both let out a small chuckle.

"First off, it is a she and second, I think she understands you and doesn't seem to like you calling her a monster," said Lysandra.

"I think we have misunderstood these creatures. It seems to know what you just said about it, Thallan, and I don't think it liked it. I think the Dusan guided this grimog to be your protector, Lysandra. I have read in some of the older books deep in the library that in the past, spirits have guided strong magical creatures to someone of importance to protect and help in their journey, whatever that may be. The spirits are looking after you," said Keir.

"Elvish texts also say similar things, now that you mention it. The Elves believe the creature sent to protect you from the spirits is a sign of importance. It has never been exactly clear. Just a bunch of riddles. I cannot remember any more about the significance of having a magical creature drawn to you as a companion and protector," said Thallan.

Lysandra remained silent, thinking of what it could mean having such a powerful and deadly companion sent by the spirits. Then she wondered what this could mean for her future.

She looked down at the grimog sitting beside her right leg. Even sitting, its head came up to her chest. She tried petting it again on its head. As soon as she touched its fur, the grimog looked up and pushed its head into her hand, as if it liked her petting it. She couldn't hide her smile.

"Keir, how exactly are we going to hide this grimog once we're back at the castle? I am not sure how people would react to seeing it," asked Lysandra.

"Hmm. You're right. We shall do our best to keep it hidden for the time being. Only those who are more loyal to myself and not my father may know of it. I know many people in the castle are still very loyal to my father and Vaxar."

"We can hide the grimog in the garden. Only you two ever go in there. If Vaxar returns he would never know. He spends most of his time in his chambers," said Thallan.

"Sounds like a good idea to me," said Lysandra.

"I agree," said Keir.

As they trekked through the snow, heading back to the castle, the grimog remained beside Lysandra. Keir slowly, over the journey, made his way to walk beside Lysandra on her left as the grimog was on her right.

Whenever Thallan tried to walk closer to them, the creature would let out a small growl, causing him to keep his distance. Thallan was not liking how Lysandra was letting herself get so close to Keir, noticing them holding hands as they walked, and now having the grimog remain at her side when he would prefer it to be killed. His worry over her safety was growing more and more the longer she remained by Keir's side, refusing to fulfill the first part of the prophecy in taking down the Dark King. He couldn't find it in himself to believe that Keir was good deep down and was simply being controlled by Vaxar.

Just before they entered the grounds of the castle, Thallan sent the guard to make sure no one would see them enter. Thallan also instructed the guard to inform Richard to ensure only loyal men to Keir would see them hide the gri-mog. They waited until Richard greeted them at the gate, let-ting them know it was safe to proceed in with the creature.

Lysandra led the way to the garden. Keir and Thallan both followed carefully behind her. Once they were in the garden, she led the grimog to an area behind some bushes filled with enough snow to hide in if someone ever came out-side or looked through the windows.

"You need to stay here. I don't know if you can under-stand me completely, but you'll be safer here. I'll see if we can get you some food, so you don't go attacking people now that you are here and not in the forest... I really hope I am making a good choice letting you stay close by me," said Lysandra.

Lysandra gave the creature another pat on the head be-fore leaving. The creature, once again, acted as if it under-stood her and remained where she told it to stay. Lysandra left the garden and reunited with Keir and Thallan, waiting in the hallway just inside beside the garden entrance.

"So, have you thought of a name for your new compan-ion?" asked Keir.

"I have not. I am sure I will think of one soon, though. It seems to understand what we say to it. Although, I fear we should feed it soon. Now that it is closer to people, we don't want to risk it needing to hunt or attacking anyone."

"Agreed. Thallan, you and Richard should get some meat for the creature and feed it. Just tell the cooks there are some men about to travel and need some meat. Afterwards, get some lunch for yourselves. Lysandra and I have some royal duties to attend to in Holbrook after lunch," said Keir.

"What are the royal duties we have to do?" asked Lysandra.

"It's a tradition I don't particularly like. We are to take a stroll through the town to display our new union. Several generations ago, my great, great grandfather created it. Hopefully, the people will be accepting of my choice of having you as the new queen," said Keir.

"I hope so too."

Keir offered his hand, and they headed off to the dining hall to eat lunch and warm up by the fire before they were to travel to Holbrook. He wanted to go to the town before the late afternoon in case a snowstorm made its way into the valley late in the day. Storms in the winter and summer were treacherous in the valley of the Thundering Eclipse Mountains.

17

A BAD DAY TO VISIT HOLBROOK

After lunch, Keir and Lysandra cleaned up from their journey and made themselves look presentable for their walk through Holbrook. Keir wore a fine dark green shirt with brown pants and his cloak. Lysandra wore her green dress to match.

Once they were ready, they mounted their horses and made their way down from the castle to Holbrook. Lysandra was already hoping that she may get the chance to see her mother and Gwyneth during their visit. She was not used to being without them for so long.

As they entered the town, all eyes were on Lysandra and Keir. She recognized many of the faces from her deliveries.

Lysandra cautiously looked around and began taking mental notes. There were two guards in front of them and three behind them, along with the guards within the town. She then kept a watchful eye on the people surrounding them. She was so focused on maintaining the fake smile and watching her surroundings that she didn't realize they had stopped.

"I thought, since we would already be here, you would like to visit your mother," said Keir.

Lysandra smiled at him before dismounting and headed into her old home as he followed. Thallan made sure the guards kept watch before entering the bakery as well. As soon as the doors were open, the smells of the bakery invited them in.

Lysandra walked in further to the back to find her mother and Gwyneth hard at work. She watched them for a moment before saying anything to get their attention. She missed waking up to the smells of them baking and eating the extras of the food they baked every day, which certainly tasted better than the food at the castle.

"Excuse me, do you have any extra baked goods I can have? The food at the castle just does not compare to yours," said Lysandra.

Eleanora and Gwyneth both looked towards her and grew excited to see Lysandra again. They quickly stopped what they were doing, and each gave her a big hug before acknowledging Keir and curtsying. He wore a smile and gave a slight bow of his head in return.

"Here, sit down. Let me get you both something to drink and eat. Oh, it is so good to see you, darling," said Eleanora.

"Thallan, have a seat as well. You know this place is safe. Besides, I see your guards out front through the window by the door," said Gwyneth as she hugged Thallan.

Eleanora grabbed a serving plate large enough to put plenty of baked goods and three glasses of warm cider on and brought it to the table. Once she placed it on the table, she made a slight gesture at Lysandra, pointing to a muffin on the plate. Lysandra's eyes grew wide, and she wore a childish smile as she realized it was one of her mother's fresh grugalberry muffins and immediately grabbed it and took a bite.

"I never realized how much I miss sneaking around here stealing grugalberries or snacking on the extra baked goods," said Lysandra.

"I think it's funny that you thought you were being sneaky. There is no sneaking around me, Lys," said Gwyneth.

"I would at least try," said Lysandra.

Eleanora laughed.

"That you did. Time and time again. Keir, when she was little, she would try to be sneaky stealing goodies. When caught, she would grab what she could and run off before either of us could stop her, giggling with her little arms full. As she grew older, she would sneak an extra muffin or grugalberry in her pockets as she made her deliveries," said Gwyneth as she laughed.

"Wait, you knew I was hiding some in my pockets? How?" asked Lysandra.

Keir joined Eleanora, laughing at the story.

"I am an Elf, Lys. I have great hearing and eyesight. Besides, I know a thing or two about children and baked goods. Thallan did the same thing when he was younger," said Gwyneth.

Thallan's face grew red with embarrassment as Keir laughed at the story. Keir was happy that they were starting to finally not be so formal around him, but he could tell there was still some uneasy tension with him being there. He only hoped that someday they would feel comfortable around him and consider him like family, as he was already considering them his.

They spent some time visiting, telling more stories and eating the plateful of fresh baked goods. After they had their fill, Lysandra, Keir, and Thallan said their goodbyes as they must set off to go back to the castle before the snow turned into a storm.

Before they walked towards their horses tied to the post

with the guards, Lysandra noticed something from the corner of her eye. She could tell it was three men with weapons who were not wearing royal uniforms. With her adrenaline rising, she instinctively used her magic, without saying a word, to cause the wet ground to become slightly frozen, causing them to slip. One of them threw a knife as they slipped and without thinking, she used her magic to cause the knife to fly too far to their left and into the ground. She could hear the guards on their horses ahead of her scramble to draw their weapons.

Lysandra spun around to Thallan and reached for his sword and pulled it from its sheath. She grabbed Keir and pushed him behind her, making sure she was in between him and the three men.

Keir, filled with surprise and confusion, looked from Lysandra to what she was protecting him from.

With the sword in hand, Lysandra stood in a defensive position, waiting and hoping that the three men would choose not to attack. She saw anger in their eyes. She recognized the man in the middle from the day she rescued a woman from a drunk man after her deliveries. Lysandra knew, deep down, their actions now have doomed their fate. She would do her best to not be their killer as she attempted to hold them off.

"Stand down. This is your only warning this time, Declan," said Lysandra.

"You chose this baker bitch as our new queen? This kingdom needs an alliance with a powerful kingdom to build the empire! We want King Erebus to wear the crown! Not this wench and piss poor excuse of a son," said Declan.

"Stand down!" yelled Thallan.

The guards pulled their swords from their sheaths, awaiting orders to attack.

The three men all showed no hesitation as they lunged after her, fueled by their anger. She dodged two of their swords as she used Thallan's sword to block the third man from striking at her chest. Lysandra, at this moment, was trying to concentrate entirely on her skills of fighting without the use of magic. She had already, at substantial risk, used her magic without thinking. She pushed the connected swords up as she kicked the merchant in his middle, then used the pommel of the sword to hit him in the head, knocking him unconscious.

Lysandra then moved quickly to stop the other two as they attempted to attack Keir. He may have been unarmed, but he was ready to attack if Lysandra gave him the opportunity.

Lysandra's eyes flickered to the guards approaching and Thallan, now armed with a bow and arrow. She could see into Thallan's eyes and knew what he was going to do. Before she could get a word out, the arrow flew right into Declan's throat.

The final man, filled with grief and hatred, attacked Lysandra violently. Their swords clashed as they fought. The guards were about to intervene when Thallan stopped them, as he was worried that they could cause the situation to become worse. Thallan grabbed another arrow and notched it, then aimed at the blacksmith fighting Lysandra, waiting for a clean shot.

Lysandra held her ground against the tall, muscular man, defending herself from his powerful swings. She was too afraid to strike at him, as she didn't want to kill him. She hoped he would tire himself out enough for her to get her chance to knock him unconscious, or to the ground at least.

Then the man on the ground regained consciousness and got up quickly and ran towards Lysandra with a knife in his hand. Thallan noticed and fired the arrow. The man fell with the arrow in his chest. Thallan quickly grabbed another arrow and notched it. With the large man's back turned, Thallan shot his arrow into the middle of his spine.

The man yelled in pain before attempting to swing once more at Lysandra, when another arrow pierced his back. He fell forward, right into Lysandra, as his body went limp.

Both Keir and Thallan ran towards Lysandra as her knees slipped in the muddy ground. Thallan grabbed the man and moved him off Lysandra.

"Lysandra, are you all right?" asked Keir, kneeling beside her.

Lysandra remained silent with her eyes fixed on the dead bodies that the guards gathered.

Many of the people in the town were watching. Some were fighting to hold back their tears, seeing friends they'd known for years die before their eyes. Even Eleanora and Gwyneth, who heard the commotion, made their way just outside the bakery to see the end of the fighting. Eleanora attempted to go to her daughter, but Gwyneth held her back.

"No. It is too risky, Eleanora. Others may try to attack. She does not need to worry about us. She knows you are here and not alone," said Gwyneth, as she held Eleanora back from running out to her daughter.

Keir placed a hand on Lysandra's as she was still holding Thallan's sword. Then, with his other hand, placed it just under her chin to lift her face up to his. He gazed into her eyes as she finally looked at him.

"Are you all right, Lys? Are you hurt?" asked Keir.

"I'm all right. I'm not hurt," said Lysandra faintly.

I never wanted this. First the soldier now Declan and those other two. I understand the soldier was self-defense. He wanted me dead due to me being the sorceress of destiny. But Declan was no soldier. *Just an ordinarily and well drunken townsperson. Was he really that mad at me for stopping him that day? How many more like him will die because of me? I'm not sure how I can do this if more die needlessly like Declan's friends that he brought to fight by his side over his anger towards me,* she thought.

Keir helped her up and took the sword from her, handing it back to Thallan. He kept his arm around her to help her feel safe.

"Thallan, tell Lysandra's mother and yours that I wish for them to stay in the castle for a while. I worry that someone may try to hurt them after what these three just tried to do. I do not wish for any harm to come to them. It seems there are some traitors still hiding in our kingdom," said Keir.

Thallan nodded and relayed the message to Gwyneth and Eleanora. They both quickly went into the bakery to clean up the kitchen, kill the fires in the ovens, and then pack a couple of bags with clothes and a basket of baked goods for Lysandra. Once they were ready, some guards helped tie their bags to the horses and had them both ride Lysandra's horse together, as she rode with Keir.

They quickly headed off towards the castle. The guards and Thallan were on high alert as they rode through town, making sure there wouldn't be a second attack. The people throughout the town bore sad and angered faces as the group passed by.

As they rode, Lysandra's thoughts were uncontrollable as she wondered about what the man said before attacking her. Then she worried about if anyone saw her using magic. Lysandra tried to remember the start of everything, making sure she did not use her hands when casting the spell, but realized she never spoke the spell or used her hands. She simply just thought of what she wanted to happen. She never knew that was a possibility. However, she knew for sure that her eyes flashed blue when doing the spell like they always did and hoped no one noticed.

It was a long, silent ride back to the castle. Once they arrived, Keir instructed some servants to prepare a couple of rooms for Eleanora and Gwyneth. Keir remained by Lysandra's side as they walked towards the royal chambers. Thallan and Richard were both ordering extra guards and soldiers to be posted around the castle and for an extra watch guard to be posted in the tower. Richard and another guard stayed by Eleanora and Gwyneth's side. Thallan didn't want to risk anything happening to anyone.

Once they made it to their royal chambers, Celia helped Lysandra change into clothes that she would be more comfortable in. Eleanora and Gwyneth, after waiting a while, requested to visit Lysandra. Keir was more than willing to let them. He tried to get Lysandra to talk, but she remained silent. She sat in front of the fire as her mother sat next to her with one arm around her as she attempted to help comfort her daughter.

Keir sat nearby, letting Eleanora and Gwyneth try to help Lysandra feel better as he realized he was new to caring for someone deeply and wasn't sure how to help. A servant entered the room and knelt beside Keir.

"Your Majesty, we have received word from Vaxar in the shadow journal," whispered the servant as he handed a folded parchment.

Keir nodded and the servant left. He opened the letter and read it. Vaxar had been chasing down General Valda of the Krogodo Kingdom, who was the person behind the attack on the Cinder Outpost. Vaxar was still searching for the general within the mountain passes and did not know when he would return.

Keir knew he should reply right away in the shadow

journal but decided it could wait as it was nothing urgent. All he would have to say was to find the general quickly. He deemed Lysandra's wellbeing more important than Vaxar's message.

Lysandra remained quiet except for the few words she eventually said to her family, asking them to leave her alone for a while. However, she requested Keir to remain by her side. Keir told Eleanora he would let her know how Lysandra was doing after dinner. Eleanora thanked him as she left with Gwyneth to see the rooms they would stay in.

Before servants delivered dinner to their room, Keir remained sitting in the chair beside Lysandra, who had fallen asleep with Astra on her lap. He had requested that the servants not bother them as much and to knock before entering for the rest of the evening. He wanted to answer the door and keep people out so they wouldn't discover Astra, who normally hid in his wardrobe underneath the warm pile of clothes he left for her.

Lysandra slowly woke up, rubbing the little bit of sleeping dust from her eyes. She looked down and smiled at Astra and gave her a few pats. The more awake she became, the more she remembered her eventful day. It was a day that held promise, starting out with a wonderful journey to see the fairies, then gaining the companionship of a grimog to the fight and ultimate deaths of people she had known since she was little.

"How are you doing?" asked Keir.

"I'm all right," said Lysandra softly.

"You knew one of those men, right? I thought I heard you say his name."

"Yes. Weeks ago, I stopped him from assaulting a poor woman while I was doing my deliveries. I may have assaulted his pride in return for what he was doing to the woman. He was drunk."

"I am so sorry. It sounds like he wasn't a good person from the start. I am truly sorry that you had to endure that today. Would you like me to get your family to have dinner with us? We can eat here. I can have the servants grab a few more chairs for the table."

Lysandra thought for a moment. She partially wished to be beside her family, but she also just wanted to be with him. Earlier, she didn't know it, but now she realized how comforting it was when he held her after the fight and on the way to the castle. She found comfort in having him by her side. She decided, though, to let her family join them for dinner, as she knew they were worried about her.

"That would be nice. Thank you. I am sure they are worried. I was just so in shock earlier and lost in my thoughts. I didn't know what to do or say."

"It's all right, my dear. We understand. I'll have a servant make the preparations. Stay here and rest, but first let me place a blanket on you to cover Astra while she sleeps. We can hide her on the bed under the cover soon."

He grabbed a blanket from the dresser between the wardrobes and tenderly laid it out on her lap, covering Astra as she slept soundly. He placed a small kiss on Lysandra's forehead before leaving to make the dinner arrangements.

18

THE DARK SORCERER'S RETURN

Dinner began an hour after Lysandra had woken from her nap. Thallan had declined the offer to eat with them. Thallan wanted to patrol the castle with Richard and make sure things were in order and the guards were all at their posts. He also wanted to make sure that the grimog remained hidden within the garden. He had three guards stationed outside the royal chambers as both he and Richard made their rounds.

When dinner was ready, Lysandra sat next to Keir and her mother sat across from her with Gwyneth next to Eleanora. The dinner started off with an awkward silence, as no one knew what to say. Lysandra and Keir were both surprised that they couldn't hear Astra snoring, as she was sleeping peacefully beneath the sheets on the bed with the door partially left open. Keir would occasionally look at Lysandra, wanting to make sure she was well. He didn't enjoy seeing her like this and wished there was something he could do to help her.

"Thank you for providing us with a place to stay after today's dreadful events," said Eleanora.

"Of course. I wouldn't want anything to happen to Lysandra's family all because of some individuals revolting against the crown," said Keir.

The room fell back into an awkward silence for a moment as they ate their stew and slices of bread.

"You are welcome to stay here as long as you like. And if there is anything that you need, the servants will help you," said Keir.

"Thank you, Your Majesty," said Gwyneth.

"Please, there is no need for formalities. You can call me Keir."

Lysandra gave him a smile for his kindness to her family.

Once they finished their dinner, Eleanora and Gwyneth left for their rooms to return to bed early for the night after the day's events.

As soon as they were alone, Astra poked her head out from under the covers and headed towards Lysandra and Keir. Lysandra saw her from the corner of her eye as she was looking out the window with Keir between her and Astra. Without giving her attention to Astra, Lysandra watched the riker move towards the edge of the bed, her head tilting side to side. Astra then wriggled her tail for a moment before lunging towards Keir, landing partially on his right shoulder.

Lysandra couldn't stop herself from laughing, as Astra surprised Keir.

"Ouch. Astra, you nearly scared me to death, little one. Watch those claws too!" said Keir as he laughed.

Astra spoke back in her own way of clattering noises as if she enjoyed startling Keir. As she situated herself on his back and shoulder, he rubbed the top of her head. She was happy getting some attention from him and getting to snuggle up to his neck.

Lysandra watched them and could see in this moment his kind heart. He cared so much for Astra. She realized that he also cared a lot for her, despite them still not knowing each other fully. She knew she needed to tell him the truth of the potion Vaxar had him taking along with her secret, but she didn't want to ruin his moment of peace and happiness. Unknowingly, she slightly crinkled her brow, pondering how to tell Keir and worrying about his reaction.

Is now the time to tell him everything? He protected the fairies all these years from Vaxar. I have only seen compassion and kindness from him through his words and actions. I only see good in him. Not an ounce of darkness. The only darkness I see is his father and Vaxar. He deserves to know. Besides, I have this feeling in my soul that this is what I am meant to do. This is how I can save him. The prophecy says I will defeat the Dark King. From what I have seen since being at the castle, the Dark King is Erebus not Keir. I was also told the prophecy showed someone in the crown bowing, in other words joining my side which could easily be Keir, thought Lysandra.

"What are you thinking about?" asked Keir.

"Hm?"

"What are you so deep in thought about? You seem to always be thinking about something lately."

"There is always something on my mind. I have a habit of overthinking."

"I wouldn't mind listening to whatever is on your mind. I can just listen, or we can talk about whatever may be bothering you."

Lysandra smiled and paused for a moment to contemplate her words.

"Actually, there is something I need to tell you. I am not sure how you will react, but it is something you need to know now. I fear if I wait too long, it may be too late, and I don't want you to find out through someone else. Just know that what I am about to tell you is the truth."

"It's all right, Lys. I'm here for you. What is it?"

Lysandra took a deep breath to calm her nerves.

"I don't know how else to say this, but...my last name is Sloane. I am the daughter of Sorcerer Krarick and the sorceress from the prophecy."

Lysandra tried to keep herself from talking too fast, as her nerves made her queasy as her hands trembled, palms sweaty.

"I could've used my magic already to take you down. I chose not to, though, because I knew something wasn't quite right. Thallan and many others have told me you are just as dark as your father, but once I met you, I quickly learned that there is good in you. Then the mention of your medicine that Vaxar has you take made me suspicious of it. So, I used some magic to test it, only to discover that it is no medicine but a potion to make you more susceptible to your father and Vaxar's orders and teachings to darken your soul. I made a potion that looked like Vaxar's but had the purpose of wearing off the effect of his potion to..."

"To free me from their control," interrupted Keir.

Keir stared at the floor in front of himself, thinking. Lysandra wanted to give him a minute, as she knew that the news would be shocking for him.

"That explains why I've felt more like myself recently. Why I felt as if a fog lifted," said Keir.

Lysandra nodded in response. The room fell silent for a few minutes as she let Keir take his time to process what she has told him. She didn't know what else to say, so she waited for him to speak.

"Why hasn't Vaxar noticed you are the sorceress?"

"Whenever Vaxar was around during the wedding, Thallan

or his mother, Gwyneth, remained by my side. Elves help mask a magical aura. I couldn't sense his and he couldn't sense mine."

"So, what are you going to do now? I've seen Vaxar use his magic, and I know I don't stand a chance against him. I am assuming you are just as powerful, considering that you took such an enormous risk hiding under everyone's noses."

"Now, I am going to go after Vaxar before he finds out who I am. I want to keep the element of surprise for as long as possible."

"And what about me?"

"You can join the fight against Vaxar and prove to the people of Lamorra that you are no Dark King. Your father is the Dark King. You can stay here. If you intend to remain loyal to Vaxar and your father, then I think I'll let Thallan have his way of locking you in the dungeons."

There were a few seconds of silence as Keir wanted to choose his words carefully.

"Well, I am not exactly happy with the fact the Vaxar and my father turned me into their little puppet... You saved me, Lysandra. The right thing to do is to remain by your side and help."

Thallan came rushing in with Richard and several other guards behind him, all with their swords drawn and pointed and Keir.

"Vaxar is back with troops and is rounding up others in the castle loyal to him. A servant overheard Vaxar telling them you're the sorceress and are attempting to take the kingdom," said Thallan.

Lysandra froze, worry filling her mind.

How did he find out? Only my family and Keir know, thought Lysandra.

"Did you hear me? Lysandra, Vaxar is here and knows who you are! We need to get out of here," said Thallan.

Keir looked towards Lysandra and saw the worry in her face with the crinkled brow and eyes blankly staring at Thallan.

"Richard, round up as many soldiers as you can loyal to me and Lysandra. Tell them Vaxar is attempting to over-throw the crown to make himself the ruler. That should get plenty on our side against his forces. Thallan stick by her side to mask her aura to help make it harder for Vaxar to hunt her down. We should head towards the garden to get the grimog and have it by her side as an extra precaution," said Keir.

"I do not take orders from you, Dark King," said Thallan.

"I love Lysandra! I don't want any harm to come to her! I am on your side!" yelled Keir.

"Thallan, you and Richard do as he says. It's a good plan. I told him everything just a moment ago. Vaxar's spell on him has completely worn off. He can't control Keir anymore. Let's get to the Grimog quickly. It can help me fight off Vaxar," said Lysandra.

Richard nodded and took a soldier with him as they rushed off to gather more soldiers and guards to fight Vaxar and his forces. Thallan, without a word, led the soldiers out of the room and into the hall to wait for Lysandra and Keir to follow. Before either of them left the room, they both grabbed their weapons from within their wardrobes and then headed out towards the hallway. Keir tried to remove Astra to keep her in the room, but she refused to leave his shoul-der, so he let her stay on him.

The soldiers surrounded Lysandra, Keir, and Thallan as they quickly jogged through the hallways towards the stairs. They started heading down the stairs when they came across a quad of men, armed and ready for a fight. The group stopped for a moment to see if the quad was friends or foes.

The captain of the quad looked at the group in front of

him and noticed Lysandra standing next to Keir. He pointed the tip of his sword in her direction.

"Vaxar has just informed us she is the wanted sorceress. She is a threat to the kingdom. Why are you protecting her, General?" asked the captain in a deep voice.

"She is no threat, Captain. I order you to stand down. Vaxar is a traitor to the kingdom. He is attempting to gain control to make himself ruler," said Keir.

The quad lunged forward. The soldiers tried to hold back the men's swords as shields clashed together. As fighting begun in front of them, soldiers arrived behind them at the top of the stairs and began fighting against those guarding from behind.

Lysandra analyzed their trapped situation in the stairwell. The commotion would certainly make enough noise for Vaxar to hear and make his way towards them. She knew the stairwell was no place to fight against another sorcerer. They would need to find a way out quickly.

Just then, as she was looking up the stairs behind her, the soldiers fighting the quad below fell before them, allowing the members of the quad its chance to strike. They quickly climbed the stairs over the dead bodies. Two quad members stood within sword length of Lysandra with her back to them. Keir noticed and moved to block them. His sword was just about to clash with one of the quad member's sword when they hit a magical shield conjured by Lysandra.

The soldier and Keir looked at Lysandra, who had her hands out towards both ends of the stairwell, projecting a magical shield protecting everyone from further attacks. In her mind she spoke the spell, "Anambulo," as she pushed her hands out further, controlling the direction of the magic toward their attackers, shoving them against the walls.

"Quickly, before they come to," said Lysandra.

Having lost a few members in the stairwell battle, the small group ran through the remaining hallways to the garden. Two soldiers ran up ahead to open the doors and guard as the rest entered the garden. Two quads were already waiting for them.

Lysandra, Keir, Thallan, and the remaining five soldiers came to a halt. Full of surprise, they wondered how the quads knew they were heading to the garden.

"I order you all to stand down! Vaxar has told you lies! He has betrayed this kingdom!" yelled Keir.

Lysandra noticed someone hidden behind the tall, large members of the quads making their way to the front while dragging something. Once in front, Lysandra had to keep her fear under control.

"Looking for your friend, sorceress?" said Vaxar as he let go of Richard, causing him to fall to the ground.

Lysandra looked down at Richard. He looked odd. As if something had drained his soul, leaving him barely alive. A large gash cut across his left cheek. Blood dripped from his broken nose, and his right eye swelled shut. Her heart ached at the sight of seeing Richard so beaten. Then she realized. Only his face had suffered from the beating. His spirit appeared drained.

Necromancy! He knows the ancient dark arts of necromancy, thought Lysandra.

Her eyes grew wide as she looked up at Vaxar, who gave her a cynical smile.

"Yes, that is right, young sorceress. I am a necromancer and a sorcerer. I am surprised that you recognized the signs of it, since I assume you grew up here in the kingdom, right under my nose. Your father was quite smart, pretending to have fled with you when you were born. That only means you learned from that dreaded codex while growing up here.

You don't have the proper training nor experience to fight me, Lysandra," said Vaxar.

"My skills might surprise you. I may not have had my father to teach me, but I have learned a lot on my own," said Lysandra, with her sword pointing at him.

"Oh, I am sure you have. But you still have much to learn. I know your father. He is much like the old sorcerer coven. They don't like any sort of magic that is too powerful or dark in their eyes. I am sure much of your book has pages torn or scratched off."

Lysandra said nothing. She didn't want to please him by saying he was right. Though she did not know there used to be a coven of sorcerers, only that there was a temple where they learned.

"I can teach you anything you want to learn if you join me. No one says that a prophecy has to come true. The future is ever-changing. You and Keir can come with me as we search for the ancient magic that has been lost and forgotten in the lands."

"No! I will never be under your control again, Vaxar! My allegiance is to Lysandra," said Keir.

"Ah! I see you have figured out the little potion. Good. You are quite intelligent for discovering that. You are far too powerful and smart to be following those old ways like your father, Lysandra. With me, you can learn and practice all that you wish."

Lysandra looked at Keir, standing by her left side. She could tell that he was ready for a fight with both hands on his sword. He stood in a stance, ready to charge at the quads and Vaxar.

"I can help you rise to a new level of power. To be above these weak souls. You can be my equal as we make this world into what it should be. You can help women in the entire realm, giving them what they need, saving them from men who used to use them for their own pleasure."

"Like Keir said, I will not join you. All you have ever done is seek power, no matter the cost. You have killed countless innocent lives. Your reign of terror is at an end, Vaxar," said Lysandra.

Vaxar let out a brief sigh.

"Then so be it. You will either die by their side or they will inevitably hunt and kill you as their fear of you grows. They won't ever truly trust you," said Vaxar.

Lysandra remained silent. She stood before him, ready to begin the fight against him.

"Kill the others, leave the sorceress to me," said Vaxar.

19

THE LONG-AWAITED FIGHT

The quads charged Keir, Thallan, and the soldiers behind them. Lysandra kept her gaze on Vaxar, waiting for his attack. She tried to better their odds against Vaxar's men and use her magic on the quad members who hadn't gotten as close to them yet.

Lysandra mentally cast the spell arboradix, then controlled the roots to trip them and stopped most of the quad members by seizing their legs. She then thought of the spell levitaortia to lift the men into the air as the roots fell to the ground. They all panicked as they floated. Vaxar watched with a smile, seeing the magic she could perform. Then, with the spell anambulo, Lysandra threw the men over the wall, beyond the castle and down the mountainside.

Lysandra kept careful watch at how her companions were doing in their battle against the rest of the quad members as Vaxar simply stood before her. Keir was fighting off a quad member to her left who seemed to be injured by Keir's sword. Thallan, to Keir's right, fought two soldiers while the others fought throughout the garden. Astra jumped to the ground and ran towards the bushes to hide from the chaos, as this was a battle she did not want to be in the middle of.

The swords clashed and the ring of steel was all you could hear in the garden. Lysandra wondered why the grimog hadn't appeared yet. She questioned if Vaxar knew of the creature and somehow defeated it. She hoped it was simply hiding, waiting to strike.

As her worries diverted her attention from Vaxar, he took notice and hurled a ball of fire in her direction. Lysandra quickly thought the spell defenetta, deflecting the ball of fire back at Vaxar. He formed a magical shield that absorbed the fire. He gave a wicked smile.

"Good. You are more skilled than I thought. You are already powerful enough to concentrate on spells in your mind instead of saying them aloud. The only thing is, are you speaking the spells in your mind or simply thinking of what you want your magic to do? I wonder. Let's find out, shall we?" said Vaxar.

Vaxar used his necromancy magic to sink the ground beneath her, causing her to lose her footing. He then threw fireballs at her. She quickly conjured the spell miraculum, creating a shield to block his attacks. She decided it would be best to keep her focus on this spell and maintain it as long as she could while also throwing his fireballs back at him. Every fireball that she returned to him changed to the blue color of her magic. Between the two of them, green and blue magic glowed in their eyes and around them as they cast their spells.

As she maintained the shield, she thought of the spell arboradix to control the roots and have them sneak up behind Vaxar and slither up and wrap around his arms. As she did, Richard started carefully crawling away, unable to stand. Lysandra wrapped the root around one arm when her concentration on the two spells nearly broke.

Out of the corner of her eye, she noticed a quad member had knocked Thallan down. The soldier was about to run him through with his sword when Keir ran in and blocked the attack. Keir swung violently at the soldier until he tripped on a large rock and Keir stabbed him. It all happened so fast that she couldn't think of a way to help, but she was glad she didn't have to, as she was trying to maintain two spells.

Unfortunately, Vaxar noticed her slight distraction once again and took advantage. He started muttering words under his breath as Lysandra was about to wrap his other arm in roots. Just as she got the roots around his arm and tried to restrain him, she felt odd. She felt weak.

Lysandra looked at Vaxar's face and noticed he was muttering. She lost focus on her spells and fell to the ground, gasping for air. She felt as if he was taking her breath away, straight out of her lungs. She tried harder than ever to focus on a spell. Any spell that she could think of as things were turning black. She hoped that Keir or Thallan would notice and try to save her.

"Lysandra!" yelled Keir.

Keir grabbed a knife from Thallan's belt and threw it towards Vaxar. As it flew, it stopped halfway, flipped around and flung itself into Keir's shoulder. He let out a loud cry of pain, causing him to fall backward from the force. Vaxar closed his eyes to put more focus on his spell.

Thallan turned to see what was happening. He saw Keir on the ground, wounded but pointing toward Lysandra.

"Help her!" yelled Keir.

Before Thallan could think of something, a large black creature lunged out of the bushes, straight for Vaxar. With one paw flung out and its claws extended, the creature slashed Vaxar's chest. Only its longest claw could reach Vaxar's chest as it landed just slightly out of reach to do more damage. The contact from the creature broke his focus, and Lysandra could breathe again.

Vaxar opened his eyes wide as he touched the wound and noticed the creature guarding Lysandra, weak from his magic. The grimog stood, glowing brighter than ever. Its claws extended, digging into the dirt as it bared its teeth. It let out a low growl at Vaxar as a warning to back off.

"You! You think you scare me, creature? I am more powerful than you! You, grimog shall pay for what you just did and for the scar you left upon my face in our last encounter!" yelled Vaxar.

Vaxar threw a large ball of fire at the grimog. The creature simply stood there without even flinching. To Lysandra's and Vaxar's surprise, the fire simply vanished and didn't seem to even hurt the grimog.

Vaxar then extended his hand toward a sword lying on the ground beside a dead soldier to control it. He made the sword swing at the grimog's head but missed and slammed it into the ground. He then had the sword fly fast towards the creature's middle, but the grimog swung its claws out and smashed the sword to the ground, breaking the blade in two. The creature kept its paw on the hilt of the broken sword. It looked at Lysandra, who was regaining her strength, then back at Vaxar. The grimog turned its body towards Vaxar and let out a loud growl and its blue glow changed to a much deeper blue that was almost black.

Lysandra saw Vaxar freeze as he lifted another sword into the air to use against the creature. She had never seen fear in his eyes in the short time that she had been around him. That's when she knew how powerful an ally she now had. Lysandra tried to get up to help the grimog against the Dark Sorcerer. She wobbled slightly on her heels as she stood beside the grimog.

"Ready to give up? You are alone, Vaxar, whereas I have friends who have joined by my side against you," said Lysandra.

"We shall see how long that lasts, Lysandra Sloane. After all, according to the soldier who told me your secret, you used magic against your so-called friends who turned against you earlier today. Soon others will follow in their footsteps. You really shouldn't have let soldiers and servants use that shadow journal for you, Keir," said Vaxar.

Vaxar used his magic to throw the sword and fireball at both Lysandra and the grimog, only for it to collide into a shield. The grimog lunged at Vaxar, claws extended. He vanished into a cloud of smoke before giving anyone or anything another chance to attack him. The grimog landed where Vaxar had stood as the smoke disappeared. Lysandra stood there for a moment, realizing what she had just done.

She used her magic without thinking of the spell. She only thought of protection, and it happened. Lysandra was so weak from Vaxar's necromancy spell that she didn't think of the spell quickly enough, but the magic flowed through her as if she did. She didn't think it was possible that Vaxar was just trying to tempt her.

How did I do that? I don't remember saying the spell. Maybe I am just tired. I didn't expect Vaxar to know necromancy. He just teleported so he couldn't have gone far. We can't let him get away. If I can stay by the grimog, she and I can take Vaxar together instead of just one on one. That reminds me, I need to come up with a name for her since we are definitely friends now, thought Lysandra.

The grimog turned to Lysandra and nudged its head under her hand to help her stand as she continued to regain her strength. The creature's glow disappeared as the threat was gone.

"Thanks," said Lysandra.

"Lys, are you all right?" asked Thallan.

He walked up to her and placed a hand on her shoulder. Lysandra nodded. Then she remembered Keir. She turned around and saw him being helped by a soldier.

"Take him to the dungeons. He will pay for his crimes," said Thallan.

Lysandra realized they were soldiers loyal to Thallan and not to the crown or Vaxar. Thallan's orders irritated her, despite her previous words to him about Keir and witnessing his lifesaving actions moments before.

"No. He is not going to the dungeons. Thallan, he was under Vaxar's control! He even admitted it before the fighting started. How many times do I need to say that Keir is good to get it through your thick head?" said Lysandra.

"Lysandra, you're weak and don't know what you are saying. Let me help you inside and to a healer," said Thallan.

"No! Enough, Thallan. I can handle myself! I don't need your help. Soldiers, let Keir go now," said Lysandra.

The soldiers froze, unsure of whose orders they were to follow. Lysandra, already annoyed at Thallan, became irritable at the soldiers for not listening to her commands and instead waiting for him to give orders. She looked at the grimog sitting beside her.

Goddess of the night, thought Lysandra.

"Nyx, protect Keir. Apparently, my word means nothing to these men," said Lysandra.

Nyx responded instantly, as if it was her name all along. She moved towards Keir and the soldiers. Afraid of her, they moved away some distance. The soldiers looked towards Thallan, waiting for orders on what to do now that the Grimog protected Keir. Then, from the bushes where Nyx hid, Astra ran toward Keir. Nyx noticed the little creature, small compared to her size, but did not seem to care that it was heading in her direction. Astra paused for a moment before going around Nyx, looking at her curiously, and then climbed up Keir's leg and back to sit herself partially on his shoulder again.

"Lysandra, what are you doing? He is the Dark King! He is evil. What if he wanted you to think that he was under Vaxar's control, only to get close to you? Have you even considered that?" said Thallan.

"He didn't even know I was the sorceress until I told him. And you heard Vaxar. He only knew when a soldier that saw me use magic in Holbrook earlier sent word to him of what he saw. Don't you trust me? Or am I still the little girl that you must protect and guide through everything?" said Lysandra.

Thallan fell silent. He felt guilty for how he was treating her. He realized he was doubting her ability, her knowledge. Thallan looked towards the soldiers and signaled for them to leave Keir.

"Thank you. Now that we've stopped fighting each other, we need to pursue Vaxar. He can only teleport so far. Keir, Thallan, do either of you know where he might go?" said Lysandra.

Keir shook his head, not knowing where Vaxar would go now that the kingdom was against him.

"Possibly towards the Krubet Kingdom. He's strangely fixated on something there," said Thallan.

"Whatever it may be, we must prevent him from obtaining the magic hidden in that kingdom. Gather as many men as you can. I will send word for Valda to see if she can join us," said Lysandra.

"Valda is already on her way here. Once I heard Vaxar was here, I sent a bird to inform her. Valda has been hiding in the forest close to Holbrook after her attack on the outpost. She insisted on being nearby in case something happened with you staying in the castle. She should be here soon. I'll gather the men and provisions and meet you at the front gate," said Thallan.

"You will not! Traitors! Leave it to my pathetic son to betray his father and join the sorcerer bitch. Soldiers, kill them all!" said Erebus.

Using the spell immolendo, Lysandra froze the soldiers in place. She then used the spell levitaortia to levitate and throw the soldiers over the garden wall.

"Thallan, have your men throw the real Dark King in the dungeon. I suggest melting down the key rather than throwing it away. We will deal with him after we deal with Vaxar," said Lysandra.

Thallan nodded and relayed the orders to the soldiers behind him. The soldiers promptly left, holding Erebus as they took him to the dungeons.

Thallan left Lysandra's side without saying another word. As he passed Keir, heading for the doors, Thallan gave him a stern look of disapproval. Then quickly looked at Nyx and kept walking towards the door.

Lysandra looked around to find Richard leaning against the bench in the garden. She rushed towards him. He was unconscious but still alive, thankfully. She quickly thought of the combination spell ceptalgo su dynanim to take away some of his pain with her magic, and she worked on healing his open wounds. Once the wounds magically sealed, Richard briefly opened his eyes, only to fall back unconscious, as he was too weak to stay awake.

"I need you three soldiers to take Richard to the healer. Tell her I've relieved his pain and closed his wounds, but I suspect broken bones. I am no healer, and I don't want to make things worse. Carefully carry him there, please," said Lysandra.

The soldiers nodded and worked together to carry him carefully. They were slow, but once they made their way out of the garden, it was only Lysandra, Keir, Nyx, and Astra left.

"Let me come with you. You need all the extra hands you can get in this fight," said Keir.

"I was already going to offer. Seeing how Thallan is acting around you, I fear if I leave you here you will be in danger of someone trying to kill you," said Lysandra.

"Well, let's go get our things from our room and meet them at the gate."

With Nyx behind them, they hurried down the halls toward the stairwell where the first group of soldiers had attacked them. As they reached the stairs, they saw soldiers binding the men Lysandra had knocked unconscious. They walked up the stairwell and through the last couple of hallways to their chambers. As they passed by the soldiers, they all stopped for a moment with worry upon seeing Nyx.

They entered their room to find Celia hiding behind the bed, near the window. She shook with fear. Keir and Lysandra both placed their swords against the wall beside the door. She stood up from hiding behind the bed, holding a dinner knife in her shaking hand.

"You're safe, Celia. The threat is over," said Lysandra.

"What about him? Th-the Dark King. And that?" asked Celia shakingly.

"He was under control from Vaxar's magic. He is not the Dark King. That is his father. And Nyx here is friendly. She won't hurt you," said Lysandra.

"You're safe, Celia. I won't hurt you. I could never do that to you or anyone here. I promise," said Keir.

Celia lowered the knife but kept a tight grip on it.

Lysandra grabbed Keir's hand and pulled him to the side, then snapped her fingers for Nyx to come to her other side. It left an open pathway for her to head towards the door to leave. Without a word, Celia sprinted around the bed and through the door, running down the hallway.

Lysandra and Keir began packing what they could to travel with. Lysandra looked at her clothes and changed into one of her new sets of clothing and packed the rest of the clothes that would be appropriate to travel in. Once she packed her clothes into her large bag, she stepped behind her changing screen to put on her new clothes. Keir noticed and did the same.

Once they were ready, Keir grabbed Astra and placed her on his shoulder again after he tended and wrapped the wound on his other shoulder. He then placed his sword at his waist and grabbed his bag. Lysandra grabbed her bag and small satchel that contained some powders and potion ingredients, along with her spellbook. She tied her sword at her waist once she had her bag draped over her shoulder. They were about to leave the room when Eleanora, holding a dagger, and Gwyneth with a bow and arrow at the ready, stepped in.

"What is he doing by your side? We heard the commotion of Vaxar with soldiers hunting you," said Eleanora.

"We've been trying to find you using the servants' hallways and stairwell to limit our chances of crossing paths with soldiers," said Gwyneth.

"It's all right. He was under Vaxar's control. And Vaxar has fled. We're going after him. Thallan is waiting for us at the front gate. You both should stay here and ease the people's worry and help run things while we're away. And before you say anything, Nyx is friendly. We ran into her earlier today on our visit to the forest and she became my new friend," said Lysandra.

"Are you sure it is safe to have him by your side?" asked Gwyneth.

"Yes. Keir is a good man, and he wants to help undo the damage that his father, the real Dark King, and Vaxar have done," said Lysandra.

"There is no way to talk you out of this, is there?" asked Eleanora.

"I am sorry, Mother. But you know as well as I that this is what I must do. We must stop Vaxar before he gets what he wants. He's hunting down magic to make himself more powerful and we don't know his purpose for this power," said Lysandra.

"I know. You just stay safe and come back to me. And you. You better prove me wrong about you and protect my daughter, understand?" said Eleanora.

"Yes, ma'am. I promise," said Keir.

"While we are gone, I think it would be best to have you both and Richard be in charge of the kingdom to keep it safe. Thallan has already locked Erebus in the dungeon. He can sit there and wait until we've taken care of Vaxar," said Lysandra.

Keir nodded in agreement.

"If you insist, but you better hurry back. Neither of us are leaders," said Gwyneth.

Eleanora and Gwyneth each gave Lysandra a hug and bid them farewell.

Lysandra and Keir made their way back outside the castle. They walked towards the front gate where Thallan waited on his horse with two other horses ready. The gates opened and a rider in armor approached Thallan. Lysandra recognized the rider. Valda arrived just in time to join the hunt for the Dark Sorcerer.

20

THE SNOWY CHASE

Valda rode right towards Thallan before she noticed Lysandra approaching. Lysandra could tell that Thallan was already speaking to her. As Lysandra and Keir approached, Valda dismounted from her horse. She gave Lysandra a smile as they walked closer to one another and then looked at Nyx, acknowledging the creature.

"I see you have made some friends since I've been gone," said Valda.

"Yes, I have. This is Nyx. And I'm sure Thallan just told you about Keir," said Lysandra.

"All he said is don't worry and to ask you. He doesn't seem to be in a good mood," said Valda.

"Long story short, he was under Vaxar's control through magic. He is now joining us in hunting down Vaxar, who is currently fleeing the kingdom," said Lysandra.

"Well, let's get going then. Thallan, you should have the soldiers over there stay here to protect the kingdom. Just the few of us should be enough, especially with Nyx here," said Valda.

"All right. But he is not going with us," said Thallan.

"We don't have time to argue, Thallan. He is safer with me. Others who see Keir as you do will try to kill him while we are away. If you have a problem with that, then stay here while we go after Vaxar. We are wasting enough time as it is. If you insist on coming along, then you'll just have to shut up and deal with the fact that Keir is coming with us. Now let's go," said Lysandra.

Valda chuckled. "You heard her, Thallan. Better make your decision quickly."

"If I am right about Vaxar, he has a small vial of a powdery substance that he uses to teleport. I have known him to use it once. I'm not sure how much he uses each time he travels," said Keir.

"Do you know how big the vial is?" asked Lysandra.

"I think two or three inches tall, and it's narrow," said Keir.

"Then I think he may have enough to get halfway to Bellehaven," said Lysandra.

"Then we should hurry to catch up to him," said Valda.

Keir helped Lysandra tie her gear and his to the horses. Lysandra tugged the hood of her new cloak over her to protect her from the snowy night air. It differed from her old cloak, but was still the same shade of dark blue. It had a clip on one side to attach to the other around her collarbone. The fabric was thick enough to keep her warm from the cold weather, lined with fur.

Once they mounted and were ready to go, they set off on the pathway around Holbrook instead of through it to avoid unwanted attention.

Valda and Lysandra led the way as Keir and Nyx followed behind with Thallan unhappily riding in the back of their small caravan through the woods. Their horses loped to conserve energy as the higher they go along the path against the mountainside, the more dangerous it became with the slick snow.

They rode for some time until they found Vaxar's tracks and followed them south. If he were to make way for the Krubet Kingdom as Thallan suspected, Vaxar would have to travel to the coast and find a ship to carry him across the Emerald Sea. Though it could be a dangerous voyage if you sailed too close to Echo Island, as there were creatures there that loved to attack ships or disappear some crew members. All anyone heard were stories of the island being dangerous, but no one knew for sure what exactly lived there. Lysandra hoped that if they could not stop him from reaching the sea, then maybe whatever lived on that island could kill him.

They continued to follow the tracks. Every few hundred yards, they would find tracks where Vaxar teleported, walked for a few feet, and then the tracks disappeared from teleporting. It was a tiresome process, trying to find the tracks in the dark with only the torchlight as a winter storm grew thicker.

The snow fell fast, and the tracks got harder and harder to find as they were covered by the fresh snowfall. They reached some small caves against the mountain that would provide the perfect shelter for the night to wait for the storm to pass as it was picking up and making their journey in the dark too dangerous.

"We should stop here for the night. His tracks will surely be gone by now with this snowfall. We know he is leaving the mountain range. Even he can't travel much longer in this weather," said Valda.

"You're probably right. There is no point putting ourselves in danger," said Lysandra.

"I'll go find some logs. Lys, we'll need you to work some magic to light them," said Thallan.

They dismounted and ground-tied the horses within the

cave. Thallan left to find wood for a fire as the others grabbed their gear from the horses and began setting up camp.

As Valda and Keir arranged their sleeping arrangements on the floor, Lysandra helped prepare food ready to cook once Thallan would return with the firewood. As she was busy preparing everything, Keir got her sleeping arrangements ready for her. He wanted to have her sleep next to him, as he wasn't sure if he could trust Thallan and Valda yet and figured he would be safer remaining by her side throughout the night. Valda noticed him setting up Lysandra's things and did the same for Thallan and placed him on the other side of her, placing herself and Lysandra in between the two men. They arranged the beds, so that everyone faced the fire, with their backs to the cave wall.

Thallan returned with arms full of firewood and laid it out on the ground. Lysandra used this as an opportunity to light the fire without saying the spell in her mind. She attempted without using her hands as she stirred the food in the pot, getting it ready to cook. Lysandra focused but couldn't get the fire to start without saying the spell as she tried to hide what she was doing, since she didn't want the others to discover what she could do.

She tried a few times before Thallan would get back with more wood to keep the fire going throughout the night. Before anyone would notice that she hadn't lit the fire, she pretended as if she was done with preparing the food and turned her full attention to the stacked logs.

Lysandra thought of the spell pyrocaustrusphere, igniting a fireball in her palm. She controlled the flame and dimmed it, so it was not so big and then carefully tossed it into the center of the stacked logs, lighting them as if they were not wet from snow.

She looked around the forest surrounding their little

cave. The snow was falling ever so delicately as it gently landed on the ground and trees. Despite it being night, the white snow provided enough light for her to see some distance. The fresh powder looked so beautiful to her with how smooth and soft it was, no matter where it landed. Winter was her favorite season.

Thallan returned and placed the extra wood just inside the cave against the wall. Lysandra ignored him as he came over to check on the stew she was cooking. He noticed her grow tense and left her be so as not to upset her any further. He went towards his sleeping arrangements and noticed that Valda strategically placed him further away from Keir and noted that it was probably for the best. After all, he could still keep an eye on him at the angle they were at.

Once Thallan sat down, Keir made his way towards Lysandra beside the fire as she cooked. Nyx, who was sitting just outside the cave, unbothered by the cold weather, took off into the woods without warning, and startled everyone.

"Nyx probably went to go catch something. I am sure stew won't appease her appetite," said Lysandra.

They were all on edge as it wouldn't be surprising if Vaxar doubled-back to attack them.

When the stew was ready, they ate in silence. Valda sat against the cave wall as she watched the tension between Lysandra, Thallan, and Keir. She could tell that Keir was no threat as he clearly looked to be in love with Lysandra and was showing so much care with anything he did around her. Valda wanted to talk to Lysandra about all that has happened since she left, but she wanted to first analyze the tension between Thallan and Lysandra before bringing up a topic that would surely cause them to argue.

"So, Lysandra, care to catch me up on all that I missed?" asked Valda.

Lysandra began telling her everything. She told her about the wedding and how they hid who she was from Vaxar. Lysandra, telling her this, remembered to thank Valda for providing the distraction to draw Vaxar away from the ceremonies and noted that he looked like a child forced to dress up and attend. Lysandra also made a mental note to return Valda's pendant. But she hid the information on the fairies and changed it to a beautiful frozen waterfall.

Thallan slightly furrowed his brow, not believing that was what was so important to travel through the snow for Keir to show her.

With her change in the story, Keir felt relieved as he too thought it should remain a secret to protect the fairies and hoped that the two of them would believe her. The fewer people who know about them, the safer they would be from the Dark Sorcerer.

When Lysandra finished, Valda thought for a moment before speaking. She wanted to weigh the options of what they should do next. It seemed too obvious to blindly chase Vaxar into Krubet.

"What are you thinking about?" asked Thallan.

"Maybe we should stop by the hills. I want Lysandra to use their magic to see if we can get some sort of information about what Vaxar is going after. Do you think that is a possibility?" said Valda.

"It wouldn't hurt to try. The hills can be tricky with providing information. According to the codex, it will only reveal what the spirits within the hills deem as something we need or are allowed to know. Often in riddles or prophecies," said Lysandra.

"Well, the hills will be on our way towards the coast to travel to Krubet," said Thallan.

Nyx appeared at the entrance to the cave from the shadows

of the night, startling everyone again. Lysandra and Valda laughed at the startled boys, who had pulled out their knives.

"Nyx, I think we need to have a talk. You're going to scare them to death if you keep disappearing and reappearing without warning," said Lysandra.

"Oh, I think the boys can handle it. They can just get used to it," said Valda.

Keir chuckled at Valda and Lysandra's remarks. Thallan found their remarks annoying.

Nyx shook off the snow from her fur and made her way towards Lysandra and laid behind her against the wall to face the fire. She curled up, keeping her head aimed at the opening of the cave. When she settled down, Lysandra patted Nyx's head. She found herself happy to have her new companion by her side.

"We should all get some rest for the night. I'll take the first watch. You guys have had a very eventful day and should get some rest," said Valda.

They all agreed as their exhaustion crept up on them. Keir laid down with Astra curled up against his chest under a blanket. Lysandra was about to lie down on her bag, using it as a pillow, when Nyx crawled towards her and curled up close beside her, providing extra warmth along with the blanket she had packed. She did not know why, but Lysandra was grateful for the love and protection from her new companion. After just a few quick minutes of laying down with Nyx, Lysandra fell fast asleep.

Lysandra woke up to the slight nudge from Valda. She groggily rubbed her eyes and before she sat up, she realized that she somehow had her head laying on top of Nyx's middle.

Nyx was sound asleep and didn't seem to notice Lysandra sitting up. Valda sat beside Lysandra, trying not to wake up Nyx. Lysandra could tell she wanted to talk, judging by how close she was. Valda shoved the stick she had in her hand into the fire. Lysandra grabbed her small bag she had sitting beside her and pulled out Valda's pendant.

"Thank you for lending it to me," said Lysandra.

"Thank you for keeping it safe," said Valda, as she placed her necklace around her neck.

There was a moment of silence, filled only by the crackling fire.

"I have to say, I am glad to see you letting your inner strength out," said Valda.

"Inner strength?"

"Being your own person and not hiding from everyone. More specifically, not taking Thallan's crap, trying to over-protect you. You are strong and only you know what you can handle, not anyone else. I could tell when we first met that you were hiding a part of yourself. So, I am glad that you are feeling free to be yourself, although there is something you're still hiding. Just know, I'll always stand by you," said Valda.

Lysandra smiled as she tried to hide that she was blushing at Valda's kind words. She knew Valda was telling the truth and wondered if she would ever truly be herself without worrying about what Thallan or others thought.

"How long will you travel with us? I am sure you have duties you must attend to in your kingdom?" asked Lysandra.

"They have been handling things there for a while now without me. I plan on being by your side for as long as you need me. Besides, someone's got to back you up against these men," said Valda.

Lysandra quietly chuckled and felt relieved as she enjoyed Valda's company.

"I think it's time I try to get some rest. Thank you for the chat," said Valda.

Valda went over to her bed to get settled down to get some sleep for the rest of the night.

During Lysandra's turn on watch, she found it hard to keep her mind from wandering and overthinking. She knew it would do no good worrying about things currently out of her control. One thing crossed her mind, but that was not a worry. She hoped that now that she was finally leaving the kingdom, she may get to meet her father. Lysandra wondered if he had heard any news of what had happened in recent days or if he'd heard that she was now leaving the Nathair Kingdom. Her mind quickly returned to worry when she remembered that Keir, her legitimate husband, was traveling by her side. She wondered if her father would react the same way as Thallan had.

Her mind continued to wander for the next couple of hours until it was time to wake up Thallan for the third and final watch. To appease Thallan's worries, they'd agreed to let Keir sleep the night through. Lysandra walked towards him and instead of imitating the kind nudges that Valda did to wake her, she jabbed her foot into his back. She nudged him twice before he woke up and noticed Lysandra standing over him. She knelt to get closer to talk to him quietly.

"Your turn to keep watch. Don't even think about doing something to Keir while he sleeps. If you do, you better run and hope I don't find your ass," said Lysandra.

"I don't understand how you could have fallen in love with him so quickly, knowing who he is," said Thallan.

"He is a good friend and deserves a second chance. After all, every dark thing he did was because he was under the control of his father and Vaxar," said Lysandra.

Thallan remained silent despite his disapproval.

Lysandra laid down and curled up against Nyx under her blanket. Thallan stirred the fire to keep it going. He looked at Lysandra for a moment, then at Keir. He had noticed the riker earlier but thought little of it until now. Thallan decided Keir must earn his trust, but for now he would stop arguing against Lysandra's decisions.

21

WHISPERS OF THE HILLS

At the first light of dawn, they began riding through the snow. The storm overnight added at least another foot, making the journey much slower than they would have preferred. The air was so cold it chilled them all to the bone. Lysandra was partially glad that they couldn't have the horses ride quickly through the slick snow, as the wind would surely cause her face to go numb. Valda had an extra pair of gloves that she lent to Lysandra to help protect her hands.

The only one who didn't seem bothered by the cold weather was Nyx. She walked as close as she could to Lysandra. Whenever Thallan got too close, Nyx would give a low growl, causing him to give up on his attempt to talk to Lysandra. Lysandra was happy Nyx didn't like him and kept him away, as she had no interest in talking to him for some time. She knew what he wanted to talk about, but wasn't in the mood for another argument.

Near midday, Nyx had taken off ahead of them, startling Thallan. They continued riding for another few minutes until they stopped at a small clearing with a few large rocks to rest the horses and eat.

As they dismounted their horses and tied them to some tree branches, Lysandra looked into one of their packs with the food. It mostly contained vegetables, bread, and small pastries, no meat, which would help them feel full longer.

She took some of the bread and pastries out and was about to distribute some to everyone when Nyx appeared out of the shadows of the snow-covered trees. She had not just one, but three large dead rabbits hanging out of her mouth. Nyx walked straight towards Thallan, who was sitting on a rock, and dropped them at his feet, surprising him. Thallan stared at her as she used her nose to nudge the rabbits closer to him.

"I think she is telling you they are for us," said Valda.

Thallan grabbed the rabbits by their ears. He stood up and looked around for a good place some distance away from their spot to skin them. Nyx stayed sitting in front of Thallan, watching him until she looked at Lysandra.

"Thallan, why don't you say thank you to Nyx? We didn't ask her to hunt for us," said Lysandra.

Thallan gave her an annoyed look before turning his attention to the creature standing before him.

"Thanks," said Thallan as he lifted the rabbits and shook them, unsure if she understood him.

Nyx stood and walked over to Lysandra to lie down beside her. Thallan was unamused by the creature's behavior as both Valda and Lysandra giggled.

"Do you want some help?" asked Keir.

"No. I do not need your help," said Thallan.

Keir nodded and sat back down on the rock near Lysandra. She gave him a kind smile as she gave him a reassuring squeeze of his hand. Lysandra felt bad for him. She could tell that all he wanted to do right now was help.

After they ate their lunch, they started riding through the snow again. Valda looked to the sky ahead and could see that another storm would make its way into the mountains, forcing them to camp for another night earlier than intended.

They camped under two large, snow-covered trees that stood side by side. Thanks to Thallan having cut and prepared the meat, Lysandra made another stew. Normally, she would try to be careful with how much meat to use for traveling, but she figured Nyx might bring them more from her hunts.

As the four of them huddled around the fire, they ate in silence while trying to keep warm with their blankets tucked tight about their shoulders. The only sounds in the forest other than the noise of them eating were the crackling of the fire and the light sound of the snow falling around them. Unlike the previous night, there was no wind accompanying this storm, which benefited them since they were out in the open.

Nyx curled up against Lysandra's back as she ate. Her body helped keep Lysandra warm enough that she was no longer shivering. Keir sat to her left, within arm's reach, as Valda sat to her right and Thallan on the other side. Lysandra pulled out her codex and began studying it once more to distract her mind, which was once again overthinking.

Valda noticed Lysandra staring at her book and fidgeting with the pendant she wore around her neck. She could see her anxiety and tried to think of something that might help. Keir noticed as well and moved to sit right next to her as he placed his arm loosely around her waist.

Valda hummed a simple melodic tune and then sang.

Lower the sails, Mount your horses!
Take the path less traveled,
Across the land and sea,
Through light and darkness.
Adventure waits for you!

Through the marshes, To the mountains,
To the dunes and icy lands,
Our journey begins.

Lower the sails, Mount your horses!
Sail on through the night,
Ride out ere break of day,
Through the storm and sun,
Your adventure has begun!

Valda's voice filled the forest, even though she did not sing loudly. It was as if the forest had opened and invited her song to travel through it so it could listen. The song helped ease Lysandra's worries, and she had stopped fidgeting with her necklace and returned it to its hiding spot beneath her shirt.

"That was a beautiful song. Where did you learn it?" said Lysandra.

"From my father. It is a special song from my family. Krogodo is a kingdom full of songs. That was only a small part of it. It is a long song. I thought only the beginning would serve its purpose right now with our journey starting. I know this must be your first time leaving your home," said Valda.

"It is. Maybe one day you can give me a tour of your kingdom if we get the chance," said Lysandra.

"One day you shall visit and there will be glorious celebrations. It would be an honor to give you a tour of my home," said Valda.

Not long after, they all climbed into bed except Thallan, who chose to take first watch. Keir asked Lysandra if they could sleep beside one another to help stay warm. She agreed.

By first light the next morning, they were off at a good pace until they came to the cliffside. They dismounted their horses. Every step required careful placement to avoid slick snow or ice. Thallan, after his last trek along the dangerous trail, had them move at a very slow pace. Keir, halfway through, slipped slightly on ice that was hidden under snow. Before anything drastic happened, he prevented himself from sliding further and falling off the cliff. Then, just a few minutes later, Valda had the same trouble. With the two close calls, they moved slower.

Once they safely made it past the dangerous cliffside, they began their descent down the mountain. It became easier to travel as the snow was not as thick. They made camp for another night in the mountains under some trees.

By midday the following day, they were finally out of the mountains, and by late afternoon, they could see Bellehaven in the distance. It was a town just slightly larger than Holbrook, with a mix of tall and short buildings with some homes and a small farm along the edge. The main road ran through the center of town, passing by bakeries, inns and taverns. They rode around the town considering that people may question the grimog traveling with them and recognize Keir. They wanted to play it safe and avoid any confrontation if necessary.

Valda led the group, with Lysandra and Keir following as Thallan rode behind. They kept a fast pace, pushing the horses to help make up for the lost time traveling in the

snow. Lysandra was grateful for the slightly warmer temperatures at the lower elevation, although the wind was still quite
cold against their faces. They camped on the open plains a
few miles south of Bellehaven against a patch of trees. The
air wasn't as cold as in the mountains and there was only an
inch of snow on the ground.

The next day, they pushed on to arrive at the Hills of the
Prophets before nightfall. As their light had faded, they all
were considering if they should stop and make camp and
continue in the morning until, at the edge of the horizon, the
hills became visible. Their spirits lifted, and they quickened
their pace until they came to the archway entrance to the
hills. They dismounted their horses and held onto their reins
as they walked through the moss-covered stone archway, entering the magical place.

Lysandra led them, using the parchment folded up in her
spellbook, which contained a small map of the hills. It felt
like a maze, as none of them had ever visited the mystical
hills. She led them around the hills, each with doors.

Within the hills, they were all connected to each other
through tunneled hallways. However, the hallways could be
a dangerous place to get lost in as the magic within the hills
and the dark spirits would trap any soul they could. Above
ground was slightly safer, as the spirits preferred to stay inside, but they were not unwilling to venture outside.

They walked around many of the hills in the dark until
Lysandra stopped. She handed her horse's reins to Keir and
approached the door. As soon as she got close, the torch
against the wall to the right of the door lit itself, illuminating
a sign below it.

"According to the map, this hill should help with foresee-
ing the future," said Lysandra.

"Let's hope this works," said Thallan.

Thallan, Valda, and Keir ground-tied the horses as Lysandra opened the door. She started to enter when she noticed the others were about to follow.

"Stay our here. I shouldn't be long," said Lysandra.

"We're coming with you. I've heard stories about this place and how its magic tries to tempt and trap unsuspecting sorcerers," said Valda.

"I wish you all could, but you can't. Nonmagical people can't enter. If you do, the magic will consume you instantly and the hills will trap you. It's called Hills of the Prophets for a reason. Hundreds of years ago, this place trapped everyone who came here. The whispered voices of those souls are mostly the prophets who studied the magic here. Sorcerers placed a protection barrier to keep out wanderers, allowing only themselves to enter. The hills claimed too many innocent people. I stand a chance against the magic, but you don't," said Lysandra.

"That's too dangerous. We should find another option to figure out Vaxar's plan," said Keir.

"For once, I agree with him. I did not know the dangers the hills possess," said Thallan.

"It will be fine. I won't be in there long and besides, the room I need to go into is just inside. Look here on the map. The room is right here, just slightly down the hallway. It's the first door on the right. Please, trust me," said Lysandra.

"We trust you. We'll wait right out here for you. Be safe. If it gets too dangerous, get out of there," said Valda.

Valda gave Thallan and Keir a stern look to have them remain silent. Lysandra nodded and entered the hill and noticed that Nyx had entered with her. She let out a sigh of relief.

"I am really glad you are with me, Nyx. This place gives me the creeps."

As the two of them entered the hallway, the torches magically lit themselves all the way down and to the other connected hallways as well. The hallways looked easy to get lost in. She kept to her map and came across the first door on the right, which opened automatically as they approached. Whispers poured out into the hallway.

"*Sorceress. Come in. Sorceress of destiny. She holds the power,*" said the whispers in unison.

Goosebumps emerged along the back of her neck, hearing the whispers. She questioned whether she should trust them. Lysandra proceeded with caution, as nothing dangerous was happening just yet. They were speaking in a very unsettling voice.

"Let's hurry, Nyx," she said in a shaky voice.

When they entered the room, torches along the wall ignited, providing light to the cobwebbed and dusty room. The cauldron in the middle of the room hung above a pit that erupted into a green fire. Then bottles and pages moved about the table and shelves on the other side of the cauldron against the wall.

"*We know what you seek, young sorceress. Would you like our help with the potion to reveal the answer to your question about the Dark Sorcerer?*" asked an eerie whisper.

"Uh. No, thank you. I think I know what to do," said Lysandra.

"Though, I don't know why you can't just tell me since you can obviously talk," muttered Lysandra under her breath.

"*You must see. Not hear. The potion allows us to show,*" said the eerie whisper.

"Oh. Well, all right, then. Can you teach me?" said Lysandra.

A book fell from the shelf. She grabbed it and placed it

on the table. The book flipped open. Pages flew to one side until they stopped on a potion. She went about the room, gathering the ingredients. She placed her ingredients on the table beside the book. Water magically filled the cauldron as she gathered what she needed. The water came to a boil and was ready for the ingredients to be added. She added liquids from vials, a crushed fig, dry leaves and twigs, and some old animal parts that she was not fond of touching. The potion changed color with each ingredient added. The voices remained quiet as they watched her follow the instructions from the book.

As the last ingredient was added, the voices returned and began chanting in unison with what sounded like a spell, but it was one she did not know of. She checked the book. There was no mention of a spell to chant for the potion.

"Hey. Uh. What are you saying? What are you doing?"

"*You can do the potion, but require our help with the spell. We keep such things secret,*" said a whisper close to her.

The voices continued chanting the spell as smoke formed above the cauldron. Once the smoke started growing, the chanting stopped. The smoke turned into a teal color, with sparks of purple flying through it. The smoke grew so large it was touching the ceiling of the room. Then a flash of purple ignited brightly from the center as images appeared.

The first image was of Keir bowing to what looked to be a woman.

"*As the prophecy we foretold, the Dark King's son would fail his father and join your side,*" said a whispered voice.

Then another image appeared. It looked like Vaxar's silhouette. She couldn't quite tell what he was doing, but it looked like he was performing some sort of a powerful spell with his arms fully extended. Then an army rose from the ground before him.

"*Now begins the battle between the light and dark sides of magic. Between the forces of Meridia and the forces of Keres,*" said a different, whispered voice.

The images of the army changed into an image of her and Vaxar facing one another. Flashes of light flowed between the two images.

"All right. So, obviously we fight one another again," muttered Lysandra.

The images changed again, forming into something large. She wondered what it could be.

"*The Dark Sorcerer will fail shall the sorceress gain the aid of old, powerful beings. But proceed cautiously, for a new prophecy exists. If you do not learn of the past, and follow her guidance, Keres will claim the lands of Lamorra,*" said one whispered voice.

"*You have gained the aid of one magical being. You must hurry to find the other and seek the hidden magic before the darkness covers it from your sight,*" said another whisper.

The smoke formed its final image. Even Nyx recognized it and started glowing in response while letting out a low growl. Lysandra's eyes grew wide. She thought they had been dead for several hundred years.

"This is what Vaxar is hunting down! A dragon!"

"*Yes. It hides within the mountains near Krubet. You must save the dragon. Vaxar wishes to destroy this powerful being,*" said a whispered voice.

Lysandra turned around and was about to leave through the door until it slammed shut. She tried to pry it open, but it would not budge. Panic set in as she feared the hills were attempting to trap her. Nyx let out a growl.

"Let me out!"

"*We are not done. There is no need to rush,*" said a whispered voice.

"Why is that?"

"*Vaxar would not be arriving at the coast in time. There is a hurricane sweeping through the sea, blocking his passage to Krubet,*" said a whispered voice.

"*With another hurricane closely behind it. The hurricane will delay him for at least a month. As the creatures from the island love to explore outside their territory to find lost travelers. He would have to wait until they return to their little island,*" said another whispered voice.

"Well, that is a relief. But can I leave now? Or is there something else that you need to tell me since I'm still trapped in here?"

"*Use this time to rest before your travel across the great ocean. For more formidable trials lie before you,*" said a whispered voice.

"Care to tell me what these trials may be?"

"*Only of your first. You must gain the trust of the dragon. We are Dusan spirits. Our instructions are to guide you. Dragons' wisdom and power surpass their age. Respect them. This dragon can disguise himself to the life around it. Be kind to it, as it has remained hidden for years. Use this information wisely, my dear. The dragon already does not like Vaxar. He despises sorcerers,*" said a whispered voice.

"What makes you think the dragon will like me any better?"

"*The dragons were loyal and protective of the last known sorceress,*" said a whispered voice.

"*You have what is needed to gain the dragon's trust and friendship,*" said another whispered voice.

The door opened behind Lysandra. Nyx quickly stepped into the hallway. Lysandra grabbed hold of the door to make sure it wouldn't shut on her.

"*Good luck, Sorceress Lysandra,*" said the whispered voices in unison.

The torches and cauldron all extinguished themselves,

leaving the room pitch black. Lysandra left the room with Nyx by her side and rushed back to the entrance of the hill.

They arrived at the doorway of the hill to find Keir and Valda sitting on the ground beside one another. Thallan was pacing behind them. They noticed her coming out and stood up.

"So, what did you learn?" asked Valda.

Lysandra told them everything the voices had told her. But as she finished, she noticed a raven perched on the hill behind her friends. It looked like it was listening intently. She knelt beside Nyx.

"Get that raven on top of the hill," whispered Lysandra.

Nyx walked off to the side of the hill, attempting to not catch the raven's attention.

"I told Nyx to go find something to eat," said Lysandra.

She knew it was no ordinary raven. It was a branwenn. They were slightly larger than a raven and more intelligent. Sorcerers could control them and used them as spies. Vaxar was not far away if he could control the branwenn.

Nyx pounced on the bird and tore its head off with her teeth. She spat out the head, leaving it to roll down the hill.

"It was a branwenn raven. Vaxar is not far away. He just heard everything I told you," said Lysandra.

"Then we should get out of this place quickly," said Valda.

They quickly mounted their horses and made their way around the hills, back to the archway. Once they were out of the Hills of the Prophets, they quickened their pace, heading south, following Valda.

"We should go just within the borders of Krogodo, where it is safe. We can stay there until it is safe to travel to the coast and gain passage to Krubet," said Valda.

They planned to ride on through part of the night to gain some distance between them and the hills and, hopefully,

Vaxar. They did not want to give him the advantage of attacking them out in the open.

After a few hours of riding, they felt safe enough to slow down and bring the horses to a trot before stopping beside a river. They dismounted and let the horses get some rest. Thallan started a fire and Lysandra got things ready to make their late dinner. Keir and Valda worked together to set up the sleeping arrangements as before.

Lysandra suddenly had a feeling, as if something dark and magical was approaching. From the corner of her eye, in the shadows of the trees from the moonlight, a hooded figure floating in the air lunged towards her as it let out an ear-piercing scream.

Her instincts kicked in and Lysandra, without muttering a spell, took the flame from the fire and threw it at the creature. The creature dodged the flame. It started its approach again. Its hands stretched out, revealing long fingers, almost like claws, with sharp nails. It wore a shredded, black hooded cloak, and appeared faceless.

It let out another scream as it tried to attack Lysandra. She pulled her sword out of its sheath as she conjured a shield, but the creature's arms went right through it. It sliced the back of her forearm as she plunged the sword into the creature.

It screamed again as the sword pierced its middle. With her free hand, Lysandra conjured a fireball and threw it right at the creature's head. The creature flew back from the fire. Its cloak ignited in flames as it screamed and flew off fast into the distance.

The others ran to Lysandra. As she fell to the ground, Valda caught her.

"What was that thing?" asked Valda.

"A...wraith. Thallan, keep the fire going," said Lysandra as she winced in pain.

"She's injured. Valda, keep holding her. I'll bandage her arm," said Keir.

He lifted her sleeve as gently as he could. Black lines extended out from the gashes and were slowly growing longer up to her elbow.

"We need to get her to a healer," said Keir.

"The closest one I know is in Krogodo," said Valda.

"Then we should start heading there now. I've heard old stories of wraiths. They are deadly and their scratches are even deadlier. She may only have days if we don't get her to a healer soon," said Thallan.

Nyx walked up beside Keir. She leaned in and sniffed Lysandra's injury before licking her arm. Lysandra winced in pain.

"Nyx, stop. It's hurting her," said Keir.

"Wait. Let her. She's a magical creature. She can probably help. We don't know what magical abilities she can do other than her magic making her glow," said Valda.

Valda helped extend Lysandra's arm to give Nyx a better reach to clean the wound. As she licked at the scratch, the black lines faded lightly as they shrank in size. She stopped and looked at Keir.

"I think that's all she can do. Thank you, Nyx. That helps. Bandage her wound, Keir," said Valda.

Once they wrapped the wound, they helped her onto the horse with Keir. Valda led in front with a torch, with Keir holding Lysandra behind her and Thallan behind them. Nyx ran beside Keir's horse, her fur slightly glowing. They rode on through the night until early morning, stopping to let the horses rest.

They were at least twelve days' ride from the border of Krogodo and thirteen days from its castle. They rode as fast as they could. The group hardly slept that morning, afraid of the wraith returning and the fear of Lysandra's wound worsening.

Later that day, they took a brief rest, letting the horses drink from a stream as they checked on Lysandra's wound. Nyx turned, head tilting from side to side. She pawed at Valda and used her nose to point toward the trees.

"What is it, Nyx?" asked Valda.

Nyx quietly whined. She stood up and walked towards a tree. She looked up and started making the most peculiar noises. It was a mix of grunts and small barks.

After Nyx stopped, hoots came from a tree branch. Wings fluttered and a kamari landed on the lowest branch of the tree. The dark rustic brown midsized creature on its muscular hind legs, sat on the branch with its front feet with sharp talons resting in front. Its long feathery tail hung almost a foot below the thick branch. It looked down at Nyx, hooting some more. The creature stopped. Then Nyx once again started her noises.

"Are they talking to each other?" asked Keir.

"I think so. Wish we could understand them," said Valda.

Nyx and the kamari exchanged conversation for another moment before the kamari flew beside Valda's bag. The kamari grabbed the bag and dragged it to Valda.

"Uh. All right. Nyx, what does this one want?" asked Valda.

Nyx extended a claw and drew a line on the ground. She pointed her nose at the bag as the kamari hooted.

"I don't know what you are trying to tell me. I wish I could understand what you are saying," said Valda.

"Wait. Nyx, are you writing? Are you saying paper from Valda's bag?" asked Keir.

Both Nyx and the kamari made excited noises.

"I guess that is a yes. Alright. I'll grab my paper and ink," said Valda.

"Nyx, what are you wanting with the paper?" asked Keir.

"This is ridiculous. We should start moving. We do not have time to try to talk to animals," said Thallan.

"Thallan, shut up. We can spare a quick moment for them," said Valda.

Nyx, ignoring Thallan's comments for once, nudged her nose at Lysandra's wound, then pointed her paw towards Valda and the direction they are going in.

"All right. So, it has something to do with Lysandra's wound. Then Valda... I'm guessing where we are going... Oh! The healer?" asked Keir.

Nyx nodded and pointed at the paper. The kamari gave an excited hoot.

"Wait. Hold on for a minute. Nyx, is this creature going to take a message to the healer?" asked Valda.

Nyx made a grunt and nodded her head.

"Nyx, you're bloody brilliant! Give me a minute. I'll write a message for the healer to meet us at the marshes. I'm still hoping those crocodiles eat those wraiths for us. It's the quickest option. I'll advise her to bring backup, just in case," said Valda, as she wrote.

"Huh. I guess you both must have some ancient druid still in your blood. I would have never figured out what they were doing," said Thallan.

Nyx looked at him. She turned her head and grunted before returning her attention to Valda.

"I think that is why Nyx got my and Keir's attention and not yours," said Valda.

Lysandra chuckled before wincing again from the pain.

"All right. The message is ready and rolled up for you to

take. Thank you, Nyx's friend. Stay in Krogodo. I'll reward you with plenty of food for your help," said Valda.

The kamari gave a hoot as it grabbed the rolled parchment and promptly took off.

"Let's make our way there. We've rested long enough," said Thallan.

They mounted the horses, and once again, started making their way towards the marshes.

22

THE RACE TO KROGODO

Two days passed since they last saw the wraith. At night, as they rode on, they could hear its screams as it hunted them. During the day, it was unsettling, with no sound or sight of the dreaded creature. They could not have the horses run, afraid of causing additional pain to Lysandra.

The black lines from the scratch continued to grow. Nyx would do her best to help ease Lysandra's pain from the magical infection. The wound did not show any signs of improvement. By the end of the second day, Lysandra developed a fever as she grew pale and weaker. She spent most of the time asleep with her head against Keir's chest as they traveled.

"How much father till we reach this healer, Valda? I'm getting worried with this fever," said Keir.

"We are getting closer. Ten days from the marshes at this pace. Maybe eleven days from the border. The healer will meet us between the marshes and the border," said Valda.

"Lysandra still asleep?" asked Thallan.

"Yes. We will need to stop soon, Thallan. Those black

veins are creeping up above the bandage again," said Keir.

"Understood. I'll find us a place that looks safe enough to stop," said Thallan.

Around midnight, the group heard the screams of the wraith behind them once more. Nyx let out a monstrous roar as she jumped in front of Keir's horse. She stared at the darkness ahead of them. Her fur glowed brighter than ever before. The screams of the wraith behind them got louder as it continued getting closer.

Then suddenly, a scream came from in front of them. Chills ran down everyone's spines as both wraiths' screams were getting closer.

Thallan jumped off his horse, grabbing the bundle of logs he had tied together and quickly made a campfire using his already lit torch.

"Keir, lay Lysandra by the fire. Everyone form a defensive circle around her. We need to protect her and take these creatures out," said Thallan.

Valda helped Keir get Lysandra off the horse and beside the fire as she shivered from her fever. Keir took out a blanket from his bag and lay it on top of her. Astra jumped down from his shoulder and sat on Lysandra's lap.

Thallan, Valda, and Keir stood with their swords at the ready, torches held out, trying to see where the wraiths were in the dark. Nyx, glowing brightly, was ready to lunge at the first wraith that would appear.

The wraiths went silent. The air went still. Nyx growled. Then the wraiths screamed louder than ever as they lunged. Nyx jumped and landed on top of one, biting the wraith's neck as she tore with her claws. The wraith slashed at Nyx, but its cursed nails had no effect on the magical creature.

Valda took her torch and stabbed it into the wraith's face, hidden within its dark hood. The wraith screamed and tried to slash Valda. It narrowly missed her. The wraith kicked off Nyx. It rose to its feet and lunged at Valda. Nyx once again pounced on the creature and sliced its fingers clean off. The wraith howled in pain. Dark red shadows oozed from the creature's hand. Nyx continued slashing and biting the dreaded creature, and Valda grabbed another torch.

"Nyx, try to pin it so I light it on fire!" yelled Valda.

As Valda and Nyx fought this wraith, Keir and Thallan fought against the other. They slashed it multiple times. The wraith screamed but continued to attack, trying to catch them with its claw-like hands. Thallan kept his torch up, burning the wraith's hands each time it got close.

Dark shadows with streaks of red stretched out from the wraiths' wounds. The shadows touched the ground and became a mixture of red and black ichor.

Amidst the fighting, the terrified horses neighed as they were being cut down. A third wraith quietly appeared in the shadows. It lunged for Lysandra, unprotected from her friends.

Astra pounced on the wraith. She slithered and scurried about the wraith's head. She scratched and bit where she could. The wraith flailed its hands at its head, trying to grab Astra.

The wraith screamed in frustration. It flung its head, trying to throw Astra off. Astra had her claws in the hood as the wraith flung its head back. She fell onto its back, pulling off the hood and digging her claws into its back. She let out an angry growl.

The others turned, hearing the third wraith's screams to see the gruesome sight of the wraith without its hood. Its skeletal head bore rotten, wrinkled flesh with deep red eyes, unnaturally enormous mouth, and massive pointy sharp teeth.

Astra climbed the wraith's back, making it back to the

creature's head. She bit and ripped the flesh off. The wraith screamed again. She got to the top of the creature's head and clawed at its eyes, blinding it.

"Astra! Jump off!" yelled Keir.

Astra jumped off the wraith, landing in front of Lysandra. Keir threw his torch at the wraith. It landed on the creature, catching its face and cloak on fire. The wraiths, all engulfed in flames from the torches, screamed and fled into the darkness.

"I wonder if they're returning to Vaxar. He'll be furious that his monsters failed, again," said Valda.

"I'm surprised they're still on fire with them moving through the air that fast," said Keir.

"That's a good point. I wonder why that is?" said Valda.

"Hopefully no more show up tonight and the fire keeps them away," said Thallan.

"Since they don't like fire, maybe that's why we don't see them in the day. They may not like the sun," said Keir.

"I was thinking the same thing. I think it is a solid theory. Still, I want to stay cautious. Who knows what else Vaxar may conjure up next that does not mind the sun," said Thallan.

"I agree," said Keir.

Nyx returned to Lysandra and whined as she pawed gently at Lysandra's arm. Keir knelt beside her and carefully removed the bandage for Nyx to help with the wound. The black lines from the scratch marks were up to Lysandra's bicep. She winced in pain as Nyx licked her arm. Sweat soaked her forehead. The black veiny lines receded back to the wound.

"Th-thank you...Nyx," whispered Lysandra.

Nyx rubbed her head against Lysandra's thigh as she let out a small whimper. Keir patted Nyx's head.

"Wraiths killed the horses. We will have to continue on foot," said Thallan.

Valda approached a dead horse. Its eyes were open from the terror it suffered. Red veins filled their eyes. From the gashes on its neck, black veins spread out across the horse to its head and hooves.

"Thallan, we may have a problem. Look closely at the horses. I think they're turning into wraiths," said Valda.

Thallan cursed in Elvish.

"They clearly dislike fire. Help me move them into a pile. We need to burn them. Hopefully that will end the process of them becoming those dreadful creatures," said Thallan.

"Nyx, look after Lysandra. I'll help them," said Keir.

Together, the three of them piled the horses and ignited them in flames. They gathered what they could carry, preparing to continue their journey on foot.

"I can try to carry Lysandra as long as I can before either of you will have to try," said Thallan.

Nyx growled and nudged Lysandra's legs.

"I don't think Nyx likes that idea," said Keir.

"I'm the strongest one here, grimog. I can carry her," said Thallan.

Nyx growled at him, baring her teeth. Thallan backed away.

"I think, technically, she is the strongest and wants to carry Lysandra," said Valda.

"Not a bad idea," said Keir.

Thallan rolled his eyes. Keir and Valda helped Lysandra onto Nyx's back. Lysandra sat on Nyx and lay her head against Nyx.

"Thank you," whispered Lysandra.

"Do you need anything, Lys?" asked Keir.

"I'm fine. Just tired," said Lysandra.

"All right, Valda. Lead the way," said Thallan.

They doused the fire, grabbed their torches, and began their journey in the dark once more. The wraiths may have fled, but they were still on high alert.

"Where is Vaxar getting these things, anyway? I've heard old scary stories of them, but everyone said they died out hundreds of years ago," said Keir.

"From what I know, they are beings from Keres's underworld. I'm guessing with Vaxar's necromancy magic, he can somehow bring them to life, in a way," said Valda.

"Necromancy is old forbidden magic. I know very little about it. I only know it deals with the dead. Ancient beliefs say it is magic from Keres," said Thallan.

Lysandra, using what strength she has left, lifted her head up to look at the others.

"Necromancy is in my codex. Only the description remains. Someone scribbled out the rest on it," said Lysandra.

"Does is say anything different from what we know?" asked Valda.

"No. What Thallan said is close to what's written," said Lysandra.

"When we reach Krogodo, we should send word to Krarick. Hopefully, he knows more about necromancy," said Thallan.

"I agree. We can also check my kingdom's archives. They may have something that can help us," said Valda.

They continued their journey in the dark of night. At sunrise till mid-afternoon they rested, getting as much sleep as possible. Lysandra started having trouble eating. If she ate any meat, she would soon throw up her meal. They had only a few fruits and vegetables that lasted her another day with how little she ate.

During their rest, Thallan would wander off, looking for

any edible berries that Lysandra could eat. He found very little. Hornfield was far behind them, and other known towns lay too far from their route.

One night, they spotted a farm in the distance. Thallan left the others beside the river in the dark to visit the farm and see if they would sell him fruit. As he approached the farm, he heard no signs of life. He quietly grabbed his sword from its sheath.

Thallan walked up to the too-quiet house. The door was ajar. He carefully crossed the threshold. The candles had burned out, wax covering the table. Blood splattered the floors and walls. He walked throughout the house, finding more splattered blood, along with ripped clothes.

What happened? Where are the bodies? This is a lot of blood for there to be no bodies, thought Thallan.

Thallan went to the kitchen and grabbed whatever food he could find, wrapping it in a clean cloth he found on the kitchen table. He left the house and walked around the farm, hoping to find anyone who may have survived.

The farm was eerily quiet and empty. He entered the barn to find the cows, pigs, and sheep ripped apart, their insides strewn about the barn floor. Thallan checked the second barn and found the horses butchered in the same gruesome way as the other animals.

I need to get back to the others. We must get far away from this cursed place, thought Thallan.

Thallan jogged back to the others hiding behind some brush and trees far beyond the farm's gates.

"Thallan, what is it?" asked Valda.

"We need to go now. There is nothing alive in the farm. Someone or something killed everything. There is blood all over in the house, and the bodies are gone. Found some fruit for Lysandra, though," said Thallan.

"Let's go then. Keir, help me get Lys on Nyx's back, please," said Valda.

They quickly left the area. Thallan and Valda both constantly checked for anything following them.

"Any idea what could have happened to the farm?" asked Valda.

"No. My only guess is some kind of animal must have killed everything. But I am confused with the barn animals ripped apart while the bodies of farm owners are nowhere to be found," said Thallan.

"Could it have been the wraiths? Since they are alive, in a way, would they need to eat?" asked Keir.

"Thallan, did you see any of those black veins on the animals?" asked Valda.

"I did not think to check. Given how gruesome the farm looked, Keir may be right. It probably was the wraiths," said Thallan.

"We need to pick up the pace and get to the marshes fast. If all you saw were the animal remains, I fear the people turned and we have more wraiths on our trail," said Valda.

The group agreed and quickened their pace. They walked throughout the afternoon and all night. They only slept during the morning to midday, hoping to get to the marshes sooner.

The next day, they took a break by a creek. Thallan again ventured off, looking for any berries or signs of people to buy food from. He walked beyond some bushes when he heard people off in the distance. He crouched down and used the bushes to help hide behind as he quietly walked closer.

Beyond a break in the trees, he spotted a large group of men camped with horses and wagons. Thallan focused his eyes on the distant camp, looking for anything that identified if they would be an enemy or a friend. Then one man stood in the sun, and Thallan noticed the Nathairian crest. Thallan sighed as he dropped his head.

He walked back through the bushes to the others, keeping low to avoid being spotted. Once he was out of sight, he stood and ran the rest of the way. Thallan scared Astra as he ran back to them, causing her to scurry around Keir's shoulder and hiss at him.

"What is it Thallan?" asked Keir, waking up from his brief nap.

"Nathairian forces. They are not far from here, just beyond the thick set of forest over there. We should start moving. I am not sure if they take your orders or Vaxar's," said Thallan.

"We better start moving. I don't want to risk finding out who they work for," said Valda.

"Most likely it's Vaxar," said Keir.

They quickly gathered their things and continued their journey south to the marshes.

Only three days remained before they would reach the marshes. The weather got colder each night. The sun warmed them very little as the wind pierced through their clothes down to their bones. In fear of Lysandra's condition, Thallan and Valda also gave her their blankets to keep her warm. Her fever worsened as the black veins crept up from the wound. Nyx whined, and the group knew it was time for her to help slow the infection. The infection slowly spread quicker each day, causing them to stop more frequently for Nyx to use her magic to fight it back to the wound.

That morning, as they slept, little Astra guarded them all, ready to wake and alert them if anything approached. The riker took her job seriously. Her ears were always twitching, listening for anything as her eyes scanned the surrounding landscape.

Her ears perked, hearing flapping wings followed by hooting. Astra scanned the sky and saw to the south an approaching kamari. Astra made her noises and slammed on top of Thallan, scurrying around him before jumping on Valda, running on top of her, then finally lunging for Keir, effectively waking them up.

"What is it Astra?" asked Thallan.

The kamari hooted and landed beside their camp. It grabbed a crumpled, rolled parchment from its claws with its large beak. It walked towards Valda and dropped the parchment before her.

"It's all right, Astra. This is a friend, remember?" said Keir.

"What does the parchment say?" asked Thallan.

"It's from the healer. She's on her way with some men to help us. She says she knows how to defeat the wraiths. Advises using the elements to keep them away. She gave examples of fire and water. Here, you can read it," said Valda, as she handed it to Thallan.

"Okay. So hopefully they will not follow us in the marshes because of the water but then again it did first attack by a river. My only guess is that these creatures are angry enough to put aside their fear of water and risk everything to get to Lysandra," said Thallan.

"If they do go after us in there, they'll have trouble trying to fight us off. The pathways are narrow, with water all around them. Just need to keep some torches with us to throw at them and worry about the crocodiles," said Valda.

"Oh. Well, that sounds just swell," said Keir sarcastically.

"Don't worry. I know how to spot those scaly creatures. We'll be fine," said Valda.

"I worry the wraiths may try to arrive in full force to stop us from the marshes. It's been days since we saw or heard them. I worry we're walking into a trap," said Thallan.

"Hmm. You're probably right. We'll need to time our entry for daytime. They've only attacked at night. The healer mentioned the elements. I'll take that as confirmation they don't like the sun. After all, they are from Keres's underworld, where it's described as a pit of darkness," said Valda.

The kamari hooted and flew away, startling everyone, even Nyx.

"Wonder what caught its attention?" asked Keir.

"I do not know. But I am tired of animals jolting away like that," said Thallan.

Valda laughed as Nyx grunted.

"I am going to count that as Nyx laughing at you," said Valda as she laughed some more.

Lysandra slightly chuckled.

"I count it as her laughing too," said Lysandra.

"How are you? Do you need anything?" asked Valda.

"Still the usual. I'm all right. Do we have any water?" said Lysandra.

"Yeah. Here's a canteen. Drink as much as you need," said Valda.

"Thank you. The sun feels unusually bright," said Lysandra.

Valda and Keir looked at one another. Worry filled their minds.

"What? Why the worried looks?" asked Lysandra.

Valda let out a sigh.

"Healer sent word back. She said wraiths don't like the

elements...and we have noticed they don't appear during the day. We also think after seeing what they did to our horses that the infection is magic from the wraiths that can turn whatever it infects into a wraith," said Valda.

"We will get you to the healer before that can happen," said Keir as he gave her a reassuring squeeze on her shoulder.

"I know. I'm sorry... I know I'm not much help," said Lysandra.

"Hey, you're wounded badly. It's all right. You're fighting against what that wraith did to you. Keep fighting. We'll get you to the healer and you'll be better," said Valda.

Lysandra gave a faint smile before yawning.

"Let's get you on Nyx before you fall asleep. We need to keep moving," said Valda.

Valda and Keir helped Lysandra onto Nyx. They gathered their supplies. Thallan approached Lysandra.

"Nyx, can I drape this bag of fruit around you for Lysandra to grab when she feels hungry?" asked Thallan.

Nyx nodded. Thallan used some rope and draped the bag to hang beside Lysandra's knee.

"Thank you, Thallan," said Lysandra.

"Eat when you can. Gotta keep your strength up," said Thallan.

The kamari returned, landing beside Thallan looking at the bag as its head tilted side to side.

"Oh, does anyone have a little piece of meat to spare to thank our kamari friend here?" asked Valda.

"I have some for it," said Keir.

"Thank you, Keir. Here you go, friend. Thank you for your help," said Valda.

The kamari gave her excited hoots before eating the piece of meat.

They gathered their supplies and began their journey

again, traveling as fast as they could. The wind picked up in the afternoon, making the air colder than before. At night, they continued, torches in hand. There was not a sound or sight of the wraiths again.

The kamari occasionally flew above them, circling around before flying off to the south. Hours later, the owl-like creature would return. It circled about and then flew off to the north. Every time it arrived back, the kamari would hoot down to them. Nyx would grunt in response.

The others wondered what the animals were saying to each other. Valda looked at Lysandra to see if she was awake. Lysandra was looking up at the kamari flying above them. Valda slowed her pace to walk beside Nyx and Lysandra.

"I'm curious. Are they any spells that help with speaking or understanding animals?" said Valda.

"Not that I know of. There is no mention of it in the codex. I hope there is magic out there that can," said Lysandra.

"Old Elvish texts said that the ancient druids had magic that gave them the ability to speak with animals," said Thallan.

"Do druids still exist?" asked Keir.

"No. They died hundreds of years ago. A war broke out between them and the sorcerers," said Thallan.

"Hopefully some of their knowledge is still out there," said Valda.

Lysandra yawned.

"Maybe one day, when all this prophecy stuff is done, we can search for ancient druid knowledge," said Lysandra.

"That sounds like an adventure I would like to take part in...if you'll have me," said Valda.

"Of course! I would love everyone here to join. It would be a much calmer adventure than this," said Lysandra.

"Then it shall be our next!" said Valda.

"I look forward to it," said Lysandra.

"Good. In the meantime, sleep. You're going to make me yawn if you keep it up," said Valda, chuckling.

Lysandra chuckled and nodded. She laid her head down on the back of Nyx's neck and quickly drifted off to sleep.

Several hours into the night, wraith screams erupted behind them.

"Shit. They caught up to us," said Valda.

"That sounds like way more than the three we last saw," said Keir.

"I'll get the campfire going. You two get Lysandra off Nyx and get the torches ready," said Thallan.

The group lay extra torches beside the fire, ready to grab. Lysandra sat beside the fire with a torch in hand. Nyx, glowing brightly, poised herself to lunge at the first appearing wraith. Valda grabbed a bottle from her bag, opened it and dipped the tips to all her arrows in them before placing them back into her quiver. She placed the bottle back in her bag.

"I'll stay here beside Lys. Nyx seems to handle these things on her own. I dowsed my arrowheads in oil. I'll light 'em from the firepit and set the wraiths on fire that way to try and take 'em out at a distance," said Valda.

"Good. Is everyone ready? They are getting closer," said Thallan.

Everyone nodded in unison.

"Here they come," said Valda.

Valda lit her first arrowhead on fire and notched it. Swords rang out from their sheaths.

Nyx lunged at the first wraith that appeared from the shadows. Two more charged at Thallan as another attacked Keir. Valda shot down two wraiths with her fire-tipped arrows.

As Valda was lighting another arrow, a wraith burst out from the shadows towards her. Lysandra, using what little strength she had, jumped up and pushed Valda out of the way. The wraith slashed her right arm as it screamed. Without a moment's thought, Lysandra conjured fire with her other hand and engulfed the wraith in flames. She then threw fireballs at the last remaining wraiths. With them fleeing in flames, she collapsed to the ground.

"Shit. Lysandra! Nyx, get over here! Thallan and Keir, be on the lookout in case more arrive. She got slashed by one. Why did you push me?" said Valda.

"I couldn't let you get hurt. I'm sorry... I'm so sorry," said Lysandra.

"Your life is worth far more than mine. Keir, toss me the bandages from your pack," said Valda.

Valda unwrapped the other arm for Nyx to check on the infection and lick away as much as possible. Once Nyx was done with both, Valda gently bandaged Lysandra's arms.

"Keir, help me get her on Nyx's back. Thallan, start gathering our stuff. We are running to the marshes now. We'll stop when we need a breather and water, but we need to get there fast," said Valda.

23

THE SHADOW MARSHES

Just before midmorning, they arrived at the entrance to the shadow marshes. They took a moment to rest before entering. Valda took watch, letting the others get a couple of hours of sleep. She woke everyone up at midday to begin the journey.

"As we go through, I'll be finding shortcuts we can safely take to quicken our journey. Be on the lookout for the crocodiles. Those things float like logs but will have a green scaly texture compared to the actual trees. They are fast, so keep your swords ready," said Valda.

"Understood. Lead the way, General," said Thallan.

"Oh! Also, watch out for the snakes. They can either be in the trees above or in the water," said Valda.

"Snakes? How big?" asked Keir.

"Do not tell me you are afraid of snakes?" said Thallan mockingly.

"Deathly afraid," said Keir, unashamed.

"Don't worry. As long as you don't purposely antagonize them, they'll ignore you. Hear a hiss, just back off slowly. You can light a torch. They don't like fire either," said Valda.

Thallan handed Keir a torch and nudged him to walk in front of him but behind Nyx as they all followed Valda. Keir awkwardly held the torch between his arm and body while using rocks to strike a light as he continued walking. After several tries, he got the torch lit and held on to it tightly.

Large trees heavily shaded the marshes. Only a few streaks of the sun's light could pierce through. The trees trapped in the moisture, making the air feel sticky, hot and heavy in their lungs. The water appeared so still it looked solid. Little bugs flew around. A few birds sang above them in the treetops. Stone bricks formed the marsh pathway, with rotten, soggy wooden planks branching off in other directions.

"How long do we travel in this?" asked Thallan.

"It can take about a day. I hope to cut that time in half," said Valda.

Thallan sighed in response as he kept watch on the surrounding water.

"Where do the wooden pathways lead to?" asked Keir.

"There are some people who live in wooden huts throughout. An odd place to live, if you ask me, but they like it here. Years ago, they agreed to the stone pathway we are on now but wanted to keep some of the wooden pathways," said Valda.

"Are they part of the Krogodo Kingdom?" asked Thallan.

"Technically, no. But the queen and king still give them the same protection and help as if they are. These people keep to themselves, mostly. Here and there, they wander into the kingdom to trade or seek help from the healer," said Valda.

"Interesting group of people," said Thallan.

"Yeah, I guess they are. They are quite kind...unless you trespass on their land around their huts. They are quite territorial," said Valda.

"Then I suggest we stay on their good side," said Thallan.

"Don't worry. I know most of them who live here. They are no threat," said Valda.

A small pointy stick flew past Thallan's head and stuck into the tree beside him as another passed the front of Valda's face.

"You were saying, General?" asked Thallan.

"Shut it, Thallan. Gyda, put your blow dart down. You're scaring my Elf friend here," said Valda.

"Ha! Thas the point, lass! Ha! Ha! Been ages since we here seen an Elf. Not many people can say they spooked an Elf, given their hearin' and all. How are ya, miss General Valda?" said Gyda.

"I'm good, Gyda. How are you and everyone here fairing?" asked Valda.

"Oh, we good. Weather gettin' a bit chilly. But we are all fine. Now what is that there walkin' behind ya?" said Gyda.

Gyda stood across the way on a soggy wooden pathway. She was a short muscular woman with messy brown hair as if she never owned a brush and sun-kissed skin despite the lack of sunlight in the marshes. Her face was filled with freckles with a few wrinkles that poked through. She wore a baggy tunic with pants held up with rope.

"That's a grimog from the Nathair Kingdom. Don't worry. She's friendly. That's my friend, Lys, on top of her. She's badly wounded. We are on our way to the healer, Willow," said Valda.

"Need anything to help the poor lass?" asked Gyda.

"Any spare fruit by any chance?" asked Valda.

"Oh, yeah! I got a small bundle of grapes you can have. Should be gettin' more from the vine any day now. Follow me, dearies. House just over yonder there. Not too far out of your way. I'll be quick to grabbin' them for ya," said Gyda.

"Thank you so much, Gyda," said Valda.

"Oh of course, General. You always helpin' and protectin' us," said Gyda.

They followed Gyda as carefully as they could. The wooden planks rocked side to side with each step, threatening to topple them into the water. A few minutes after walking along the wooden pathway, a small hut came into view. It sat above the water against the surrounding trees. Vines crept around the sides that fell from the trees.

"Wait here. I'll get the grapes for ya," said Gyda.

Gyda entered her hut through the creaking front door. Thallan looked around and saw another hut a way down. A man stood in front of it, watching them from afar. Thallan placed a hand on his hilt, uneasiness setting in from the unusual place.

"Here ya go, darlin'. Is there anythin' else you need?" asked Gyda.

"Thank you. Do you know of any shortcuts towards Krogodo?" asked Valda.

"Oh yeah! Come in here, I'll show ya on the map I got," said Gyda.

"Stay out here, guys. I'll be back in a moment," said Valda.

Valda followed Gyda into the hut. There was a small table beside the narrow bed. Gyda grabbed the box from under the table and slid it out. She fished through the box for the map.

"I have it marked here. You can take this. Haven't used it in ages. Know the way by heart now. One of the others showed me years ago. Wrote it down when I was still new to the area. Just follow those there markings and you'll be out of the marshes...oh, I say sometime after nightfall, but before midnight, I thinks," said Gyda.

"Thank you so much, Gyda. You are a lifesaver. Visit the castle sometime soon. Tell them I sent you. I'll give you loads of coin for your help," said Valda.

"Oh! Don't worry 'bout it, dear. I'm just glad to help ya. If ya set on givin' me somethin' then...hmm...I know! A new pair of boots! These are gettin' a bit worn," said Gyda.

"All right. I'll get you a nice pair of boots," said Valda.

"It's a deal then, lass," said Gyda.

The two of them stepped back outside. Thallan was staring at the man across the water, who was watching them. Keir knelt beside Nyx, checking on Lysandra.

"Oh, ignore ol' hermit over there, Elf. Old man is just curious. Guy is like a father to me. He just making sure I'm safe. He's the one here that dislikes strangers the most, so he's always watchin'. Just gotta ignore him," said Gyda.

"Thank you for your help," said Thallan, as he bowed to Gyda.

"Oh, you a prim and proper Elf. My apologies for spookin' ya. And you are more than welcome. You best be going now and get that poor woman to the healer. May Meridia protect you on your journey," said Gyda.

"Thank you, Gyda," said Valda.

As they walked down the wooden path, Gyda waved goodbye as did the old man across the water. The group waved back.

"Did she show you a quicker way out of here?" asked Thallan.

"Yup! She gave me her map with our path marked out. We will stay on the stone path for a little while, then we will take a wooden path off to the right that cuts straight through some of the mucky waters and thick vegetation, then the last bit will be back on the stone path. She said we should be out of here before midnight," said Valda.

"That's a nice shortcut. Your friend back there was nice. Unique accent," said Keir.

"Yeah. All the people here in the marshes have those thick accents. Her accent is not the worst I've heard. She's originally from one of the small villages along the coast before moving here," said Valda.

"Why would she move from the coastline to...well, this place?" asked Keir.

"Not sure. Most people here want more of a solitary lifestyle. I think she left because of the violence from the coastal towns. There are a lot of drunk sailors there," said Valda.

"Hmm. I don't blame her, then. I'm grateful for her help," said Keir.

"As am I. Of course, after learning she was not intending to poison me with those darts of hers," said Thallan.

Valda laughed.

"Yeah, I saw her. I thought she was going to shoot a snake or crocodile that we didn't see. I didn't know she was trying to scare you... But that was funny. Did you really not see or hear her?" said Valda.

"No. And I would appreciate it if you do not gallivant it throughout the whole marsh, please," said Thallan.

Valda and Keir both laughed.

"How is Lysandra?" asked Thallan.

"She's weak and tired. Wounds don't need cleaning from Nyx just yet, but soon," said Keir.

"Let's try to get to the wooden path as quickly as possible before then," said Valda.

Valda led the group through the marshes. As the sun sank closer to the horizon, the group lit their torches. They walked as quickly as they could through the marshes. The group reached the wooden path for them to take as the sun touched the horizon.

Thallan kept watch as Valda and Keir helped Nyx tend to Lysandra's wounds. Lysandra winced in pain as Nyx licked the black veins away. Keir held her, trying to provide comfort. After Nyx was done, Valda gently rebandaged Lysandra's arms.

"Do you want anything to eat or drink?" asked Valda.

"N-no thank you. I'm just c-cold," said Lysandra.

"Let's get you back on Nyx and I'll wrap a blanket around you," said Keir.

They started walking along the wooden pathway once Lysandra was on Nyx. As the sun disappeared, the birds ended their songs, and the frogs began theirs. The air cooled but kept the sticky feeling.

Suddenly, the frogs went quiet. The bugs disappeared. Then the crocodiles jolted in the water around them as they swam away.

"Valda, what could scare them?" asked Thallan.

"I don't know," said Valda.

The group halted, frantically looking around.

"Nyx, are you seeing or smelling anything?" asked Valda.

Nyx inspected their surroundings. Her fur did not glow, and she showed no other signs of seeing anything concerning.

Multiple screams erupted in the distance behind them.

"Shit! I was hoping they wouldn't go in here. Let's run!" said Valda.

The group ran, following Valda as she led the way. They made it to the stone pathway and began following it south.

"Almost out of here!" yelled Valda.

More screams echoed off the water, closer than before. The group quickened their pace. Lysandra closed her eyes tightly in pain from Nyx's running. It was getting unbearable for her. She grabbed the knife from her boot and sliced the rope that held her onto Nyx. Lysandra fell onto the stone pathway.

"Valda! Wait! Lysandra fell off Nyx," yelled Keir.

"Pick her up and keep running. The wraiths are getting closer," said Thallan.

"Here, Thallan. Start shooting them. The arrows are still soaked in oil. Just use your torch and light them," said Valda, as she tossed her quiver and bow at him.

"Keir, get over here. Hold my torch so I can light these effectively. Valda, get her back on Nyx. This is not a good place to be for a fight against these things," said Thallan.

A flaming arrow flew past Thallan's head and struck a wraith in the face on the pathway across the water. The wraith screamed as its arms flung about its head. Several more arrows flew through the air, hitting other wraiths behind it.

"Valda, get out of there! Now!" yelled a cloaked man with several others around him.

"I'm trying! The sorceress is wounded! She fell off the grimog that was carrying her!" yelled Valda.

"Do not move her! I shall come to you. Ludvik, cover them as best you can," said a woman from behind Ludvik.

"Yes, ma'am," said Ludvik.

The woman carrying a satchel quickly made her way to Valda.

"Elf, what are you gawking at me for? Help the men shoot those wraiths down! Fire does the trick, but try to knock them into the water. It'll fill their bodies and expel the darkness from them, ending the wraiths' lives," said the woman.

"I'm so glad to see you, Willow. She's hurt on both arms now from the wraith's claws," said Valda.

"Thank Meridia we found you in time. Alodie, help me unwrap these bandages. Valda, dear, you can help the men.

Same for you, grimog. Get those cursed things in the water," said Willow.

Nyx whined at Willow, not wanting to leave Lysandra's side.

"It's all right. If I need help, I will call for you. Now go help shove those things in the water for me, will you?" said Willow.

Nyx nodded and jumped into the water. She swam towards the wraiths. Then she lunged out of the water and slammed her teeth deep into a wraith. She jumped back into the water, landing on top of the wraith, forcing it to stay below the surface. Black shadows exploded out of the water and vaporized into the air. Nyx felt the body grow limp.

She moved her attention to the next wraith and continued to forcefully pin each wraith underwater until they stopped moving.

As the others fought the wraiths, Willow and Alodie worked hard to eradicate the infections in Lysandra's arms. Alodie poured water across the wounds to clean them. Willow grabbed herbs from the satchel and carefully rubbed them across the gashes on her arms. Black oozed out of the gashes and vaporized into the air. Clean blood poured out of the wounds, pushing the last of the infection out.

Alodie rubbed the herb mixture on the clean bandages she had laid on the ground. Willow cleaned up the blood that dripped from the wounds. Alodie handed a bandage with herbs to Willow for her to wrap one arm as she wrapped the other.

"There you go, sweetie. The infection is gone. Just rest now," said Willow.

"Valda, she's ready to be moved," said Alodie.

"All right, good. The grimog is drowning the last wraith," said Valda.

"How is she? Will she be all right? Were you able to get rid of the infection?" asked Keir.

"Yes, yes. She will be all right. Just needs rest now. Infection is gone," said Willow.

"Thank you so much for your help. Both of you," said Keir.

"Of course, dear. Anyone else wounded?" said Willow.

"No. She was the only one," said Thallan.

Nyx got out of the water and shook herself dry beside Thallan.

"Oh, really, Nyx? I know you did that on purpose," said Thallan, as he sighed.

Everyone laughed as Nyx approached Lysandra. Valda gave Nyx some head pats as she walked by.

"Ludvik, come over here and help carry her to the wagon, please?" said Willow.

Nyx growled in protest.

"Oh, hold on. Grimog wants to carry her. We'll meet you at the wagons. All right, let's gently put the sorceress on the Grimog," said Willow.

With Lysandra back on Nyx, they followed Willow to the wagons. They made it out of the marshes and to the top of the hill and to the wagons, where Ludvik and his men waited for them.

"Wait, they are rangers?" said Thallan as he pulled his sword from its sheath.

"Whoa! Thallan, it's all right. Put the sword away. Rangers are from Krogodo," said Valda.

"They are rangers! I do not care where they are from. Rangers are wild men. They cannot be trusted," said Thallan.

"Thallan, all rangers are from Krogodo. They are essentially like part of our army in a way. I was a ranger before being promoted. Ludvik is my oldest brother," said Valda.

"She's telling you the truth, Elf. We are no threat to you. We are friends," said Ludvik in a heavy, deep voice.

Thallan slowly put his sword back into its sheath.

"My apologies, then," said Thallan.

"Don't worry about it. There's a good reason why we haven't fought against those accusations that people have spread about us. Provides an excellent cover," said Ludvik.

They all carefully helped lay Lysandra down in the back of the wagon on some hay. Keir sat next to her, holding her hand. Valda sat across from him as Thallan sat next to her. Ludvik and his men sat in the other wagon.

A loud screech jolted them. They all looked up to find a large gryphon flying above them, with a figure on its back. Nyx growled at the gryphon as her fur flashed its glowing color.

"Oh, that bloody man. He was supposed to stay at the castle. Go on, men! Get the wagons moving. We should not be sitting here in the dark. Best get far away from the marshes. May be more wraiths," said Willow.

The men cracked the reins and had the horses trot south to Krogodo. Nyx followed beside Lysandra's wagon.

"Is that a gryphon? I didn't know they existed," said Keir.

"They live with the dwarves in the hills by their mountain home. That is the only one you can find outside of there. It is a companion to Sorcerer Krarick," said Thallan.

"They are magnificent!" said Keir.

Thallan ignored him. He rested his head on the wooden railing behind him, shutting his eyes, and soon drifted off to sleep.

Valda soon fell asleep, too, exhaustion overtaking her will to stay awake. Keir remained awake as long as he could until he eventually drifted off to sleep, still holding Lysandra's hand.

They woke as they heard the commotion of the town before the grand castle of Krogodo. Entering through the front gates, the town bustled with people trading and buying from merchants perched at the sides of the main road.

The buildings were log-and-plank structures with a hay and moss mixture for the long, pitched roofs. The land looked very lush for the start of winter, with only a few brown patches throughout. Wooden signs hung from buildings along the main road of business, from taverns and lodgings to blacksmiths and bakeries.

A bard greeted them with a song as they passed by. He stopped playing his lute and flipped his hat towards the rangers as he bowed. Two of the rangers tossed coins to the bard.

"Thank you, dear sirs! May Meridia smile upon you!" yelled the bard.

He returned to his lute, singing and dancing along the main road, entertaining the people.

Built on top of a short hill was a large, single-story castle overlooking the town, a mix of stone and fine wood. It was small compared to the Nathairian Winterstone Castle, but it gave a more welcoming atmosphere to the kingdom. Large, round wooden pillars held up the roof that hung over the front steps. Intricate woven carvings were on the pillars and the wood above the doors painted in gold.

On either side of the pointed, overhanging portion above the front steps, grand Gjallarhorns sat atop the roof. The Gjallarhorns were of a lighter shade of wood with gold weaving designs painted all over it. Large gold-painted images of Krogodo warhorses adorned the front doors.

The front doors opened into a large room with tables and firepits with cauldrons scattered throughout. Two large thrones sat in the middle of a raised floor on the far side of the room, with four smaller thrones around them. Multiple hallways branched out to the side and behind the throne, leading to many bedrooms and the large kitchen. The Krogodo flags draped down from the ceiling.

Nyx carried Lysandra as they followed Willow down a hallway to the right of the large room. She led them to a room with an enormous bed in the middle, framed by two nightstands on either side of it. A fireplace took up the far side of the room, with two small windows illuminating a small table with two chairs.

"This will be her room. Help me get her onto the bed, please," said Willow.

An older woman entered the room, smiling at everyone as she walked to Willow.

"Ah! You've made it! Thank Meridia and the gods! Willow, how is the sorceress?" asked the older woman dressed in long tan dress and brown robes with greyish white hair partially braided down her back.

"She will be fine. Infections from the wraiths are gone. Gashes on her arms will need to heal, with lots of rest. Your herb mixtures worked perfectly, Gladyss," said Willow.

"Oh good. Then let's all give her some peace and quiet to heal and rest," said Gladyss.

Nyx growled at the mention of leaving Lysandra.

"Oh! Who are you, dear?" asked Gladyss.

"This is Nyx. She is Lysandra's friend. Would it be all right if she and I say here beside her?" asked Keir.

"No! I am not leaving you alone with her," said Thallan.

"Oh shush, Elf. You, my dear, must be King Keir Nathair?" asked Gladyss.

"Yes, my lady. I care deeply for Lysandra and, like Nyx, don't want her to be alone," said Keir.

"Hmm, well, there is a joining room there that you can have just through that single door there to the left of the fireplace. You two can stay here so long as you don't disturb her. She has been in a great deal of pain from those wraith infections and will need lots of rest," said Gladyss.

"Thank you, my lady. We will stay in that room then with the door open to hear if she needs anything. If she wakes, where can I find any of you three?" asked Keir.

"We will be on the other side of the room, here to the left. Queen and king agreed to let us stay close by in case she needs us," said Alodie.

"We ladies usually stay in our house in the town, closer to the people. I will travel to and from here as needed. Gladyss and Alodie will stay here until the sorceress fully heals," said Willow.

"Thank you so much for your help," said Keir.

"Of course, dear. Oh, Thallan is your name, right? Sorcerer Krarick will want to speak with you. He should be in the main room, back down the hall by now. That man took off from here flying on that gryphon of his. He should be back now. Talked about you before leaving," said Gladyss.

"Thank you, ma'am," said Thallan.

The healers, Thallan, Valda, and Ludvik left Lysandra's room, shutting the door behind them. Willow led Thallan to the main room when Krarick appeared down the hallway.

"Where is she?" asked Krarick.

"In her room. Don't you dare go in there, sorcerer! She needs her rest after the injuries she suffered from those wraiths. Leave her be," said Gladyss.

"She is my daughter. I will see her if I please," said Krarick.

"No, you will not. Ludvik, have men stationed by her

door and Keir's. Only the healers, yourself, and Valda may enter," said Gladyss.

"Excuse me? You cannot prevent me from seeing her. I must check the wounds myself," said Krarick.

"Doubt our skills as healers still? Ask your Elf friend here who you spoke so highly of. The infections are gone. She needs rest. All that remains are the gashes from the wraith's claws, which will take time to fully heal," said Willow.

"Krarick, she speaks the truth. Infections are indeed gone. Lysandra is sleeping right now. Her grimog companion and that man, Keir Nathair, are in there with her," said Thallan.

"You left the Dark King in there with her alone? We cannot trust him! He should be in the dungeons or dead!" yelled Krarick.

"Enough! No one will enter her room. Ludvik, get your men to guard her room, now. Krarick and Thallan, wait in the main hall. You can both discuss your grievances with the queen and king. Keir is not the Dark King. I should think after our eventful trip, Thallan, you would have learned that by now. Keir is a good man with a pure heart. He is under the protection of the crown! I will deal with either of you should you harm him in any way. Understand? Now off to the main hall for both of you," said Valda.

Krarick and Thallan left for the main hall, anger filling their faces. Valda let out a sigh of relief as they walked away.

"General Valda, your parents are waiting for you and I in their study for an important meeting. No need to rush. They knew it would take a moment to get the sorceress in her room," said Gladyss.

"All right. Shall we make our way there then? I can clean up after," said Valda.

"Yes, my lady. The girls can help the sorceress if she wakes," said Gladyss.

Valda and Gladyss walked side by side down the long hallway and down two more hallways to the left before arriving at the royal study.

24

WELCOME TO KROGODO

Valda opened the door to the study and let Gladyss enter first before following and shutting the door behind her.

The room was large with two tables on one side, bookcases behind each. A round table with seven chairs sat in the middle of the room. The other side of the room had a fireplace with a table and two chairs in front of it. Torches lined the room on the pillars and walls, as there was only one window directly across from the door.

Gladyss handed Valda a rune rock and pointed at the bottom of the door. Valda propped the rock against the door and the rune glowed a vibrant maroon color.

"Room is silenced. No one outside this room can overhear," said Gladyss.

"Thank you, Gladyss. It's good to see you again Valda. I'm so happy you are home safe," said Queen Simona.

"Yes, your mother and I were worried when Gladyss got your message. I am glad that both you and the sorceress arrived safely. How is the sorceress doing?" asked King Priamos.

"She is doing fine. Just getting her rest. It will take some time for her arms to heal. She will heal quickly if her father stays out of our way and we can continue applying the herbs," said Gladyss.

"You'll have to thank Lysandra when she wakes. She's the reason I didn't get sliced by one of those wraiths. She pushed me out of the way as I was lighting my arrowhead," said Valda.

"A very noble action. We are grateful for her bravery at protecting our daughter. I'm glad your healers got to her in time, Gladyss. If the sorcerer continues to get in your way, alert us. We will have him escorted out of the castle. He may be a guest, but he must remember his manners," said Simona.

"Yes, Simona," said Gladyss as she bowed her head.

"Now onto other important matters. Valda, you remember Dritan?" asked Priamos.

"Oh yes! It has been a long time since I've seen you. How has it been traveling with the sorcerer?" said Valda.

"It is good to see you too, my lady. Actually, that is why I asked to meet with you all immediately once I heard of the sorceress's arrival. I have discovered something that involves her safety," said Dritan.

"What did you find?" asked Valda.

"The last few years, Krarick hasn't needed my help. I've noticed over the years since seeing him after his daughter was born how stressed and focused he has been trying to get Vaxar away from the Nathairian forces. We all believed he was trying to keep the sorcerer distracted and away from possibly finding his daughter," said Priamos.

"Yes, we remember his reasoning for wanting our aid to distract or draw out the Dark Sorcerer," said Priamos.

"Well, I made the trek to the old sorcerer's temple, Strommeth. Most of it is in ruins from that Nightshadow War among the sorcerers many years ago. But upon my investigation, looking for anything that may help Krarick in this fight, I found their archives, or library. I'm not sure what they called it. Anyway, the temple caved in around it. After crawling through the rubble, I was in. I found these," said Dritan.

He pulled out a book and several scrolls of paper and a chest from his sack onto the table between them all.

"This book is one of their codices. In particular, this one is the laws and rules of the sorcerers set by their first leaders ages ago. It's quite extensive. I read through it and found this page. Right here it states that no woman born with magic may live. Then in these scrolls, I found information on the device in this chest here that the elder sorcerers would use to find soon to be born sorcerers to take and train them to use their magic. It also told them of the baby girls. They would arrive exactly when the baby is born and, using this scroll as a guide, would lie to the parents, depending on the situation, to explain why the child must be killed, aside from their simple rule of no women being allowed to practice magic," said Dritan.

"They have been murdering babies all these years?" asked Simona.

"Is there any explanation why women are not allowed to be sorceress?" asked Priamos.

"The codex states that women are dangerous with magic. Their unchecked emotions make the magic uncontrollable. It states magic in women is dangerous as it refuses to be tampered with and will cause harm to others," said Dritan.

"That is a lie. Those shite men just wanted magic to themselves. Lysandra has full control over her magic and is in no way a dangerous threat to anyone but the Dark Sorcerer," said Valda.

"I agree. If a sorceress is not to exist, then why did

Krarick not end his daughter's life while she was a baby?" asked Simona.

"In the codex, there is a strict law that a sorcerer must aid and stand by any child of prophecy should there ever be one. Sorcerers must not hinder prophecies in any way. I suspect the prophecy given before her birth prevented Krarick from killing her. So, instead, he abandoned her in the dangerous kingdom, so close to the enemy. We all questioned his reasoning. He left her behind, hoping fate would work in his favor and end her life. He hasn't been trying to distract Vaxar, he's been trying to get Vaxar alone to kill him without soldiers complicating the fight," said Dritan.

"Oh, my Meridia. It makes so much sense. Years ago, when I first met Krarick, he asked where the male healer was and has never been kind to me or the others since," said Gladyss.

"Oh, no. Would Krarick attempt to kill Lysandra once she fulfills the prophecy?" asked Valda.

"After learning this, I'm afraid there may be a high chance. Krarick is faithfully loyal to the codices. He was quite angry for a while because he forgot one of them years ago in his home before he left," said Dritan.

"We must protect Lysandra," said Valda.

"I agree. Valda, you shall stay alongside her and keep her safe from Krarick as she continues her destiny to save our lands. Safely bring her here when her task is complete. We offer better protection here when we can outnumber her father," said Priamos.

"I would add Thallan as another person to protect her from," said Dritan.

"Thallan?" asked Valda.

"Yes. He is incredibly loyal to him. Thallan joined the Nathairian forces as instructed by Krarick to keep a better watch on Vaxar and the Dark King. Thallan's father was an old friend of Krarick's who died in the Nightshadow War. The Elf looks to Krarick as a father. He will do anything Krarick tells him to," said Dritan.

Valda sighed.

"I'll protect her from both of them, then. Keir will help alongside Nyx," said Valda.

"Is Keir not the Dark King?" asked Simona.

"No. He never was. His father is the Dark King. Keir has a pure, good heart. Not an ounce of evil in him. Vaxar and his father tricked him when he was young to drink a potion that allowed him to be under their control. Lysandra discovered the potion and made one to undo its effects. She freed him from their control. Dark King Erebus is sitting in the Nathairian dungeon. Besides, Keir is madly in love with Lysandra. He will not let anyone hurt her," said Valda.

"As the prophecy stated of the prince bowing to her," said Gladyss.

"He should know of what Dritan has informed us. Tell him when you can. Gladyss, give her a spare silencing rune rock when you can, please. Valda, also tell your siblings of this news and have Ludvik and his men be on constant watch around Krarick and Thallan," said Simona.

"Yes, Your Majesty. I shall get that rune rock ready for Valda," said Gladyss.

"I'll let my siblings know," said Valda.

"Good. Thank you, Dritan, for this valuable information. Meeting is done. You may remove the rune from the door," said Priamos.

Valda rushed throughout the castle until she found her three brothers and younger sister. She checked their rooms, the kitchen, the main hall, and the stables. Valda grew tired and went to her room. She opened the door to find them all in the last place she thought of looking. In her room. She promptly shut the door behind her and placed her hand over her mouth, signaling them to be quiet.

She peeked out into the hallway, checking for anyone nearby. The hallway was empty. She shut the door, locked it and placed a rune rock against the bottom of the door and locked it before turning to face her siblings.

Her room was half the size of the study. A large bed sat in the middle, across from a small table with two chairs. A window opposite of her door let light in on a dresser and a wardrobe. To the left of the window, in the corner, was the fireplace. She had only a single nightstand on the left side of her bed. Drapes hung down the front two posts of her bed.

Ludvik and Quinn sat at the table as Percival and Kyler were on her bed. Valda's abrupt arrival startled them.

"I have been looking everywhere for you all! What are you doing in here? Wait, hold that thought. I'm happy to see you all, but first I need to catch you all up on the meeting I just had with mom and dad," said Valda.

"We wanted to give you time to talk to Mother and Father. We overheard they wanted to speak with you. Also, we were all excited and wanted to hear about your adventures. But tell us about the meeting," said Ludvik.

Valda quickly shared the news from Dritan and the instructions from their parents. She then caught them up on her adventures of what had happened since she had left for Nathair Kingdom many months ago.

"I will order some men to keep watch on those two. I'll continue to have some men guard her room as well," said Ludvik.

"I can see what knowledge our temple has on the first sorceress. I'm curious why she lived, learning that awful rule the sorcerers follow. We really don't know much about her.

318

It may be helpful for us to protect Lysandra and as well as for her to learn about the last sorceress," said Percival.

"I'll help Ludvik and the rangers," said Quinn.

"Not sure what I can help with. Tell me where you need me," said Kyler.

"Thank you. Sounds like a good plan. Kyler, you can stick by me in the meantime," said Valda.

They all left her room. Valda and Kyler walked down the hallway towards Lysandra's room to check on her. As they got closer, Valda noticed the guards were no longer outside, and the door was opened. She sprinted to the door to see Nyx glowing brightly and growling at Thallan and Krarick. The two ranger guards stood behind them, no weapons drawn. Keir stood behind Nyx, fear in his eyes.

"Somebody better explain fast what is going on in here?" said Valda.

"An argument, General. We were trying to help calm and move them outside to avoid waking the sorceress," said a guard.

"He should be in a dungeon, General Valda. Why is the Dark King allowed in here?" asked Krarick.

"Thallan, have you not told him what has happened?" asked Valda.

"I did. We both agree the Dark King needs to be locked up," said Thallan.

"Oh, for the love of Dusan! Both of you out of this room or I tell Nyx to have some fun tearing you apart and end up waking up Lysandra. Keir is under Krogodoan protection and will not be harmed. Go to my parents, Krarick! They will explain things to you," said Valda.

"Your parents?" said both Krarick and Thallan in unison.

"Yes, my parents. Queen Simona and King Priamos.

Now get out of this room before I tell Nyx to bite your arses," said Valda.

Nyx growled and chomped her teeth at them as she took a step forward. Krarick and Thallan backed up and left the room. They stopped in the hallway.

"You are a princess?" asked Thallan.

"And General. If you go into her room again without permission from myself, the healers, or any member of the royal family, I will personally throw you in our dungeons. Understood?" said Valda.

They both nodded and left, heading towards the main hall. Valda returned to the room and waved at the guards to leave.

"Are you both all right?" asked Valda.

"Yeah. Thank you. I am sorry for causing so much trouble," said Keir.

"Don't worry about it," said Valda.

Gladyss knocked on the cracked door.

"Miss Valda, this is for you. Also, my thanks in kicking those two morons out of this room," said Gladyss as she bowed before leaving, shutting the door behind her.

"What is that? Also, did I hear you are the princess?" asked Keir.

"Yeah, I'm the princess, and the heir. I have two older brothers who have both abdicated from the throne. My eldest brother enjoys being a ranger. My second oldest brother likes the temple. My younger brother is a ranger. And my younger sister here is learning combat. This is Kyler, by the way. So sorry, honestly bad at those manners," said Valda.

"Hello, Kyler. It is an honor to meet you," said Keir as he bowed.

Nyx approached Kyler and sniffed at her before rubbing her head against her thigh.

"It is an honor to meet you as well. And who is this? You are the softest thing!" said Kyler.

"That's Nyx. She's a grimog from mountains near the Nathair Kingdom. She's Lysandra's companion. Looks like she likes you, Kyler. Also, to answer your other question, Keir, this is a rune rock with the silencing rune carved into it. Place it here and no one outside this room can hear us talk," said Valda.

"Why do you need the rune rock in here?" asked Keir.

"Because we need to inform you of some very important information we just learned," said Valda.

Valda sat down with Kyler and Keir beside the bed as Lysandra remained in a deep sleep. Valda told Keir everything she learned from Dritan. Kyler sat next to Nyx and continued petting her. Nyx eventually laid down next to her and fell asleep.

"Thank you for telling me. There is no way we can just leave for Krubet without them, is there?" asked Keir.

"I don't think so," said Valda.

"We will do whatever it takes to keep her safe from them, then. I can't lose her," said Keir as he looked at Lysandra.

"You won't. We won't lose her," said Valda.

"You both want some food? I'm getting hungry. I can grab us something," said Kyler.

"Actually, yes, please. It has been a long time since either of us ate," said Valda.

"Be right back!" said Kyler, and she jumped up to her feet, patted Nyx one more time, and took off to the kitchen.

"She's sweet," said Keir.

"She is. Kyler is the gentlest of all of us. I'm excited to see where her path leads her later in life," said Valda.

"I can see her doing great things, helping others with her immense kindness," said Keir.

"I agree," said Valda.

The next day, Gladyss let Krarick and Thallan into Lysandra's room, once they had calmer heads. Gladyss had them sit in chairs near the door. Keir, Valda, Kyler, and Nyx sat on the other side of the room beside the windows. Keir sat closest to Lysandra's bed as he read a book that Percival loaned to him after their talk at the previous night's dinner. The book was about the ancient religions still practiced in Krogodo.

Thallan had grabbed the codex out of Lysandra's pack and gave it to Krarick. He immediately began rereading his old book. Gladyss sat in front of the bed in between them all, knitting. The room was still and quiet. The only sounds were Gladyss's knitting needles clacking together and Kyler happily petting Nyx.

Nyx jolted her head up from the floor, sniffing the air. She then stood and walked over beside Keir and looked at Lysandra. Gladyss stopped her knitting and watched Nyx.

Lysandra moaned slightly as she turned her head. Her eyes slowly opened to see Nyx, Keir, and Valda before her. She smiled at them. Keir knelt beside her, caressing her hair from her face.

"How are you feeling?" asked Keir.

"Better. Arms still hurt, but I feel better," said Lysandra. She started to move to prop herself up.

"Slowly, miss. You got some nasty wounds there on your arms. Will take a bit to heal. The infection is gone. Keir honey, help her sit up. Would you like some food and drink, Lysandra?" said Gladyss.

"Actually, yes, please. I'm famished," said Lysandra.

"I'd imagine so. You've hardly eaten in days. I'm glad you are feeling better, Lys," said Valda.

"I can go get her food and drink, Gladyss," said Kyler.

"Thank you, dear. By the way, miss, I am Gladyss. I am a healer here alongside Willow and Alodie who are in town at the moment," said Gladyss.

"Thank you for your help. It's so good to see you all. Where are we?" said Lysandra.

"We are in Krogodo," said Thallan. "The Sunoak Castle."

Lysandra turned to see Thallan standing beside someone she did not recognize and had not said a word. She stared at him as his glare felt uneasy.

"Hello, Lysandra. It is so good to see you finally. I have not seen you since you were born," said Krarick.

"Really? Nice to meet you, then, but who are you?" asked Lysandra.

"Sorcerer Krarick," he said. "Your father."

ABOUT THE AUTHOR

ALEKSEI PARKER is a fantasy adventure and sword and sorcery author. She is a proud New Mexican living with her family. She grew up in love with reading fantasy adventure and science fiction novels. While she loves a good fantasy story to escape into, she also spends time learning all she can about Ancient Greek and Norse Mythologies. She enjoys stories of all mediums, from films, games, and comics to books. Sorceress of Destiny is her debut novel.